Crashing Into Tess

Other Works by Lilly Christine
Coming Soon
"Crazy On Daisy" (McGreers #2)
Eva Smashing & Dashing

Works by Christine Griffin
Aria of Sylvania

Crashing Into
TESS

LILLY CHRISTINE

Cover Art by Libra Press Graphics

LIBRA PRESS

ISBN-13: 978-1492704447
ISBN-10: 149270444X

Libra Press is a division of Equilibria, LLC
Crashing Into Tess copyright 2013 by Lilly Christine

This is a work of fiction.
Names, characters, places and incidents either
are products of the author's imagination or are used
fictitiously. Any resemblance to actual events or
locales or persons, living or dead,
is entirely coincidental.

For publisher information, contact equilibria.llc@gmail.com.
Contact the author at LillyChristine13@gmail.com

Endless Thanks
to
Noor and Flor,
for agreeing that I could do it,
Patty Jo, for all those encouraging Thai dinners,
Robin, for your care and enthusiasm
and Lani at StoryWonk,
for kickin' feedback.

I wrote this book
for all of us searching
"Wide Open Spaces" for the "one".

~

May we find our heart's desire.

1

"Wide Open Spaces"

Balancing an acrid cup of cheap motel coffee and an overnight bag, Tess Bamberger tugged the leash clipped to Rhiannon's collar, frowning at the cold drizzle falling from a bleak, predawn sky. "C'mon girl, I'm getting wet!"

Unlocking her rental car, she tossed her bag in amongst duffels, books and computer equipment, almost blocking the car's rear window. Her retriever-collie mix hopped across the driver's seat and curled up on the passenger's seat. "Good girl, Rhiannon. Just one more day." Ignoring muddy paw prints, Tess climbed in after her.

She'd driven endless miles of straight, grey-ribboned highway since leaving her parents' gracious Tudor-style Villanova home two days earlier. Golden-tasseled cornfields of Ohio and Indiana had turned to wheat and soy across long, lonely stretches of Illinois. The sketchy radio reception had been unbearable; angry talk show hosts alternated with terrible church music.

Then she'd found Rhiannon, alone and hungry, wandering a Missouri interstate. The matted, three-quarter grown pup had lunged into her car to gulp the remainder of Tess's turkey sandwich; the radio switched from static-y fifties oldies to her sister's favorite Stevie Nicks song. "It was fate, wasn't it, Rhiannon?" Thumping her tail, Rhiannon nosed Tess's elbow, then laid her chin on a denim clad thigh, gazing up with adoring chocolate brown eyes.

They passed through Kansas City at mid-morning. Steady drizzle turned to torrential downpour, and spray from passing eighteen-wheelers thumped against the windshield, obliterating the road ahead. Tess jumped with nerves each time, clenching her teeth and continuing on. *I'm driving to a job that pays less than half what I would have made in Montgomery County, and I didn't even consider Dad's offer to buy into that Main Line emergency clinic.*

Was I just being bullheaded to prove that I could do this? And am I trying to prove it to my parents or myself?

As the sky darkened, Tess's sense of unease increased. Her headlights were barely visible through a bleary windshield. Just after ten o'clock, garish lights of chain motels around Colorado Springs beckoned. Feeling numb and anxious, Tess reached down to the hip pocket of her worn Levi's, touching the outline of the apartment key Doc Harnes' wife Bea had sent.

"No sense stopping for another cheap motel room, Rhiannon. Green Junction can't be too much farther, now."

*****

Jake McGreer nursed a ginger ale at the bar at Green Forks Tavern. From the jukebox, Kenny Loggins complained about the fine timing of Lucille's departure. Thursday nights, the pool tournament was the only action in town. It was late, he realized; the last pair was setting up to break.

"What happened over there with your cue stick tonight, Jake?" Alice teased from behind the bar. "Losing your edge?"

"Maybe I am. Wanna go out after work, help me get it back?"

"Oh, yeah, that would go over big with Lotts." Rolling her eyes, she wiped down the bar. "C'mon, a smart guy like you with two big ranches and a million head of cattle—the ladies must be lining up for dates."

Jake glanced over his shoulder to the almost empty room. "Sure, they're takin' numbers."

"Don't tell me you haven't had offers." Arms crossed, she leaned her curves against the bar, curiosity shining in her green eyes.

Count on her to dig into this stuff. "Well, there are always offers, Alice. Mostly girls from high school, divorced like me. It's awkward. You can't just date in Green Junction without raising expectations."

"You ought to be with someone, Jake… mend that broken heart."

2

Scowling into his empty glass, he wished he'd changed the subject sooner. "Not with my luck. I need another round of alimony payments like a hole in the head. How about a shot?"

Alice had taken bottles from the shelf. Swiping amber whiskeys, clear vodkas, rums and gins with a damp cloth, she frowned, "You know you don't drink, knucklehead. You're a great guy and a real catch. There's somebody perfect for you out there. You'll bump into her when the time is right."

Jake shook his head. "That's probably the last thing I need." Alice eyed him sympathetically. He ran a hand through his thick, dark curls, ready to talk. "I fetched Cassie from school today and took her out to the ranch. We saddled up for a trail ride, then I helped with her homework. After dinner, we went back to Vicki's place." He swallowed. Steadying his voice, he continued."She gets this look on her face just before she hops out of my truck. Watching her walk into that dinky apartment just about kills me, Alice." He picked up the empty glass then set it back down on the bar and sighed. "Maybe I should have tried harder, stuck it out, but the fighting really got to Cassie at the end."

Alice eyed his reflection as she set the bottles back on the shelf. "You've done everything possible for that little girl, Jake. You're a great dad." She turned to him, cocking an eyebrow. "Fathers are getting custody a lot more these days, y'know."

He shrugged. "I can't start up with the lawyers again. That's just hell. I'll take my three long weekends and Thursday nights for the time being, see how things go."

"Hang out and keep me company while I lock up, Jake?"

"Sure, Alice." He lifted chairs and set them seat-down on the tables so Lotts could mop up in the morning.

Alice turned to the last few guys at the pool table. "Last call, guys! Anybody want a draft before I shut down the taps?" She pulled a few more beers and gave the game's winner fifty bucks cash. After closing out the register, she swept behind the bar. "What time you up in the morning, Jake?"

"Usually before five."

"Wow, burnin' the midnight oil then, huh?"

"I just have a load of cattle to run down to the south ranch in the morning. I don't sleep much these days, anyway." He took his insulated cotton duck jacket from the coat hook by the booths and set his hat on his brow, dead even. "Toss me your keys, Al, I'm gonna start my truck. I'll warm your car while I'm out there."

Outside, it was raining a chill, sleety drizzle. Back inside, he helped Alice with her coat, waiting while she set the alarm and locked the door. The hum of his diesel engine was audible under gusts of wind. It was just after midnight.

"Cripes, it's only the last week of September," Alice said. "Too early for this frozen sleety stuff. Take it easy getting home, okay?"

"Sure, Alice. Have a good night."

His ranch was in the foothills, fifteen miles out of town. Rain would make visibility poor, and it might be snowing in the elevations. He'd better step on it.

*****

Closing in on midnight, the back and forth windshield wipers lulled Tess into a daze. All day she'd pushed away the doubts that plagued her. *I wanted an adventure. This is it,* she thought, stroking the silky fur on Rhiannon's belly.

Tess felt the car slip into lower gear. The little four-cylinder engine whined as it climbed mountainous terrain. Suddenly, she was alert and on edge. The rain was turning to sleet, curdling on the road in front of her. *These tires are probably worthless.*

Descending a steep incline, her wet brakes squealed. Barely able to see, she slowed to a crawl. Her headlights bounced off sheeting curtains of white. Finally, she made out a sign: *Green Junction, Exit 19~ 5 miles.*

The last five miles of the journey seemed to last forever. Wind gusted on the exit ramp, catching the side of the car and tugging the steering wheel in her hands. She managed the curve, but the little car pitched into a steep downhill grade. Unable to see the road through the whiteout in front of her, Tess tapped the brakes. The car fishtailed. She braked again, but her car was sliding

4

through a tunnel of white now, out of control. A stop sign loomed, coming fast.

Tess stood on the brakes, and the car spun, sliding sideways. From the left, she heard a loud horn and the blast of a diesel engine. Her screams echoed a screeching roar. Headlights flashed across her dashboard as a big truck slammed into her door, jamming it into her left hip and shoving the flimsy car sideways.

When the truck finally came to a standstill, Tess's head whipped sideways, smacking the metal on the edge of the car door. Flashing lights whirled, the dark vortex closed, and then there was nothing.

*****

Outside the truck, gusting wind sent frozen pellets down Jake's collar. A head of curly blonde hair was slumped on the steering wheel of the little grey car he'd hit. A white dog inside nudged the girl's face, but she didn't move. *She's unconscious—or worse. The doors are locked. This rig could catch fire any second.*

Grabbing an extinguisher and flares from behind the seat of his truck, he dialed 911, counting the seconds until the call center picked up. "Hey, Sherry, this is Jake McGreer," he breathed, trying to control rising panic. "I'm at the intersection of exit 19 and Broad Street." Setting flares on both sides of the road, he relayed the particulars of the accident. "Send a fire truck, too, just in case," he finished.

"You got it, Jake."

Pounding the driver's side window, he tried to rouse the girl. The car's windshield wipers squeaked madly; its engine raced to a high pitched whine. *If I disconnect the battery cable and shut the engine off, at least the car won't catch fire.* He fiddled with the badly mangled hood but couldn't get to the latch. *Damn!* He pounded the hood with his fist. Interminable seconds passed. As he returned to the girl's window, panic twisted his gut. "Hey! Wake up. C'mon, sweetheart, you're scarin' me!"

Freezing rain pelted his face as he grabbed a tire iron from the truck, ready to break the windshield. But the girl was picking her head up now, slow and groggy. *Thank God.*

"I'm Jake. I'm trying to help you," he shouted. "Can you turn your engine off?" Responding unsteadily, the girl twisted the key. The little car quieted. "Can you unlock the doors?"

The locks clicked up. He opened the passenger door. Whining nervously, the dog jumped out.

"Stay, Rhiannon. Stay here," the girl cried, a raw edge of panic in her voice. "I-I picked her up on the road. Sh-she doesn't know anything yet."

"I can take care of the dog," he soothed, kneeling so he could see the girl. "Are you okay?"

"I think so." Blood covered her sweatshirt. "I-I guess I bumped my head on the side of the door." Her voice had a wondering kind of drowsiness, which frightened him. She took her hand away from the side of her head. It was sticky with blood.

"The ambulance is on its way. Look, I'm worried about your neck and spine. Can you wiggle your toes?" he asked.

"Yeah, my toes are fine," the girl nodded, still in a daze. "Really, I'm okay."

"Let's let the ambulance crew decide that."

He looked up the slippery road behind them. "Can you put your hazards on in case someone is coming off the highway? Move real slow... That's it, just take it easy," he coached. When the hazards were blinking, he said, "I'll go get the dog. What's her name?"

"Rhiannon."

Jake clapped his hands, calling the butter-colored retriever. The pup bounded over, following him to the truck. Rooting on the dashboard, he found a half stick of beef jerky. The silky pale dog jumped up into the cab, wolfing it down as Jake dug behind the seat for his first aid kit. "Good girl."

Ducking back into the car's passenger door, he clicked the overhead light on. "How are you doing?" he asked gently, leaning in to study her eyes. *At least her pupils are contracting.*

"Really, I think I'm okay." The girl's voice was still shaky. "Best I can tell, the cut isn't too deep. There's a lot of blood, though."

Jake tore the wrappers off gauze pads, handing her a stack. "I hit you pretty hard. You were unconscious for a while. You must have a bad concussion, and the way that's bleeding, you'll need stitches. The hospital's forty miles back, in Salida."

The girl was gazing at him through wide-spaced blue eyes, set on high cheekbones. She had full lips, a pointy chin, and too much blonde curly hair full of blood. He'd seen the car's out-of-state license plates; her back seat and trunk were full of gear. "Are you from around here?"

"No." The girl shook her head and took a deep breath. "I'm just getting into town for a new job. I'm Tess. Tess Bamberger. I'm sorry, what did you say your name was?"

"Jake McGreer. I have a ranch a few miles out of town."

Her left hand pressed gauze against the cut on her head. Blood ran down her forearm, but she held her right hand out to him. "Well, you're the first person I've met here, so hi."

He wrapped his hand around her ice cold fingers. "Sorry we're not meeting on better terms, Tess."

She took the gauze away from her head. "Me too."   Eyeing her worriedly, he handed her another stack of bandages. *At least she's not screaming at me, blaming me for the accident, the way Vicki would.*

A police car pulled along the shoulder, lights flashing. Ronald Karachek was in the driver's seat. He'd hoped Sergeant Fuller would be on. Ron's day job was Department of Agriculture inspector. He was a part-time local cop, full-time pain in the ass, and the last person Jake wanted to see.

"Hi, Ron."

Ignoring Jake, Ron shone his flashlight over the truck, slowly examining the damage; the dent in the bumper, the busted passenger headlight. Chest puffed out, he came to the open passenger door. "What happened here?" Ron snarled, sticking his blinding light inside the car.

Tess leaned forward. "I came off the highway too fast. I didn't expect the curve, lost control on the hill, and slid through the stop sign. It was my fault."

"You hurt?" The officer asked, flashing the light over a pile of blood-soaked gauze pads.

"She's got a gash on her head, and she blacked out for few minutes," Jake offered quietly.

"I asked her, not you. Step outta that car, Jake," Officer Ron demanded curtly. Obliging, Jake stepped to the shoulder. "Where you coming from, buddy?" Ron growled, shining the blinding flashlight in his face.

"Thursday night pool tournament," Jake said evenly, squinting from the light.

"Have a seat in your truck. I'm givin' you a breathalyzer."

"You're kidding me."

"No, I ain't!"

"Ron, we've got a concussed girl here, and no sign of the emergency crew. Let's stick to priorities, huh?"

"My priority is fully investigating this accident scene. Now, go sit in your truck," Ron snarled.

Cursing under his breath, Jake opened his truck door. *This is some hell of a night. Karachek's been trying to nail me since eighth grade football tryouts when I was quarterback and he didn't make the team.*

The fire truck pulled up, the ambulance right behind it. The ambulance crew chief motioned for Jake to back his truck so they could get to Tess, but Jake waited for Ron's nod before he complied. *Can't afford to tick off the idiot with the badge.*

While first responders worked on Tess, Ron waved the fire crew back to the station. Then he gave Jake a breathalyzer test. "Inconclusive," Ron gloated, packing the kit up.

"You're full of it, Ron. I drank two ginger ales tonight. Alice will vouch for me," Jake protested.

"I expect she will," Ron smirked, walking back to the police car. With a wide smile, he opened the door to the cruiser. "But will the judge believe her?"

Refusing to take the bait, Jake watched the ambulance crew pry the car's driver side door open. His headlights flashed on Tess's skinny-legged blue jeans and white hoodie, all covered in blood. She held an ice pack to her head.

"How is she?" he asked, once the medic had fastened a cervical collar around Tess's neck.

"She's refused transport to the hospital," the paramedic said under her breath, looking concerned. "Nothing's broken, but there's a slim chance of cerebral hemorrhage. We don't want to take any chances, Jake. Her parents are next of kin, but she doesn't want us to call them."

"She was unconscious when I found her. She needs a CAT scan," Jake agreed, squatting down next to the medic, at eye level with Tess.

"Tess, you have a head injury," he said gently. "I don't want to upset you, but if it's serious, every second counts." Still dazed, her gaze wandered. Trying to make eye contact, he said, "Tess, I feel some responsibility here. Why not let the crew take you to the hospital for some tests?"

Her blue eyes turned to him, glistening with unshed tears. "How will I get back here, Jake? I haven't seen my place yet, I don't know my way around, all of my stuff is here in the car. . .What about Rhiannon?" Her voice broke. Dropping her eyes, she bit her lower lip, struggling to keep it together.

"Look, nothing is as important right now as making sure you're okay," he said softly, taking her hand. Her fingers were still ice cold. "Your dog is in my truck, she's fine. If you take the ambulance to the hospital, I'll follow your car to the tow yard to make sure your stuff is secure, and Rhiannon and I will come to Salida right behind you. I can give you a lift back here when you're finished with the doctors. How's that sound?"

"I'm not sure . . ." Their eyes locked for a moment, then Tess looked down. When she met his glance again, she looked annoyed. "Look, honestly, Jake, I don't know you. At all. And you just hit me. I mean, I appreciate what you're trying to do. . ." she sighed, "I just didn't ask for any of this."

The paramedic jerked her thumb towards Jake. "My cousin went to school with this character. Believe it or not, he usually knows how to drive. Why don't we take you in, and let him bring you back? He's a safe bet, I promise."

"C'mon, Tess, this is really important. Even Ron the cop will vouch for me, and he hates me. We need to be sure you're okay," Jake said gently.

Tess looked around. The emergency crew all nodded encouragement. She put her hand to her forehead, squeezing her eyes shut. "Okay, if you promise this guy is cool to drive me back here, I'll go to the hospital."

"That's a good move, hon," the medic said, laying a hand on Tess's shoulder. The crew wheeled a stretcher around. Jake watched Tess swipe at tears and felt a tug in his chest. *She's tough, just like Cassie.* "Where's your cell phone, Tess?" he asked.

She dug into the little bag at her hip and handed it to him. After the crew had strapped her on the stretcher and tucked a blanket over her, Jake bent to her. "My number is under Jake, and I called myself, so I have your number, too," he said, putting the phone in her hand.

"Thank you," she half-winced, trying to smile. Her head and neck were in a head stabilizer, her pupils dilated with pain.

"I guess the crew has contact information for your parents?" he asked. The medic nodded confirmation. He turned back to Tess, touching her shoulder. "I'll see you when you finish with the doctors, okay?"

"Yup," she nodded, sniffling. He squeezed her cold fingers as the crew hoisted the stretcher into the ambulance. "And don't worry. You need to get checked out, but I'll bet you're okay."

The ambulance took off, bright red lights flashing against the black sky. Ron Karachek glared from the patrol car. Rhiannon's whining turned to muffled yelps. In his truck's warm cab, Jake waited for the rollback, stroking Tess's dog to quiet her. Once the smashed car was locked in the tow yard, he headed back to the highway, starting for Salida. *2:33 a.m. I sure won't be worth much when morning rolls around.*

2

"Rescue Me"

Motionless in the neck cuff and head stabilizer, Tess watched the lights on the ceiling blink as the ambulance bumped along the highway. *Mom and Dad are really going to freak if they find out about this one.*

After the CAT scan, she waited on a stretcher in a busy emergency room, an ice pack under her neck and another against her head. The nurse bustled over. "Good news, Tess. Your scans check out fine: nothing broken, no internal bleeding. Doc wants to put sutures in your head, so I'll just shave a little around the cut, okay? Don't worry about how it will look, Hon. You'll be able to flip your hair over to cover the scar."

"Uh-huh, I've got plenty of hair," Tess volunteered weakly.

"That's the spirit."

As the electric razor buzzed, she closed her eyes, taking deep breaths, waiting for the pain medication to take effect. The nurse patted her arm. "Doc will be here any minute."

"Okay."

She floated in and out of a haze, drowsy with pain and fatigue. Then she looked up, and a doctor was peering down at her. Tall and bald, he had kind eyes and a silver mustache. "I'm Doc Verwey. Tests are clear. How's your pain, Tess?"

"Still pretty intense."

"Headache?"

"Sharp and throbbing. My neck hurts, too."

"It's going to be tender and bruised for a while yet," he said, probing gently. "I've diagnosed you with neck strain and head injury, whiplash in common terms. You have a concussion. You're going to be sore for a few days at least. Once I've sutured your head, we can let you go, but you'd better take it extra easy for a while."

"I start a new job on Monday."

"Oh really? Well, you should plan to rest all next week and follow up with a family doc. Your employer will have to be sympathetic. This is going to sting, now." He injected lidocaine near the cut. "What are you doing for work?"

"I'm a vet. I finished school in June and came out west to join Doc Harnes' practice in Green Junction. This is my first real job."

"A rural vet, serving ranchers? That's hard work, young lady. Very physically demanding." Tess felt pressure as he tugged the sides of her cut together with sutures. "What led you down this path?"

"I've spent my whole life fascinated by anything with four legs."

"Where did you study?"

"University of Pennsylvania. I worked with the large animal surgical team at New Bolton as a resident this past summer, and left Philadelphia on Tuesday morning."

"That must have been an adventure, driving cross-country and all."

"It ended with a real bang."

The doctor chuckled. "Well, you haven't lost your sense of humor, anyway. You'll need that the next few days. Here's a prescription for pain reliever. Good Luck, Tess."

A busty young orderly helped her into a wheelchair, pushing her out into the dingy waiting room. Increasingly ill at ease, Tess glanced over the orange plastic chairs and the torn linoleum. *What if Jake's not here?*

A stringy-haired, skinny woman in a fuzzy bathrobe and slippers sat next to a huge man in a Harley jacket. She glanced at Tess and looked away.

In the far corner, a lone figure stretched out in a chair in front of a dark window, cowboy hat tipped over his face. Muscular arms cloaked in a faded cotton duck jacket crossed his broad, flannel-shirted chest.

Nervously, she glanced over the man's long, denim-clad thighs, the expensive-looking brown boots on his feet.

12

"S'that him?" the orderly asked, snapping her gum.

"I'm not sure." Tess stood up. She felt dizzy, her hip pinched with pain. She bit her lower lip and sat back down. *This is super awkward. Crying now would be lame, so just keep it together.*

The man shifted in his seat, pushed his hat back, and looked at her sideways. He had high cheekbones and a narrow jaw, rough with almost-beard. "Tess?"

"Hi, Jake," she answered, relieved.

Red-faced under his tan, he came towards the wheelchair, appraising her with an anxious smile. "You okay? You look better."

"The CAT scan is clear. I have a concussion and whiplash," she told him.

Jake looked younger than she remembered, less sure of himself. He held his hat in his hand, his contrite eyes liquid brown. "I feel real bad about the accident. Sorry I wasn't able to avoid you."

She shrugged. "I lost control of the car. The tires are probably junk."

His eyes flashed regret. "It's a hell of a welcome to town for you, though."

"I came for an adventure, but this wasn't quite what I bargained for."

"I guess not," he winced.

"Look, you made me come to the hospital. And you're here now, Jake. I appreciate that."

A slow, friendly smile spread across his face. Tapping her knee, he said, "I'll bring the truck around."

Tess checked Jake out as he strode out the door. *If I had to drop into a tailspin and land in Oz, at least the Lone Ranger came to rescue me. A Lone Ranger with a really, really cute butt.*

A big green truck with a single headlight appeared at the curb, its engine humming loudly. The sky was still dark, but she could see Rhiannon leaping around the cab, wagging her whole body.

Snapping her gum, the orderly jerked the wheelchair through the door. Holding her ice packs in place, Tess stood up, catching her breath at the pain in her head and hip. Jake was just coming around the hood of the truck.

"Hey, I was on my way in for you," he said, grabbing the slipping ice packs and opening the truck's passenger door. He held her elbow as she climbed into the high bucket seat.

Excited, the retriever licked her face. Tess wiped dog spit from her cheek. "Ugh, hi, Rhiannon."

Jake laid an ice pack at her neck then helped with her seatbelt, his sturdy hand over hers. "All set?" he asked, searching her eyes. In the dark, the bulk of his square shoulders was distracting.

"I'm okay," she smiled. Neil Young's "Harvest Moon" played softly from the CD player. His truck was new, the heated bucket seat cozy and warm. It smelled of leather and tobacco. She settled back as Jake slid into the driver's seat, slamming his door. As he pulled onto the highway, she said, "Thanks again for coming for me."

"I just wish an air bag had gone off. I feel real bad about the accident. Where am I taking you?"

"349 East Chambers Street, in Green Junction. Do you know where that is?" she asked anxiously, sliding her fingertips to her hip pocket, feeling for the key.

"Sure, the old Sherman place."

"What's it like?"

"The house? It's a big white Victorian, built before the turn of the century by a man named Carson Sherman. Green Junction is a rail transfer hub for wheat and cattle, and the Sherman family operated the rail yard."

She liked the friendly twang in his voice. *He sounds like a cowboy.*

He continued, "The last surviving Sherman sold the old house to Elmer Freethy about ten years ago, and he cut it up into rental apartments. There's a yard in front, lots of windows. Plenty of room, but it'll be drafty come winter. The neighborhood is quiet and safe. My daughter and her mom live right around the block."

Tess ran her hand down her dog's back. "I hope the landlord won't have a problem with Rhiannon. I picked her up on the highway in eastern Missouri. She's come this whole way with me."

"Rhiannon put up a fuss when the ambulance pulled away, didn't you girl?" he asked, scratching between the dog's ears. "She's already real attached to you, Tess. Elmer probably won't mind Rhiannon if nobody complains. Run it by the other tenants in the building first. Where are you working?"

"At the vet clinic. With Doc Harnes."

Jake's brow wrinkled. "Last I heard, Doc was going to sell the practice and retire to Florida."

Her chest pinched. "Nobody said anything about that. I've been counting on this job, at least until spring. Doc's wife Bea found my apartment, and Alice, the woman who works there, helped me with everything else over the phone."

"Alice is a friend of mine. She works days at the clinic and helps her husband Lotts out with their bar downtown at night. Maybe I heard wrong. If Doc brought you on board, he'll likely be around for a while yet. He's a good man, and a great vet. Where'd you come from?"

"Pennsylvania."

He glanced over at her skeptically. "Girl, you've come a long way for a job in a vet's office."

He doesn't know I'm a vet, yet. But if things work out, I'll see him on ranch calls. Stroking Rhiannon's pale silky coat, she let Neil Young and the hum of the diesel engine distract her from a throbbing headache and worries about her new job.

The barest glimmer of eastern light was just visible above the jagged mountaintops when Jake took the Green Junction highway exit. As he navigated the tight curve, she saw a ribbon of black rubber tread marks criss-crossing the road. *Ugh.* They approached the stop sign. "Look, it's where we met," Tess blurted.

Clearing his throat, Jake tapped his fingers on the steering wheel. "Are you always this funny, or does it have to do with the head injury you sustained last night?"

Quirking her lips in a half-smile, she raised an eyebrow. "What head injury?" Jake grinned back, flashing teeth that were even and very white.

Rosy morning light shone on a fresh row of well-kept brick Victorians with fancy gingerbread porches as the truck crossed the intersection, starting down a residential street. At the next intersection, he paused. "Tess, the body shop doesn't open until seven. I know you need your stuff, but the tow lot's still locked. It'll be another hour at least."   As his voice trailed off, she heard the nervous staccato of his fingers on the steering wheel. He turned to her. "You want breakfast? The diner's open."

*****

Two blocks from the diner, Ron Karachek heard tires crunching gravel outside the Green Junction Police Station. Hastily, he tucked the auto accident report into a folder, stuck it in the filing cabinet, and poured a cup of fresh coffee.

The back door swung open, and Sergeant Fuller came in, fifteen minutes early for the morning shift. When Ron set the mug on his boss's cheap brown Formica desk, the Sergeant said, "So Jake McGreer hit a girl out near the interstate last night, huh?"

"Yup," Ron said, trying to hide his smile. "On his way home from the pool tournament, just after midnight. Musta been tipsy."

Fuller's brow furrowed as he shuffled papers on his desk. "Tipsy, you say? That's not like Jake, especially with all the nonsense over his daughter. He's a careful guy with a lot to lose. You're sure about this?"

"I've got the printout from the breath-lyzer right in the file, next to the report. Says .038—darn close to the legal limit. He shouldn'ta been at the wheel of his truck," Ron gloated. Sergeant Fuller's eyes met Ron's dead on. "It's all in the report," Ron insisted.

Fuller set his jaw. "I better double check the calibration on the darn thing. How's the girl?"

"She blacked out, guess you heard that on the scanner last night. Has a Pennsylvania driver's license, but she was in a rental car. Ethel and the crew got her to Salida for a CAT scan. Seemed like Jake was going to bring her back when they finished with her at the hospital. Don't think she has any family 'round here."

Looking over his ledger, Fuller picked up his phone. "I'll do some digging, find out how she made out."

Ron shuffled into the hallway to clock out.

Sergeant Fuller raised his voice to make sure Ron heard him. "And I'll ask Alice what Jake was drinking last night."

"You do that," Ron called, nodding to his boss as he headed to the locker room to change for his day job.

******

Tess sopped a last bit of egg with her whole wheat toast, flashing Jake a flirty little smile. He blushed and slid his hat on his head, looking away. *Judging by the way people here are checking us out, he hasn't been seen around town since his divorce.*

All through breakfast, he'd glanced her over worriedly, asking if she was okay, assuring he'd help her get settled. She hadn't mentioned her parents were attorneys. The waitress took their plates, refilled Jake's coffee, and laid a check on the table. Tess snapped it up. "I got it," Jake insisted, grabbing for his wallet. "C'mon, Tess, you're hurt. Let me get breakfast."

"No way!" She dug out her credit card and slapped it on the bill. "You spent all night taking care of me, and now I've guilt-tripped you into helping me with my errands. The least I can do is buy your bacon and eggs."

Jake raised an eyebrow in disapproval as the waitress scooped the check up. His tanned face crinkled around his eyes. "Well, then, Nancy gets a real good tip." He laid a ten on the table. "You want to order something for later, since you won't have anything to cook with?"

"Very thoughtful of you," she smiled. "After we check out my apartment, I plan to hit the Goodwill. I hope to have pots and pans and dishes by lunchtime."

Amused, Jake slurped his coffee. "There's no Goodwill in town, but we do have a thrift store on Third Street, pulls from all five churches. It's too far to walk in your condition, and with any luck, you'll have a load to haul back to your place. I'll take you there after groceries."

"Thanks!"

Standing, she grabbed her blood-stained hoodie from the hook at the top of the booth. He stood up to help with her sleeves, the rough stubble of his cheeks close. She smelled leather and soap. Her brow crinkled. "I really shouldn't tie up your whole morning. Should I call a cab or something?"

His face burst into a grin. "A cab...in this town? Fat chance, Tess. There's not a taxi service outside of Denver." His grin widened as he pushed the diner door open for her. "We're surrounded by ghost towns out here. Where did you say you're from?"

"Pennsylvania," she hedged.

"Where in Pennsylvania?" he asked pointedly as they crossed the parking lot.

She winced as he opened her door. "Philadelphia?"

His grin widened. "Hah, I thought so. You're a city girl. Not for nothing, but what made you pick Green Junction?"

"I wanted something different," she said, lifting her chin. It was hard to admit to a real cowboy she'd wanted to escape the suburban bubble she'd always felt swaddled in.

"A challenge?" He didn't even try to hide his amusement.

"The work Doc has for me seems interesting," she said defensively, climbing up into the truck with as much dignity as she could muster.

"Oh, it'll be a challenge, girl," he agreed, moving around to open his door. He turned the key in the ignition. "Winters are cold here, and this town can feel real isolated once the snows come. I hope you're not disappointed," he said, glancing her way.

18

"I won't be. And even if I am, I'll stick it out. I'm only committed until spring."

*****

Bright morning sun angled across the diner's parking lot, melting all traces of the previous night's ice storm. Pulling out onto the street, Jake said, "It gets real snowy around here, come winter time, y'know."

Looking out the window, Tess finger-combed her blonde curls absently. "I know. I'm thinking maybe I'll buy a four wheel drive truck, not as big as yours, though. I'll talk it over with Doc."

Jake glanced at the clock on the dash, annoyed at the concern he felt for her. "It's after seven. We'll head over to the body shop. Dave Burns runs it; he's probably got some used cars you can look at. Dave's an honest guy; he won't rob you."

When he parked there, Tess asked, "Can Rhiannon stay here with you?"

"Sure."

He opened the hatchback of the demolished rental car, and she dug through soft, hippie-flowered duffel bags. "I'll just change inside."

After she left, he surveyed the new computer equipment and fancy teal sport luggage. *What does a city girl want with a four wheel drive pickup? She belongs in a shiny little BMW coupe.* Trying to resist the lemony-sunshine appeal of her, he stashed her belongings in the bed of his truck and waited.

Tess crossed the lot with Dave, looking over his inventory and motioning with her hands. He smiled. She'd changed into a clean white fleece vest, matching ribbed turtleneck, and stretchy fleece yoga pants that hugged her curves. Then she was floating towards him, curly blonde hair flopped over the white bandage on the side of her head. There was a wide smile on her pale face, and something in his chest tugged.

Leaning over, he opened her door. "Hey, how'd it go?"

Rolling her eyes, she climbed up onto the seat. "I reported the accident to the rental company. They won't have a replacement car until the middle of next week—can you believe it? And Dave doesn't have anything for me right now, either." She eyed him carefully. "Are you sure you want to do all this other stuff today? It can probably wait."

"I drank three cups of coffee at the diner, Tess. No turning back now. I'll call the ranch to get my guys started and crash when I get home." Shaking his head, he started the engine. "I mean, I can sleep. Enough crash talk."

She smiled at him, her wide blue eyes saucy. "I was just thinking about a new CD. Maybe some Crash Test Dummies?"

He shook his head, unable to help grinning. "Yeah, that goes well with a head injury."

*****

Why can I not stop flirting with this guy? And these bad jokes... He must think I'm desperate. Tess's cell buzzed. Fishing it out of her little bag, she looked at the display. "Ugh. My mom. Excuse me, I have to take this." She cupped her hand over the speaker to shield the noisy truck engine. "Hi, Mom."

"Good morning, Contessa." Her mother's crisp voice put her immediately on edge. "Are you in Colorado Springs, at the hotel?"

"Can you see William Penn?" Tess replied. *If she finds out about this accident, I'm doomed.*

"Very funny, Tess," her mother said drily, not at all amused. Noelle Bamberger's center-city law firm specialized in urban zoning and land development. From her office on floor eleven of a Market Street high-rise, Noelle shared a view of City Hall with Tess's father Richard, a partner in a patent and intellectual property firm. His office was on floor twelve.

Omissions are a sanity measure, here. Fake perky, Tess. Feeling her throat tighten, she said, "I'm actually in Green Junction, Mom. I made it to town about an hour ago, and I just had a big healthy breakfast."

"Well, you got an early start, didn't you?" her mother said approvingly. *Earlier than you can imagine, Mom.* "How is your new place?"

"Ah-h, I haven't seen it, yet. I'm heading over there now." Tess flashed Jake a cheeky grin. "It's sure to be a great little crash pad."

Unable to help grinning, he shook his head.

"A what? I hope it's not some kind of roach motel, Contessa. The furniture shop is set to deliver your bed sometime this afternoon, so call right away if there is a problem with the apartment. I can stop the delivery and book you a flight home."

Tess rolled her eyes. "I'm sure my apartment is fine, Mom. Can you have Shirley give the furniture people my cell number and ask them to call beforehand?"

"Yes, but there's plenty of room on your credit card if you want to fly home, Contessa. I still can't imagine how that place is at all suited for you."

Tess tried to keep annoyance from her voice. "Thanks, Mom."

After Noelle picked up her printout of rural ranch jobs lying on the kitchen counter last June, she'd poured herself a double gin and tonic and stewed until Richard returned from his golf game. That night at dinner, they'd offered to finance a partnership in a small animal emergency clinic on the Main Line. Noelle had not hidden her disappointment when Tess turned it down in favor of the Green Junction job. First she'd been disparaging, then downright caustic. As Tess's departure loomed, Noelle made snarky references to "Tess's Trip to the Wild West".

But that's all behind me, now, she thought, glancing at Jake. He was a nice distraction, his angular jaw slightly bristled, strong brow and chiseled nose etched in the sunlight, reddish brown hair curling at his collar. *I just got to Colorado, and I'm already hanging with the Marlboro Man. Wait 'til I tell Sammi.*

"I'll be out of the office all day, dear. I have client briefings then a deposition. Shall I check in with the rental company? How much longer will you need the car?" Her mother's voice brought Tess crashing back to reality.

"B-Better let me handle the rental company, Mom," she said with as much assurance as she could muster. *This is way too dicey to get sidetracked by the magazine ad next to me.* "I'm looking at trucks today."

"But what if you change your mind about that place? Your father won't appreciate having to ship a vehicle back to the east coast, you know."

"Mother, as both you and Daddy are aware, I've promised to be here until spring. I'll need four-wheel drive and good tires before the bad weather hits, and I can drive the truck home next summer. Look, I hate feeling like I have to explain myself to you. This is my decision. I need the truck. I'll be in touch, okay?" she asked impatiently, hoping her mother would take the hint.

"All right, dear. I'll check in at lunch time to see how you're doing."

"Bye, Mom, love you," Tess said, ending the call. Glancing at Jake, she sighed, slightly embarrassed. "Sorry about that. She's called five times a day since I left Philadelphia."

He glanced over to her then back at the road. "She's your mom. She cares about you."

"It doesn't always feel like caring," Tess exhaled. "I don't usually fib, but both of my parents are huge micro-managers. My sister Samantha is absolutely perfect, and lately, they've focused way too much on me. It's a bit much, actually. They're freaked I moved out here. It will be a huge adjustment for them."

"It'll be a huge adjustment for all of you. You're far away; I'm sure they're gonna miss you," he said easily. "Is your sister in Philly?"

Tess shook her head. "Manhattan. She does PR for a think-tank. She's a brilliant writer, but my parents persuaded her to do something practical, so she puts together newsletters and press releases, handles all of their website content. I guess she likes her job. Do your parents live in Green Junction?"

"My dad lives at the ranch with me during the summer, but he'll stay in Texas this winter at my uncle's place. The warmer weather suits him," Jake said evenly. "I've been managing the ranches here for the past eight years."

"And your mom?" Tess asked.

"Mom died when I was ten."

Did I seriously just complain about my parents to him? Caught off-guard, she grasped for something to say. "I'm so sorry. That's sad, Jake. You were just a little kid."

"There's never a good time to lose a mom, I guess," he said.

*****

When Jake pulled in front of Elmer Freethy's big white Victorian on Chambers Street, pink-streaks of sunlight hovered above the Sangre de Christo Mountains, casting the morning in rosy brilliance.

Tess dug into her hip pocket for her key, and he noticed her hands. They were pale, fine boned and elegant, her fingers long and thin. *Piano hands. That's what Aunt Olivia calls hands like hers.* He opened her door, steadying her as she stepped down. "You sure you're okay?"

"I'm fine," she assured him with an eager smile. "C'mon Rhiannon, this is home. Let's go check it out!"

Tongue lolling, the dog hopped from the truck. Jake grabbed the ice packs and discharge instructions from the seat and followed Tess up the green painted steps of a deep covered porch. Turning the key in the old-fashioned lock, she pushed against the gleaming oak entry door.

In the hallway, a curved wooden stairway led to the second floor. As Tess unlocked the door to the right, he inhaled baby powder, antiseptic, and something lemony, clean and light.

In the apartment, tall living room windows faced the front porch. Her footsteps echoed on recently refinished wood floors, then she stepped into the room beyond: a kitchen tiled in black and white, occupying the old sun porch. A wide smile lit her face. "Wow, this is really super! Come see it, Jake!"

The windows at the front of the eating nook had a view of the Sangre de Christos on all three sides. "It'll be bright and sunny in the morning," he agreed. Next to him, Rhiannon wagged her tail enthusiastically.

Tess walked down the hall and into the bedroom, calling, "Can you believe there's a claw-foot tub in the bathroom? My sister will be so jealous. . . How many girls get claw foot tubs in their first apartment?" Her voice trailed off, and she came back towards him. "What day is it?"

"Today's Friday." She was right in front of him now, blonde, curly ringlets almost at his fingertips, eyes glistening, pink cheeks smooth. He put his hands in his pockets. "It was a long drive, huh?"

"Ridiculously long, and it got a whole lot more confusing last night," she admitted, shaking her head. "I start work on Monday, so I have to get settled in here."

He cleared his throat. "You've got time."

"I guess so. I'm feeling much better since I've seen this place, anyway." Her full lips were rosy, a little chapped, and she was still smiling. "Can we head for the grocery and drug store, now? Do you mind?"

"Let's go," he grinned, opening the door.

3

"New Vet In Town"

The sun hit the dashboard of Victoria Scalamagotti-McGreer's white Acura as she zipped into the shopping center, late for work.

Cassie had missed the starting bell at school, but she'd taken a call from Ronald Karachek, and the news had been good.

She passed her ex-husband's green diesel pickup, idling in front of the supermarket. The bumper was banged up, and the headlight was missing. Her eyes narrowed as she watched a thin girl get out, long blonde curls bobbing. The girl grabbed a cart and headed through the glass double doors. Jake pulled into a parking spot.

Hah! I've got news for you and that little mermaid, Jake. That police report is my ticket out of here! Once I show the judge you're a drunk, you'll be bankrolling my new life in sunny California. If you're lucky, you might see Cassie at Christmas and Easter. Two weeks in summer, too, if you'll agree to cover my cruise.

Parking in front of the bank branch, Vicki smiled at her reflection in the mirror as she unclasped the large black alligator purse that matched her stilettos. She opened a mint tin, popped two little yellow pills into her lipsticked mouth, and washed them down with the can of diet Coke in her console. *Breakfast of champions. . .These will hold me until lunch!*

*****

Idling in the fire lane, Jake watched Tess walk into the pharmacy, admiring the way her knit pants hugged her willowy thighs and curvy little butt. *Focus, Jake. You're getting carried away, here.*

He swallowed, pulled into the nearest parking spot, and called the ranch. "We'll have the cattle loaded and be on the road in the next forty-five minutes," his foreman Larry said, "Why don't you just stay put?"

It was just what he wanted to hear. Drowsy in the sunlight, he tilted his hat and leaned back for a nap. He was enjoying Tess's company. Two ranches kept him busy, but it wasn't the same as being needed, taking care of things… the way it had been when Cassie was around. *I could fall for Tess in a heartbeat, but she's only here until spring.*

When Tess came through the automatic doors with a cartload of groceries, he pulled the truck to the curb. "Look, just climb in and relax while I load this stuff," he offered, opening her door. She rolled her eyes. "What?" he asked.

"I feel like my Dad's mother, Granny Esther. My grandfather does everything for her. I'm not ancient, you know."

"You're not ancient, but you are banged up. You'll need to take it easy the next week or so, Tess," he said gruffly, feeling the blush crawl up his neck.

They let Rhiannon run in the park, and he took her down Main Street to show her the library, courthouse, and the movie theater.

"So you think I'll find some good stuff here?" she asked when he pulled to the curb at the thrift store.

"Best show in town for a girl with an empty apartment," he answered.

She hopped from the truck, flashing him another killer smile. "I might be a little while."

"Take your time. I'll be here."

Unable to stifle a grin, he pulled his hat over his face and leaned back, absently stroking Rhiannon. Twenty minutes later, the passenger door swung open. Tess's blue eyes gleamed with excitement, her hair a shining halo. She looked like an angel, floating on adrenaline and endorphins.   "I scored big! I got this great set of old restaurant china from this place called the 'Halfway Hotel.' The lady inside, Gertrude, said it came from somewhere up near Pike's Peak. There's a little pickaxe and miner's pan on every piece!"

He smiled as she rambled on, breathless with enthusiasm. "I found drinking glasses and mugs and a cast-iron frying pan and a tea kettle and a pot or two to get started, and they've got a gorgeous oak dresser and chest of drawers. Do you mind helping me get it all over to my place?"

"Might as well load the truck up while we're here," he said agreeably.

In the store, Gertrude was wrapping at the counter. She greeted Jake with her sweet, steady smile.

He tied the dresser and chest of drawers behind the cab then started on the boxes lining the floor between the aisles. When Tess was next to him in the truck again, he cocked an eyebrow. "I sure bet the thrift shop appreciates your arrival."

"Do you think? And this is just the tip of the iceberg. I'll be their most loyal customer over the next few months."

"I bet you will."

On their way to her apartment, she said, "There's so much sky here. I didn't know what to expect, but it's all so gorgeous and amazing."

He looked at her eager face and couldn't help smiling. "I hope you think so in February when the sky is dumping two feet of snow on top of the four already on the ground and most of the mountain roads are impassable." He pointed to the mountains. "That range to the south is the Sangre De Cristo, and to the west are the Sawatch Mountains. See those street signs?"

"Yes."

"Are they up that high in Philadelphia?"

"No way."

"They have to stay visible above the snow piles the plow throws up in winter. The streets are wide just so there's plenty of room for snow."

"Hmm, I'll keep that in mind when I pick out my vehicle."

"Look around and see what people are driving. Get something with high clearance and four wheel drive, and plan to keep plenty of weight in the back if you're driving into the mountains in winter. Make sure to figure in for good snow tires, too."

"Thanks, Jake. I will."

He pulled into her driveway, unloaded groceries and boxes onto the porch, then carried her dresser and chest up the stairs. He parked, threw the forty pound bag of dog food over his shoulder, and rounded the corner. Up on the porch, Tess was picking up her printer. Rhiannon was underfoot, her tail wagging.

"Why don't you just relax and tell me where to put your stuff? You're supposed to be taking it easy, remember?"

She flashed him a hesitant smile. "Are you sure you don't mind? I've got everything sorted into piles."

Setting the dog food down, he said, "I don't mind. You stay here and let me carry everything in."

He hoisted the dresser. Drawer in hand, she followed him to the bedroom, motioning where she wanted it. Sliding the drawer into place, she turned to him and said, a little breathlessly, "Thank you so much. For all of this. You're really helping me out here."

"It's no problem. I'll feel better knowing you're settled in." His fingers itched. He wanted badly to reach for one of her corkscrew curls. "Do you have a boyfriend, Tess?"

She looked up at him wide-eyed and shook her head. "No, no boyfriend."

He moved closer, letting a hand drop to her waist. Her skin was warm and taut, better than he'd imagined. *This is exactly what I said I wouldn't do.* "How old are you?" he sighed.

"Eighteen."

Startled, he pulled away.

She giggled and slugged him gently. "Silly, I'm twenty-six."

He cocked an eyebrow. "You look younger than that."

"I hear that a lot."

Touching her hair, careful of her bandage, he asked. "Ever been in a serious relationship?"

"Not really serious. I was with my college boyfriend for three years, but he dumped me when he went to law school. My blood type is A positive, want my GPA?" she whispered, moving closer.

Her chin tilted up to him, so close now. He couldn't stop his lips from brushing against hers, soft and tender. "Tess?"

"Hmm?" she murmured, running a forefinger along his collarbone.

He groaned softly, trying to resist. "Tess, I don't usually kiss women I barely know."

She tucked her head against his chest. "Me neither, Jake."

"You don't kiss women you barely know?"

"Not usually." She smiled up at him, shaking her head. "Or men either. But you're the person in Green Junction I know best."

"I'm the only person you know in Green Junction, Crash," he murmured, letting a hand fall to her waist. He kissed her for real then, his mouth hot on her pink lips. When he felt her twitchy little tongue tease his, he felt his heart catch. He came up for air, breathing hard surprised by the effect she had on him. "So you're not afraid to go after what you want, either, huh?"

She met his eye. "I wouldn't say that. You've taken really good care of me since last night. I like being with you. It feels safe."

"Oh, I'm safe. And there's plenty of time to get to know me if you decide to stick around Green Junction," he said, dropping his hands, which felt empty without her.

"I'm here for the duration," she said with certainty.

"That remains to be seen. You haven't even put a day in on the job." He plucked a curl, then, unable to resist, pressed his nose into her hair, breathing the scent of her again, lemony and soft and fragrant. She tightened her hands around his back, her fingertips pressing on the tight muscles at his rib cage.

"I should leave before we get in trouble here," he murmured.

"We're already in trouble," she told him softly, kissing his chin. Unable to resist, he found her mouth again.

"Daddy?" a shrill little voice called from the front yard. "Daddy, are you here?"

Red-faced, Jake pulled away and walked quickly to the front of the apartment. Boots tapping down the porch steps, he asked, "Cassie? It's Friday. Why aren't you in school?"

*****

Tess followed Jake out. A cupid-faced girl with two long reddish-brown braids was leaning a turquoise bike against the front steps.

Small but sturdy, she was built like a little gymnast. She crinkled her freckled nose at Tess, flashing a lopsided grin. "We had a half day today. Teacher in-service. It was on the calendar. Mom had to take a half day from work, and she is 'Not Happy.'"

"Why didn't you guys let me know?" Jake asked easily, putting a hand on his daughter's shoulder. "I would have gotten you from school. Cassie, this is Tess. She's just moving in, so I offered her help getting settled," he explained. "Tess, this is my daughter Cassie."

"Hi, Cassie," Tess said, extending her hand. "Looks like we're neighbors, huh?"

"Yup." Grasping Tess's hand, the little girl shook it vigorously, her amber-olive eyes steady. "Nice t'meet ya, Tess. What happened to your head?"

"Oh. I-I bumped it," she answered, touching the bandage self-consciously.

Cassie screwed her face up, red-brown braids swinging against her back. "Does it hurt?"

"Well, yes it does, a little. More throbbing than hurting, really, but I'll be okay," she said. "Want to see my place? I have apple juice."

The little girl nodded, so Tess opened the front door. Rhiannon slipped out in a white flash, eluding her grasp. "Hey, Rhiannon! Come here!"

Ignoring her, the dog bounded towards Cassie, leaping up and licking her face, which the little girl managed surprisingly well.

"Well, this is Rhiannon," Tess laughed. "I hope you like dogs."

30

"Yup, I do. She needs to learn to behave herself, though." Cassie grabbed Rhiannon's collar. "Sit, Rhiannon!" Busy sniffing, the dog ignored her. "I said, SIT!" Holding Rhiannon's collar, the little girl neatly scooped the dog's bottom, and Rhiannon sat. A satisfied Cassie met Tess's eye. "We really should give her a treat now, don't you think?"

"We definitely should," Tess agreed. Tearing into the dog food bag, she handed the little girl a handful of kibble. "That's some dog training you just did. I'm very impressed. Will you give us lessons?"

"Oh, my dad taught me everything I know about dogs," Cassie answered breezily, shrugging her shoulders. "Horses, too. I help out at the vet office."

"At the vet office?" Tess asked, surprised and pleased. "So we're neighbors and colleagues?"

"Tess is here for a job at Doc Harnes' office, Cassie," Jake said, touching his daughter's shoulder. To Tess, he explained, "Doc's wife Bea is Vicki's aunt. Cassie spends some time there."

"Vicki is my mom," Cassie added helpfully. Tess nodded as the little girl continued. "I help Alice file. It's all alphabetized; we do it by owner's last name. At first I messed it up. Now Alice has me organize the pile starting with A. Then she helps me put them in the drawer."

"I'll bet you're a big help," Tess offered.

"Yup, I guess I must be, 'cause Doc Harnes always gives me five dollars," Cassie answered proudly. Scolding Rhiannon to sit again, Cassie made her take treats politely. Then she eyed the front door. "Want to show me your place now, Tess? I'm thirsty. I could use some apple juice."

*****

Jake brought Tess's gear in while Cassie took a tour and had apple juice. When he passed through the kitchen, his daughter was helping Tess put away groceries. They chattered amiably as cupboard doors opened and closed. *Well, Cassie found a new friend. It never takes her long.*

When he'd finished setting up Tess's laptop and modem, Cassie was stacking thrift store finds on the kitchen counter, unwrapping and admiring each one, while Tess filled the sink with hot, soapy water. "How 'bout I make you guys some lunch?" she offered, dunking a stack of plates in the dishpan.

"Hmm, what do you have?" Cassie asked, eyeing Tess curiously.

"We'll stop for pizza, Cassie," Jake interrupted, shooting his daughter a quelling stare. "Thanks, anyway, Tess."

Her hands in sudsy yellow gloves, Tess turned off the water and hit him with her killer smile. "But you both really helped me out here. I want to feed you." Leaning slim hips against the counter, she looked at his daughter, her clear eyes wide. "What do you like for lunch, Cass?"

"Um, well, I like pizza. You really need to try Mamma Boccini's pizza. Even Aunt Olivia thinks it's good, and she's not really a pizza person. But at home I like apples and tuna sometimes, and . . ."

Jake set his jaw. "Cass, Tess just got here. She's got a lot to do. It's time for us to leave."

Ignoring him, Tess narrowed her eyes with a smile. "Do you like root beer floats?" she asked Cassie.

Cassie's eyes got round. "Oh, yeah, I really, really like root beer floats. Do you have the stuff to make them? Can we have some root beer floats, Dad?"

"I need to get you over to your mom's, kiddo. She has no idea where you are," he said, tugging one of his daughter's braids. "Let's ask Tess what kind of pizza she likes and bring some back."

"There's all kinds of pizza at Mamma Boccini's. What do you like, Tess? Mostly I get regular with pepperoni, but sometimes I like the broccoli and cheese, and once Trudie and I split a piece of ham and pineapple," Cassie gushed. "It was good. I think you'd like it, if you're feeling adventurous."

"Mmm, regular with pepperoni sounds great. Thank you." Tess followed them to the porch with Rhiannon padding behind. Jake lifted Cassie's bike into the back of his truck.

"I'll have root beer floats next time, I promise," Tess called, waving as Cassie climbed in.

After they returned with pepperoni slices and iced tea for Tess, Jake parked the truck at the curb near Vicki's apartment and waited while Cassie packed for her weekend at the ranch. To kill some time, he dialed Alice at the veterinary office.

"So you trashed Tess's rental car, picked her up from the hospital and gave her the Green Junction Welcome Tour? Then Cassie showed up, and you both helped her move in? You're quite a guy, Jake," Alice cackled.

"Hey, it was okay until Cassie tried to weasel lunch out of her. That was a bit much," he laughed, feeling guilty about what he'd been doing with Tess when his daughter showed up.

"So, what's she like?" Alice drawled. "She seemed real sweet on the phone, very smart and together. Is she cute?"

"She's a pleasant-enough person," Jake answered in the most neutral voice he could manage. *If I say anything more, Alice will see right through me.* Cassie had spoken of nothing but from Tess from the time she climbed into his truck, and he couldn't stop thinking of her, either—all saucy and upbeat, with her teasing eyes and luscious lips. The thought of the silky skin he'd felt when he touched Tess's waist made him hard all over again.

"I feel a little guilty for asking you to stick around last night," Alice was confessing. "If you'd left earlier, you'd have missed Tess and Officer Ron and his breathalyzer test."

"How do you know about the breathalyzer test?"

"Sergeant Fuller called, wanting to know what you drank last night. I told him ginger ale and water and you left stone sober, don't worry. Geez, that Ron Karachek's got it in for you! Be careful, Jake." When he said nothing, Alice took a deep breath. "Okay, I'll fill in Beatrice and Doc on Tess's situation, call her later to check in, and have Lotts put feelers out at the bar for a truck?"

"That would be great, Alice. Four-wheel drive, probably new-ish, I'd say. Real clean. Look, this is my weekend with Cass, so I'm off duty as far as Tess is concerned. Can you look out for her?"

"Like one of my own. I'll see you during the week, okay?"

"Sure. Bye, Alice."

*****

That afternoon, the mattress guys delivered a brand new, top-of-the-line, queen-sized CertaRest, compliments of Tess's mom and dad. She put her new tea kettle on to boil and dug through her bags. Pulling out lavender and white polka-dot flannel sheets, she made up the bed, topping it with the patchwork quilt her grandmother had made for her college graduation.

She set out towels and soap and shampoo in the bathroom, found slippers and hung her robe, made herself a cup of chamomile tea, and stood back to admire her new room. Quarter-sawn honey-gold oak gleamed in the late-day sun, the carved designs around the knobs etched in shadow. The antique chest and dresser were her first-ever furniture purchase, and she could still see Jake's broad, flannel-clad shoulders setting them in place.

Better make the apartment comfy now, before the snow flies. Sounds like I'll be spending plenty of time here this winter. She added "head board" and "bed frame" to her furniture list, then, "nightstands, lamps, dining set, sofa, coffee table, Jake."

He better show up again. Not much goes on here, and I'm too young to start collecting cats. Plus, he's really nice to kiss.

Tess put her teacup in the sink, grabbed dog treats and a tennis ball, stuck her cell in her pocket, and snapped the leash on Rhiannon. She explored town from the sidewalk, walking the stiffness out of her hip, inhaling crisp autumn air.

She thought about Cassie, then Jake, kissing her. *Stop that!*

The sky, an incredible, piercing blue, was punctuated by jagged, white-capped mountain peaks. Below the mountains, rolling foothills were doused with yellow and orange foliage, splashes of russet and brilliant red amongst tall stands of evergreen.

Cattle and horses and sheep and pigs must be grazing in the fields up there, on the ranches I'll visit soon for work. Smiling with anticipation, she arrived on Main Street.

Town Hall was on the circle, a grand old brick structure with a domed tower, next to the court house. Turning left, she walked past the library to the park. Kids shrieked on the playground, laughing and running as their mothers sat nearby. Crossing the soccer fields, Tess let Rhiannon off her lead. She tossed a ball, which the dog grabbed in midair, racing to the far end of the park. Her cell buzzed, and she looked at the ID. *First local call, other than the mattress guys...*"Hello?"

"Hi, Tess? This is Alice," said a familiar, peppy voice. "From Doc Harnes office?"

"Oh, hi, Alice. I got into town late last night. It's great so far." *No need to mention the smashing impression I made at the intersection last night.*

Alice had set up her phone interviews. Doc had gone to great lengths to assure himself of Tess's suitability for large animal work in general and rough ranch work in particular, asking complex questions that required detailed technical answers. However, he had provided only cursory information about the town and the practice. Alice filled in all the necessary details, answering questions patiently and thoroughly.

"I heard. I guess you've met Jake?" Alice asked brightly.

"Oh. Yes, I have," Tess winced, thinking of his warm kisses. *Stop that!* She focused on Rhiannon, who was still tearing around, tongue lolling.

"I'm so sorry you got hurt. Everyone in town knows how treacherous that intersection is."

"Thanks." Tess felt her face burn with embarrassment.

"Doc and Bea don't want you to feel pressured about starting work right away, so just plan on taking it easy the next week or so, okay?"

"That's nice, Alice, but I'm really looking forward to getting started," she countered enthusiastically. "Besides, I won't have anything else to do."

"Okay, but I have to tell you, Bea's already heard about the accident. She made an appointment for you with Doc Estes here in town early next week, and she asked if you'd call them tomorrow to check in. Bea's like that. I think you already have Doc's cell and home phone, but I don't want you to feel overwhelmed. Is that okay with you?"

"It's very kind that you're all so concerned. I'm genuinely touched," she answered.

"Can I bring you dinner? I'm solo; my husband Lotts is working tonight. Mamma Boccini's, the Italian place on Main Street, has chicken parmesan on special tonight, and they have a great lasagna."

"Dinner would be great, Alice. I love lasagna."

"I just need to finish here at the office and feed the dogs at home. I'll grab dinner and swing over to your place afterward, okay?"

"That's perfect. I look forward to it, thank you."

"See you in a bit, Tess."

Tess switched off her cell with a rush of gratitude. Snapping Rhiannon on her lead, she smiled as she walked back to her new apartment. *I might just have spoken to my new best friend. . . My hip feels better, and there's time to take a bubble bath in my claw-foot tub!*

At six-fifteen, it was dark outside. Towel-drying her hair, Tess switched the porch light on for Alice and turned up the heat. Fifteen minutes later, a blue Subaru wagon pulled up to the curb, and a petite, curvy woman with short, spiky red hair got out, waving.

"Alice?" she called from the porch, feeling shy.

"Yeah, it's me. Hi!" the woman chirped, popping open her hatchback and pulling out a pair of folding chairs. "I brought along a bistro set I use on the patio in the summertime. Can you use it?"

"I don't have a kitchen table yet, so that will be great!" Tess felt like hugging Alice, but that seemed too familiar yet shaking hands was too formal. *Anyway, she has chairs in her hands.* She grabbed the chairs while Rhiannon tore around her yard. "Meet Rhiannon. I rescued her on my way out here. She's a bit hyper, getting settled in and all."

"Hi, Rhiannon, aren't you a lovely girl?" Alice's voice was high-pitched and chipper, even as Rhiannon thumped against her knees.

In the small, bright kitchen, she set the table up while Tess opened chairs. "Perfect size. Thank you again, Alice."

"My pleasure. And it does look nice," Alice agreed, surveying the little kitchen, her green eyes sparkling. "Welcome to Green Junction, Tess. How are you feeling?"

"A little stiff and sore but really happy to be here. And I'm thrilled to finally to meet you."

"We'll have fun together. Do you like the place?"

"It's awesome!" Tess raved.

"Bea was determined to find you something right in town since winters are so long around here. Both Bea and Doc are really tickled that you came all the way from Philadelphia for a job in Green Junction. Bea keeps calling you 'Our Philadelphia Girl'."

"Oh, golly, how will the locals feel about that?"

"Don't worry, I don't think she'll say it to anyone outside the office. I've been here for over six years, and she still calls me their 'Louisiana Girl'."

"So you are an import, too? That helps," Tess smiled, digging through her bags for a linen table cloth and tossing it on the bistro table.

"Not only am I an import, I'm a Southerner to boot. I dropped the drawl, though, as best I could."

Tess set out the napkins her grandmother had given her, arranging new glasses, plates, and silverware while Alice brought in dinner. "I got cheesecake for dessert. It's homemade on Fridays. And I brought a split of champagne for a housewarming toast and some beer and wine coolers to stock your fridge."

"You didn't have to do that," Tess said, pleased all the same. "Is everyone around here so thoughtful, or did I just strike gold with you and Jake?"

"Well, I promised to keep a look-out for you, kiddo. You're new in town, and I know how that can be," Alice said cheerfully. "But Jake is one of a kind. He's a complete sweetheart, and he's just been through a killer divorce. It's too bad you guys met under such stressful circumstances."

Tess couldn't help blushing.

"Ah, so that's how it is. Well, Jake is the best catch in Green Junction, as far as I'm concerned. I don't think you could do any better here."

"He does seem like a great guy."

Feeling her face flame, Tess popped the champagne cork, pouring bubbly into two glass Denver Broncos mugs from the thrift store. Handing Alice a mug, she said, "Salut. It's so great to have company my first night here."

"To your total and complete success in Green Junction, fabulous times ahead, and a winning season for the Broncos," Alice grinned. They clanked mugs and drank.   Champagne was one of Tess's weaknesses, and from the smell of dinner, Momma Boccini's would soon be another.

*****

To: NBamberger@SKLLaw, RBamberger@RGBLawcom
From: Tess.Bam@vmailcom
Subject: LOVING my new place!
Date: Friday, September 23, 9:14 PM

Dear Mom and Dad,

The bed arrived, and it's super comfy! Thank you, thank you, thank you! Alice, my new friend from work stopped by tonight with takeout, and Bea and Doc have invited us to dinner on Sunday at their place, so my social calendar is already filling up.

My apartment is amazing, so no worries, Mom. It's an old-fashioned Victorian, right in town, with a wide front porch and plenty of gingerbread. I took a hot bubble bath in my claw-foot tub, soaked the kinks out from my long trip, and I'm already online. Mom, thanks so much for suggesting I set up my electric and Internet ahead of time~that was a good call.

Green Junction is a tiny, historic town, surrounded by gorgeous mountains ~ I hope Sam can come out for some skiing this winter. Please give Buster a treat for me. I miss you both, but I am fine.

Love, Tess.

She pressed "Send", shut her laptop and dialed Samantha's cell. *It's only 6:30 in New York. I can't wait to fill Sam in on life in Colorado!*

*****

Jake and Cassie had a standing invitation to Saturday night dinner at Aunt Olivia's stately brick Georgian on Talbot Street. They'd just enjoyed an excellent meal of roast beef, mashed potatoes, and glazed carrots. Jake sat in front of the library fireplace, paging through local newspapers.

Tonight, Cassie had invited her best friend Trudie along. Listening to their chatter, he smiled. The girls were playing in Aunt Olivia's guest room, which was full of things that Cassie and her friends loved; a real china tea set, trunks full of hats and shoes, fancy dress up clothing specially altered for six year olds, and a big old-fashioned dollhouse that had been Aunt Olivia's as a girl.

"No nightcap with friends tonight, Jake?" Olivia asked from the hallway, coming down from getting the girls settled.

"I think I'll stay in, Aunt," he answered, pretending to study the headlines.

Alice was taking Tess to Green Forks tonight to introduce her around. *Best keep my distance for the time being.* He couldn't forget the way she'd felt in his arms, but her welcome had gotten way more involved than he'd intended.

Vicki had never stopped complaining about poky old Green Junction, reminding him what she missed about California. He wouldn't put himself through that. He'd wait to see if Tess made it through winter before kissing her again.

Aunt Olivia brought the silver coffee service in, set it on the little table, and took the sateen damask wingback chair next to him. "We had our Ladies Auxiliary luncheon today. Bea Harnes said the vet they were expecting arrived Thursday night." She handed him a filled cup set in its fancy bone china saucer.

So Tess is a veterinarian. Why hadn't she mentioned what her job was? Two small dessert plates, each with a slice of chocolate layer cake, sat on the tray, dessert forks and napkins at the ready. His aunt handed him a plate, and he took a napkin from the tray. "She's a young woman—a very nice girl from a fine Philadelphia family."

"Really? A lady vet, now that's a first for Green Junction," he mused politely, in the most detached voice he could manage.

"It certainly is. She studied at the University of Pennsylvania. Apparently she's very bright." Aunt Olivia's refined voice warmed with approval. Jake remembered the *Penn* stamped on Tess's white knit pants. *They hugged her firm little butt so nicely.* He put a forkful of cake in his mouth to hide his grin while his aunt continued. "Apparently she smashed her car getting into town, poor thing. Bea doesn't know exactly what happened. I do wish they'd do something about that exit ramp coming off the highway. It's a disgrace how many accidents have happened there."

"It is." He put his cake plate down quickly and picked up the newspaper to hide behind. The baby powder scent of Tess's curly blonde hair came back to him, and blood began to pool in his abdomen. He tried to focus on the article about the new sewer plant improvements.

"Bea got her a place in Elmer Freethy's Victorian over on Chambers Street near Cassie and Vicki. She's already been to the thrift store to outfit her apartment. Gertrude said she was absolutely delightful."

"Hmm, really?" Gertrude was tight-lipped. He was glad she hadn't mentioned he'd been helping Tess.

"Now, she'd be a lovely role model for our Cassie," Aunt Olivia said, plumping the pillow behind her innocently. "Perhaps I'll invite her to join us for dinner next Saturday night. I hate to think of her getting lonely here, not knowing anyone."

Jake lowered the paper, raised his eyebrows, and eye-balled his aunt. Glowering slightly, he warned, "Auntie O, while I appreciate the generous intention of your meddling, you will do no such thing. I can't imagine a more strained attempt at matchmaking than a dinner date with you, Cassie, and the new girl in town." His aunt was a headstrong woman, but she did respect him. "I've already met Tess, and I'll likely be bumping into her again at some point. Meanwhile, Cassie is certain to see her at the veterinary office."

He put his head back behind the newspaper, but not before he caught the gleam in Aunt Olivia's dark, intelligent eyes. "Wonderful!" his aunt enthused. She'd tried her best with Vicki during his marriage, which he'd appreciated, but since the divorce, she'd been dying to pair him off with someone new. Aunt Olivia had discriminating tastes. Much as she schemed, she just hadn't been successful in identifying appropriate prey.

"I'm sure with the social whirlwind you and your lady friends enjoy, you'll meet Tess soon enough," he growled from behind the newspaper. "I'll let you know if things progress to the dinner with family stage."

"Delightful," she trilled. "That's certainly something to look forward to. Make a bit of an effort, Jake, won't you? I'd like to be able to count on having her for dinner before Thanksgiving." He could not miss the unmitigated glee in Olivia's normally regal voice, and he was glad the newspaper hid his grin.

"In the meantime, perhaps I should get Buxie and Susie in for their annual exams," she mused. Aunt Olivia had kept a pair of English Springer Spaniels for as long as Jake could remember.

They ran fat on table scraps. "I'm sure Doc won't mind if the young lady sees them."

"There you go. If I know you, you'll have met Tess before your Wednesday afternoon bridge game." *Hold on to your silver tea set, Auntie. Tess will knock your damask tablecloth sideways.*

*****

Nervous for her first day of work, Tess hustled out to Alice's Subaru wagon on Monday morning, feet crunching through the crust of snow that lay frozen on the ground.

"Morning, Tess. Ooh, that coffee smells good," Alice said, motioning to Tess's raisin toast and travel mug of coffee.

"Thanks for doing this so early," Tess said, trying to stop her teeth from chattering. "I'll bring you some breakfast tomorrow."

"I thought we'd go over some things at the office before Doc comes in so you could get your bearings," she chirped. Tess nodded gratefully.

Pulling onto the street, Alice continued, "On a normal day, Doc comes in at seven-thirty or eight. Small animal office appointments start at nine on weekdays and Saturdays, but he takes emergencies early. After lunch, Doc goes out on farm calls. Sometimes he's out really late, depending on what's happening. Some weeks, you'll have an afternoon or two off, but you could get slammed on weekends. Springtime is lambing and calving, so it's crazy busy around the clock. This year we'll have you around, which will be a big help."

"Okay." Tess clutched her travel mug, "I'm hanging on every word."

"You're a quick study. I got that right away," Alice said with an approving smile.

"I'm really excited to be here. It's fun. Nerve wracking but fun."

"You'll be fine. There's a lot to absorb, so Doc wants us to be careful we don't overwhelm you. You're just supposed to hang out in the office this week, maybe ride with him on a few farm calls if

42

you're feeling up to it, but no pressure… all in good time. Your appointment with Doc Estes is tomorrow. I think Bea mentioned it at dinner last night?"

"She did. Bea and my mother are clones from the same mother cell when it comes to trying to run my life."

"Well, at least you're used to it. Drove me nuts at first, and Bea will probably be worse with you. You're young and single, and she'll rationalize that your mother expects it of her."

"I'm used to meddling."

"I had my share when I first got here. You will rediscover the luxury of anonymity in Green Junction, I assure you. It's a small town, and everyone is in your business. It can be a little intense."

Tess took a deep breath. *Might as well spit it out.* "Doc told me he needed a vet full-time, Alice, but Jake mentioned something about Doc retiring. Doc hasn't said anything to me about retiring."

"Oh, boy, see how the gossip goes around here? Here's the story: Doc was a widower when he married Bea. She was the town librarian, never married. When they got hitched, Doc promised he'd retire in five years. That was twelve years ago. Doc's daughter is in Florida, with his grandkids. He's had a standing invitation to join a small animal practice there part-time. His idea was to bring you on board to see if you like it. If you do, he'll stick around two years or so until you're settled. When you find another vet you both like, he'll hand the practice off to you."

"Really?" The prospect was both exhilarating and completely intimidating.

"I doubt that Doc will say anything about it, at least not for a while, so no worries. He knows your commitment is only until spring, and he wouldn't ever want to pressure you. Doc is close-mouthed and careful, but Bea is the complete opposite. What Doc thinks of as top secret, Bea has shared with the whole town. If anyone asks, you could just say that you are here to help until spring, and Doc hasn't discussed future plans with you."

"Got that. Doc isn't much of a talker, but he is really nice."

"Oh, yeah, Doc is great at what he does, and he's very patient about explanations. Even if you forget and ask the same question twice, he won't mind. He'll go into great detail about animal care, but the other stuff is Bea's department."

"Doc made me want this job, but, honestly, you made me feel like I could do it, Alice," Tess said. "You gave me the courage to make the big leap. I might still be in Philadelphia, bored stiff. This is a whole different world."

"I could tell how competent you'd be right off the bat. We need someone like you here. It will be an adventure, I promise you that." They'd arrived at the low brick building where the veterinary clinic was housed. Alice shut off the engine and turned to her. "There is something I want to ask of you—really for my own sanity, but for all of us, too. Doc is working too hard for a man his age, and Bea will flip if he keeps it up. He can't keep going like this. You might not want to hurt Doc's feelings, but I'm asking you to promise to tell me right away if you realize this isn't the job for you."

"I'm going to love it. I know I will," Tess answered.

"You might, but ranch calls are pig shit and cold weather and biting wind and chapped cheeks and freezing feet. It can be grueling. You'll either like it or hate it; it's as simple as that. The next six months will tell. You have amazing credentials, and you can go anywhere. If this isn't your cup of tea, we can bring someone down from Fort Collins in the spring. I want to be straight with you because you've already taken the leap. This might be the ride of your life, but if you decide you want a different colored parachute, just say the word and I promise to get you out of here gracefully, okay?"

Tess looked at Alice's sober face, appreciating her forthrightness. "I won't bail on you, Alice, but I do get it. I hope I love it. I think I will, but I promise to let you know if I'm not happy."

"Life is too short to be miserable, and you are too talented not to have the exact life you want. It will be challenging as hell when you are up to your ears in cow poop and placenta after your fourth or fifth difficult calving of the day on only two-hours sleep in a month of seventy-five farm calls. You'll know by spring if it works for you." Tess nodded intently, grateful for Alice's comforting smile.

Unlocking the back door, Alice hung their coats. "Welcome to Green Junction Veterinary Clinic, Dr. Bamberger. Let's get you started." She showed Tess through the waiting room and office, into the examining rooms, surgery, infirmary, and dispensary. Tess looked through the set of large-animal surgical tools Doc had ordered for her. "Let us know whatever else you want," Alice called from the reception area.

Doc arrived at eight. He was a large-framed man, very tall, with a furrowed, kindly face, a shock of white hair, and an easygoing manner. "We've got a smooth morning here, Tess. This afternoon I head out to Tarleton's horse farm. There's a two-year old to geld and a pregnant mare to ultrasound. You're welcome to ride along if you're up to it," he offered.

Tess worked with Doc all morning on small animal appointments, becoming increasingly more at ease as the day moved on. He introduced her to his clients, and she observed as he checked for ear mites, inoculated six-week old puppies, advised diet changes for a pair of overweight schnauzers, and adjusted medication on an elderly cat with a heart condition. Then she helped Alice with blood work, familiarizing herself with the lab.

Bea bustled in at eleven-thirty, beaming. "I brought cheese steaks, in honor of our Philadelphia Girl's first day!" As Bea began fussing over her, Alice shot Tess a knowing look. She helped Tess fill out paperwork, and they ate lunch at the table in the dispensary.

Afterwards, she rode with Doc west out of town in his big white truck. "A four wheel drive truck is a good idea," Doc said, his large frame filling the seat next to her. "If you find one you like, the practice will buy you a tool box for it and tires for the winter. Make sure to keep plenty of weight in the back. I use sand bags." Tess nodded nervously, her headache still a dull twinge. *There is so much to learn here.*

The Tarleton horse farm was a beautiful modern facility, with a large indoor arena and acres of rolling pasture. Snow was slowly melting in early afternoon sun. Doc introduced Sherri Tarleton, a petite woman with chapped cheeks, a pouf of strawberry blonde hair held in a barrette, and an earthy laugh.

Sherri nodded appreciatively as she took Tess's hand. "So pleased to meet you, Dr. Bamberger. I'm so glad Doc Harnes finally has back up. You've come from New Bolton?" Tess nodded. "That's as good an equine care facility as exists. Warm welcome to Green Junction. I've got a pair of sons who will be happy to know that you're in town, too."

"Thank you," Tess blushed. "It's lovely to meet you."

Sherri led her mare into the aisle, talking local horse gossip with Doc while Tess set up the ultrasound equipment. Donning a plastic glove, she got to work.

"There it is," Doc said when the tiny equine fetus appeared on the monitor. "Nice work, Tess. Looks like your mare's bred, then, Sherri. She's two months along. Come May, she'll throw a fine foal."

Next, Sherri led them to the young colt's stall, and Tess assisted with the gelding. Doc offered encouragement as she moved around the horse, injecting the sedative and suturing the incision. She felt calm and confident working with him, pleased by his obvious satisfaction in her work.

4

"Cowboy Take Me Away"

On Tuesday morning, Jake pulled his truck into a parking space at the medical plaza, his neck and back stiff and sore, and headed into Doc Estes' office.

As he stepped up to the registration desk, a blond, curly-haired woman in an Irish wool sweater spoke animatedly to the nurse as she stepped backwards. Turning abruptly, she bounced against his chest. At his nose was a pile of corkscrew curls, all baby powder and lemony scented. "Tess?"

"Jake!" A blush spread across Tess's face. "Hi. Sorry about that."

"I can't get away from you, can I?" He tried to laugh it off, but his attraction to her caught him and a curl of desire welled in his belly.

"I guess not," she said with a puzzled look, taking a seat along the back wall.

Jake gave his name to the receptionist. He took a seat far enough away to resist Tess's allure, but close enough to be sociable. "So why didn't you tell me you were a vet?"

Glancing over with a shy smile, she lowered her magazine and tucked a lock of hair behind her ear. "I didn't want it to get around that the new vet was a city brat who couldn't drive in bad weather," she whispered.

"You were in a rental car with bad tires, Tess. Everybody around here knows that exit ramp is a death trap once it gets cold. It's the most dangerous spot in town."

"So, how are you feeling? Are you all right?" she asked, concern in her voice. She gave him a smile, open and inviting—and just a little bit curious.

Staying casual, he picked up a six-month-old copy of *Field and Stream.* "I'm fine. I'm just here for x-rays. I have this thing with a

disc; my back gets stiff. Too much rodeo-ing in my younger days."
He shifted in his chair. His brain may have decided to avoid
entanglements, but his body wasn't cooperating in the least.
"How's Alice?"

"She's great. I started at the clinic yesterday. I was there this
morning, too. I really like it. Doc's so great. He gave me the rest of
the day off, but I'll probably go back later, learn more about how
the office works." Her face glowed with enthusiasm.

He could not banish the memory of kissing her, and the curl of
desire intensified. *I am such a fool.*

"I got the notice about a presentation on freeze branding at the
Rancher's Alliance meeting on Monday. Looks like you'll be
giving it. Good for you, jumping right in."

"Oh, right," Tess blushed. "With Ron. It's just a PowerPoint
the Ag Department puts out. Doc asked me to do it. Honestly, I'm a
little nervous about it. I don't know where the Grange is, and I
haven't done all that much freeze branding."

"Just outside of town. Doc will show you. Don't worry, you'll
be fine. It's not a tough crowd."

"We missed you Saturday night at Green Forks."

"Yeah, busy weekend," he said nonchalantly, trying to focus on
the elk hunting article. Just as he'd adjusted to the sensations in his
torso, a wave of longing crossed his chest.   *What is it about her,
anyway?* He'd been out of circulation for a long time, not meeting
anyone new. Tess was pretty, but he'd always dated pretty women.
He shifted in his chair, relieved when the nurse finally called her
name and she went in the back.

She came out a few minutes later, signing something at the
desk. "What's happening with that Tacoma Lotts found for you?"
he asked from across the room.

"How do you know about my Tacoma?" She moved towards
him, pink chapped lips smiling, brow furrowed.

"It's a small town, Crash. I was at the bar Sunday night, and
Lotts filled me in. I know the guy who's selling it, Aaron. His
brother left town for a sales job in Atlanta. He left the truck for
Aaron to deal with."

"Well, you know lots more than I do. I haven't seen it yet. I'll have Dave check it out before I buy it like you suggested, though."

"Good girl."

"You saved my butt last week, Jake, and you and Cassie got me pizza. I owe you lunch." Her big blue eyes danced invitingly.

"You don't owe me lunch, Tess. I smashed into you, remember? You still have my number?"

"In my cell," she waved the phone.

"Call if you need anything," he said, eyeing her over the top of the magazine.

Pulling a down vest off the coat tree, she eyed him quizzically. "Okay."

She waved as she stepped through the door. Relieved, he settled back in the chair, trying to convince himself he was right to have turned her down for lunch. *There's no way I will have it this bad for her the next time I see her.*

*****

Tess walked home from the doctor's office, trying to brush off hurt feelings. The weather matched her mood: damp, grey and chilly. *Why wouldn't he get lunch with me?*

Morning frost had turned to midday haze, and the temperature hovered at the freezing mark. The sidewalks were slippery, and the cold air made her head pound. *Ugh, have I made a fool of myself already?*

As she walked towards Mamma Boccini's, homey smells of yeast and tomato paste, warm and familiar, grabbed her from the street. She ordered a slice and a soda, and took them to a small table. There, gooey flavors of mozzarella, salty, tangy prosciutto, basil and spinach boosted her spirits.

At home, Rhiannon was waiting. Tess took her for a long walk. Then, unable to resist the lure of lavender polka dot flannel, she crawled beneath the covers. At half-past two, her cell buzzed, startling her awake.

"Hi, Tess! Lotts called. Aaron can bring the Tacoma down today, if you want," Alice chirped. "Doc will be here, too. I can come get you anytime."

"Thanks." She felt a rush of gratitude for Alice. She already felt like family.

"So what did Doc Estes say?" Alice asked when she pulled to the curb an hour later.

"Not much, it's just a strain. She suggested the chiropractor."

Alice nodded. They drove in silence, the radio playing softly.

"Jake was there," Tess blurted. "I bumped into him in the reception area, like a total dork. He wouldn't get pizza with me, but he said to call if I needed anything. I don't get it. Maybe he just feels guilty about the accident?"

Alice shot her a look of sympathy. "Oh, honey, I don't think it's that."

"What else could it be?"

"I think he's scared," Alice said, braking at a stop sign.

"Really? I just didn't want to eat by myself." *Well, more kissing would be nice, too.* "You're certain he doesn't have a girlfriend?"

Alice shook her head. "There's nobody else, I'm positive. Jake falls kind of easily, and I'll bet he's already a little head-over-heels for you. He got burned so badly in his divorce, he most likely feels safest keeping his distance. Lotts told me he's always asking for you."

Tess remembered how he'd been in the diner. *Shy and a little nervous.* The idea that she'd scared him off made her face burn. But then she thought of when he'd touched her. *He hadn't been scared then. Or shy. At all.* "You said he was the best catch in town, Alice."

Alice's eyes were understanding. "He is. But just take it easy and give him some time. I'll teach you billing codes when we get back to the office, okay?"

"Oh, billing codes? That should get my mind off Jake," she laughed.

*****

50

Dear Mom and Dad,

I looked at a pickup truck today: It's everything I need, four wheel drive, high off the ground, less than fifty thousand miles, and really nice inside. Doc Harnes offered to buy a toolbox for the back and put new snow tires on it for me. It has heated seats, so I'll be set for the winter. Once I have a truck, I can start doing farm calls on my own, so I really hope this is the one. The mechanic checks it out tomorrow.

I'm taking small animal visits at the clinic alone now, and I've gone out on a few farm calls with Doc. Work outside the clinic setting is challenging, but Alice is a huge help, and I'm learning so much.

It's already cold here, and it snows a little bit every night, just an inch or two. I set up firewood delivery for next week. I'm glad I brought those insulated coveralls along. I know how you love those, Mom. Besides being a total fashion statement, they are super warm.

Mom, if you can mail the rest of my winter clothes that would be great. Hug Grandma for me~ I called and told her about Mamma Boccini's. Knowing how much I like to cook, she's glad someone is feeding me ~

Love you both Oodles, Your girl, Tess

*****

Friday morning, Tess worked in the clinic, and her afternoon ranch calls lasted well past dark. Tired, dirty and still in the mountains, she was heading for home when her cell buzzed.

"Hey, bet there's a hungry vet heading towards town about now," Alice's voice called cheerfully. "I just called Mamma's. Eggplant parmesan on special, and fresh napoleons for dessert. How about I bring dinner over to your place?"

"Homemade napoleons in Green Junction, Colorado? Yum, *mia nonna bella* will be so happy for me."

"You have an Italian grandmother?"

"Nonna Maggie. Northern Italian. She lives in South Philly, in the house where my mom grew up. Every Sunday, she takes the train from the city to make us dinner, lamb or beef or veal, homemade pasta and her own gravy. It's a tradition."

"Hmm, just like our Friday night dinners, from Momma's," Alice teased.

"I'm always one for tradition," she giggled.

Alice arrived with dinner as Tess was kicking off her boots and dirty coveralls. "Wow, it smells like heaven. You and Mia Nonna, si così generoso! You both feed me," she laughed, grabbing silverware and napkins from the drawers.

"Nonna Maggie sounds like my kinda girl," Alice answered, sorting through the bags on the counter.

"I adore her. My table cloth and napkins are from her hope chest, from the old country, and Nonna Maggie made the quilt on my bed. She makes fresh mozzarella and grows herbs in tubs in her little garden. I hope she can come visit next summer, with my parents. She'd love to meet you."

Steam escaped from the containers Alice was opening. "Oh, before I forget: Jackalope dinner, next month at the high school, Doc and Bea's treat."

Tess dished up dinner, handing Alice a plate of eggplant and chicken. "Jack-a-what? I thought Trick or Treat was next?"

Alice laughed as she sat down. "It is. A Jackalope is a mythic creature: a jackrabbit with antlers. The taxidermists make them up around here as a gag. There's one down at the bar, I'll show it to you. They do fundraising dinners with game dishes, elk, antelope, rabbit, and so on, and call them Jackalope dinners. Rotary is hosting. The whole town will be there. Doc and Bea are excited about introducing you to everyone."

"Bea's not wearing a costume, is she?" Tess asked, grabbing Pellegrino from the fridge and pouring it into the glasses Alice had set on the table.

"Nope, that's the Hallowe'en Dance at the Elks Club," Alice said patiently. "That's the last Saturday in October, three weeks away. Better put that one on your social calendar, too. We'll need to come up with costumes."

Tess put a fork loaded with chicken and eggplant in her mouth. "Yum, will the food at the Jackalope be this good?"

"Well, I'm not a big game eater, so I pretty much stick to the smoked trout and wild rice, but you can try rattlesnake jerky if you want," Alice offered diplomatically, digging into her salad.

"Rattlesnake jerky?" Wrinkling her nose, Tess shrugged. "When in Rome, I suppose. I should probably give it a shot. It'll give me something to talk about with the ranchers."

They ate the better part of dinner silently, enjoying the food. Finally, Tess pushed her plate back. "I was hungry. I start running again tomorrow, now that my hip is better."

"Has Cassie stopped by?"

Tess smiled. "She was here yesterday. We looked at my vet books and I made her a root beer float. It's clear her dad adores her, but I get the feeling she doesn't get much attention from her mom. She's such a great kid. Next time, I want to take her to the library, but I can't figure out if I should ask her mom. I don't want it to seem like I don't think she's doing her job."

"Mmm," Alice said noncommittally. "This is Vicki's weekend, so we'll probably see Cassie at the clinic tomorrow. Did you set up your bank account?"

"What?"

"Your bank account. Did you set one up here in Green Junction yet?"

"I get my first paycheck next week, I'll do it then. Why?"

"Vicki's the manager at the branch near the shopping plaza. Avoid it. She knows that Cassie and Jake helped you move in, and she's got you marked. She can be lethal."

Tess got up to make coffee. "Are you kidding me? What problem could Vicki possibly have with me? We're neighbors. Cassie stops by to visit like it's nothing."

"Green Forks Ladies night was Tuesday." Alice set the new pickaxe cups and saucers on the table with the sugar bowl. "Twice a month, mixed drinks two dollars. Lotts usually works. As you can imagine, he's much more patient with the single girls than I am. He wasn't feeling well, so I covered the bar. Vicki came in with a bunch of friends. She knows we work together. You'd think she'd appreciate the time her kid spends at the office with us and play nice, especially since she's Bea's niece, but that's not Vicki. I heard much more than I wanted to know, Tess. I'm telling you, open your account on Main Street. Out of sight, out of mind. You don't want to give her any ammunition."

"Thank you for that. It's sad for Cassie, though. Was her mother always this way?" Tess asked, pouring fresh coffee.

"Vicki? I wish I had something nice to say, but Vicki is just miserable as far as I can tell. I've only been around since right after Cassie was born, but best I can figure, she took Jake for all she could get from the start. The worse it got at home, the more Lotts and I saw of him at the tavern." Alice poured milk and sugar in her coffee and stirred. "The custody situation with Cassie just tore him apart, but things seem to have settled down in the last six months." Flashing a devilish grin, Alice said, "Jake usually stops in Friday nights around seven-thirty when Cassie's at her mom's, for a beer with Lotts. Let's head to Green Forks after dinner."

"Oh, to add fuel to the fire?" Tess rolled her eyes. "I'm not even sure I should make the effort, Alice. He hasn't called."

Alice sipped her coffee. "Hey, Doc made me promise to do what I could to keep you around. I take my work seriously, and Jake's the best Green Junction has to offer." Then, at the look on Tess's face, she said gently, "He'll come around, don't worry. This coffee is great."

54

"My sister sent fresh roasted beans and a grinder from New York as a housewarming gift. I'll give you some to take home. Lotts will love it."

*****

On Monday afternoon, Doc introduced Tess at the regular business meeting of the Rancher's Alliance. The crowd of more than two dozen ranchers included two female sheep ranchers and a woman who raised dairy goats.

After chatting with everyone and listening politely through the meeting, Tess faced the room, nervously narrating a PowerPoint presentation on freeze branding. Jake stood in the back, as appealing and friendly as he'd been at Green Forks on Friday night. He gave her a big smile of encouragement when she began, but by the time Ron had circulated the sign-up sheet for an on-ranch demonstration, he'd disappeared.

I have to just forget him. Ignoring a stab of disappointment, Tess packed up the projection equipment and carried it to Ron's truck.

"You did a nice job with that presentation," Doc said afterward over coffee at the diner.

"Thanks, Doc. It was great to meet the ranchers. I don't have much experience with an actual branding operation, so it was a relief that the questions were easy."

"You can get practical experience this week if you want it. Jake McGreer has some late season calves he's branding on Thursday. He'd like you to stop by, if you're interested. You can learn the technique he uses now, before the spring rush. You been over to his place?" Doc asked in his now familiar laconic drawl. She shook her head. "You'll see the very best procedures. He runs a clean, professional operation."

"I thought he didn't sign up because he wasn't interested in freeze branding."

"The McGreers have been freeze branding for ten, twelve years, at least. His dad always had a real forward thinking, independent streak, and from the looks of things, Jake's following suit. They're both smart men and damn hard workers. No one at the place works like Jake. That is the way it is with most of the successful ranchers around here, you'll find. It's six, seven days a week, easy," he said.

"Thanks for suggesting it, Doc, I'll definitely go. It'll be great to see a real operation in full swing so I'm ready for calving season in spring."

"Good for you. Every bit of experience helps," Doc said approvingly, putting a five on the table.

*****

Thursday morning, long before dawn, Tess dressed in work clothes, warmed up her new maroon pickup, and got on the road, arriving at the gates of the McGreer Ranch at quarter after six.

Her headlights caused sparkling in the pasture stretched out on either side of the driveway. There had been a light dusting of new snow in town, but up in the mountains, four inches of heavy, slippery snowfall lay across the driveway. She slipped the truck into four wheel drive, took a deep breath, and started down the snowy lane.

Just as Alice said it would, the road forked, with a big hay barn to the right. As she drove over a knoll, Rhiannon barked excitedly. Ahead, young cattle milled in portable pens, bawling in the early light. Two men tossed them flakes of alfalfa.

This is it.

Feeling out of place, she got of the truck to a biting wind. Jake's truck pulled up, and she swallowed hard, uncertain about seeing him on his home turf. *I just hope he doesn't make any more city girl comments.*

*****

In the half-light before dawn, Jake surveyed Tess's heavy work jacket, shapeless insulated overalls, and tall pack boots. Her curls
56

were pulled back into a braid that fell down her back. Unable to keep from smiling, he handed her a travel mug of coffee. "Welcome. Are you warm enough?"

"Once I start moving I will be," she answered cheerfully. Pink light brightened the eastern sky, and in the cold, her blue eyes shimmered. Curls escaped her fuzzy sky-blue wool cap, framing her cheeks. *Angel in coveralls. And still too damned cute. Maybe I'll just have to get used to it.*

"We'll start the calves through the crush shortly. We de-horn and brand heifers first, and we'll castrate the steers after lunch. You can try all the jobs if you want. That's what Doc sent you here for, right, to see how this is done?"

"He spoke highly of your operation. I want to understand all of it before spring," she said politely, stamping her feet to warm up. "I've never seen this done on a large scale."

"Ah, not much to it; it's routine ranch work. You'll get the hang of it in no time. Feel free to warm up in my truck anytime. There's a special heater in my cab." She returned his smile with less sparkle than he remembered, and he felt guilty about kissing her and not calling. *At least she doesn't hold a grudge.*

At the pens, he introduced Larry and Ralph. "You want to let Rhiannon out, see if she'll tag behind Van and learn how to round up cattle?"

"Sure, if you want to give it a try. Let me know if she gets in the way, though."

"We'll know soon enough."

The sun was rising as Ralph guided Tess through the de-horning process. Van helped Jake rally the heifers into the crush, with Rhiannon tagging behind. While Tess de-horned, Ralph and another helper did the freeze branding. Freeze branding was annoying to the animal but not painful, and far more humane than the old electric heat branding.

Larry took the young heifers down the chute afterward, opening the gate to let them graze in the pasture. By eight-thirty, the sun had burned through the cloud cover, and the snow began to melt.

"You cold?" Jake asked her.

"Not so bad."

"You can sit in the truck a few minutes, warm up," he offered, wishing she would.

"I'm okay, thanks," she answered.

At mid-morning, with everything going smoothly, he asked Tess if she wanted to switch places. Jake clipped, swabbed with alcohol, and held the timer, while Tess did the branding. He admired the way she worked with the animals, confident and unobtrusive, smooth and neat and efficient with the equipment. *She'll make it to spring, anyway.* The thought cheered him.

By noon, they'd finished all the heifers. The temperature had climbed to the mid-forties, and sunshine melted the snow. "Tilda has lunch fixed at the house. If you head over with me, Tess, I'll show you the ranch."

She nodded, so he whistled for the dogs. Van jumped in the bed of his truck eagerly, grinning his dog grin, with Rhiannon right behind, muddy from work.

Tess climbed into his warm cab and took her jacket off. "How long has your family been here?" she asked, smacking her lips with bee balm.

Distracted, he put the truck in low gear, starting up the muddy roads before answering. "My great-great grandfather got the original ranch in the 1880s, from a gold-miner who'd lost his family to typhoid, adding more land as others abandoned their sections. The McGreer family has been ranching here ever since, gradually adding land as it became available." He started towards the house, taking the long route. "The utility company was going to charge an arm and a leg to run electric out here back in the forties, so Grand-dad stuck with water and wind power. Pops was never too keen on the utility companies either, so the ranch has always been off the grid. We have a windmill, and the creek's been dammed for water power since the twenties."

"Hmm, forward thinking ancestors," Tess commented.

"They were independent. They just figured out how to fend for themselves, being so far out of town during the Depression, then

World War Two, when everything was rationed." He pointed to the low glass houses behind the ranch house. "These were my Gran's greenhouses. Tilda and Aunt Olivia keep them going year-round with help from the ranch hands when I can spare them. You ready for lunch?"

"I am hungry," she nodded, looking across the pastures, to the mountains. "Your place is so interesting, though. It's really beautiful out here, Jake."

"I think so. I'll take you to the creek on horseback next time, show you the dam, but for now, let's get something to eat."

She followed him into the house through the back door. They kicked their boots off and hung outerwear in the mudroom. Under his overalls he wore jeans, but Tess's legs were clad in fleece tights, and she wore a fuzzy blue turtleneck, and bulky wool socks.

Working in the cold with the animals, he could pretend she was one of the guys, but back in close quarters, he felt that undeniable pull again. *Oh, hell. Who am I fooling? She's more irresistible than ever.*

*****

Tess followed Jake into the red-tiled kitchen, where a paisley-aproned woman was preparing lunch at a six burner gas stove. "Tilda, this is Dr. Bamberger, Tess. She came out today to help with branding."

"So you're the new vet in town. Nice to meet you, Tess." Tilda squeezed her hand, smiling warmly. She had a weathered, pleasant face, and sparkling grey eyes. Her black hair, worn in braids pinned over her head, was tinged with silver. On her feet were beaded moccasins, and her apron covered a calico prairie skirt. "I've got lunch set up in the dining room. The others are in there waiting. There's a big green salad and plenty of chili. Help yourself."

"Thanks, Tilda." Tess smiled.

She wasn't at all surprised to find Jake's house roomy and rambling, tastefully decorated with expensive things. He led her through a butler's pantry to a big rectangular table in a sunlit dining room where Larry and Ralph were already seated. A wall of windows faced the mountains. She glanced up at exposed beams, a sloped ceiling, and an elaborate, hand-crafted copper chandelier. *Why is it that everything about him is both understated and larger than life?*

Jake held out a chair, seating her in front of a plated salad set on a brightly woven placemat. He poured them all ice water then dished her a big bowl of chili and took the chair next to her.

From across the table, Larry passed a basket of corn chips and a bowl of shredded cheddar cheese. Ralph nudged a jar of chilies and a bowl of guacamole her way. Tilda set a pitcher of milk and an insulated carafe of hot coffee on the table and sat down to join them.

The large room was full of western art: framed landscape paintings of the high plains and mountains, a bronze Remington horse and rider sculpture, a stretched leather hide etched with images of buffalo and Sioux hunters, woven baskets, and clay pots.

Through a set of wide French doors to the right, she saw a giant stone fireplace. Flanked by book shelves, it filled the entire far wall of a vaulted great room. In front of the fireplace, a colorful, woven Navajo wool rug was framed by comfy leather couches.

Fascinated, Tess sat quietly, eating, looking around, and listening to the ranch talk. After they'd eaten, she helped clear the table, thanked Tilda for lunch, and followed Jake into the mud room.

"You want to stay here, rest a little while?" he offered quietly. "We started so early this morning, you must be tired. Why don't you take coffee into the living room and just relax for the afternoon while we finish up? I can light a fire for you."

Pleased, she tried not to read too much into the offer. "That's really thoughtful, but I feel like I should get back to work. Maybe another time, okay?"

Back at the crush, Rhiannon was getting the hang of herding. Jake had taught her the same commands he used with Van. By two o'clock, they'd castrated most of the steer. Jake turned to her.

"You've seen enough of this to last you, I imagine. We've only got another hour here. I hate to tie you up. It's been a long day, and you've worked all this week already. Don't you want to get going?"

"Honestly, if I get an emergency, it's probably closer for me to take it from here, Jake. Doc's had me on call since noon. I really don't mind sticking around, unless I'm in the way. Alice said she'd page me if Doc needed anything."

He smiled at her, his dark eyes glowing. "That's fine, Tess. Cassie will be here soon. I know she'd like to see you."

5

"Crashing Into Tess"

An hour later, Tess watched Jake walk to the door of the old woody-sided Wagoneer she'd seen parked at the house. Cassie hopped out and waved to Tilda as the jeep pulled away. They walked towards her, hand-in-hand.

"Sorry I wasn't there to pick you up after school today, Cass," she heard Jake say.

"That's okay; Tilda brought me oatmeal raisin cookies and a thermos of cider for a snack. We brought some for you, too, Daddy. Can I ride Sparky? I don't have much homework, and I haven't been on him since Sunday."

Jake tugged one of his daughter's braids. "It'll be a little while until I can help you today, hon. We have to finish this branding."

Recognizing Tess in her shapeless overalls, Cassie said "Hey, Dr. Tess is here! Hi, Dr. Tess!"

"Hi, Cassie," Tess said brightly, "Bet you didn't expect to see me here, huh?"

"No, but I'm really glad you surprised me!" Cassie hugged her, offering a cookie.

"Oatmeal raisin, yum. Thanks, Cass," Tess said, squeezing the little girl's shoulder.

"Where's Rhiannon?" Cassie asked.

"She ran off with Van." Jake grabbed two cookies from the bag.

"So, Dr. Tess, after we looked at your books last week, I decided I want to be a vet when I grow up. I'm already good at helping out at the clinic, and the blood stuff doesn't bother me at all. Did you work really hard in school?" Cassie asked, munching a cookie.

"I did," Tess nodded, brushing a crumb from her chin. "Grade school and high school and four years of college and then four more years of vet school. Twenty years of studying and tests, Cass, but here I am."

"Wow, twenty years? I'm only six. That's a really long time to be in school. Can I show Dr. Tess Sparky, Daddy?" Cassie asked.

"Well, that's up to Dr. Tess," Jake said, glancing at Tess.

"Sparky is my pony, Dr. Tess. You really have got to see him. I got him last year. Sherri Tarleton helped Daddy find him. Even she likes him, and she's really picky," Cassie explained proudly.

"I'd love to meet Sparky, Cass," Tess said.

"You're sure you don't mind?" Jake looked a little skeptical.

"Mind? Not at all. Cassie and I will have a blast," she answered.

"We get along great, Dad," Cassie added assuredly, taking Tess's hand. "I stop by her place sometimes, when my mom wants a rest. I like Alice a lot, but Tess is my favorite grown up friend."

Jake grinned. "Okay, Cass, since Dr. Tess is willing to tag along and keep an eye on you, you can get Sparky out of the paddock and groom him and tack up. I'll be up when we finish here," he said, shooting Tess a grateful smile.

"I'll show you to the horse barn, Dr. Tess," Cassie offered, tugging her hand. "Let's take your new truck. I really like the color."

The horse barn was fancier than Tess expected, as nice as the Tarleton's, but smaller, with just twelve stalls. A grey pony and a larger taffy-colored palomino shared the fenced paddock closest to the barn. A chestnut, three bays, a pinto, and two appaloosas grazed further off.

Cassie led her into the tack room, grabbing lead ropes for the ponies. "I'm in Pony Club, and I'm learning to barrel race," she said proudly. "My dad teaches me how to ride. The grey pony is Sparky."

"Sparky is a pretty pony, Cassie." Tess held the gate as the little girl clipped the lead shank on him. "You're so lucky. I wanted a pony more than anything when I was your age."

Cassie halted Sparky in front of her, letting Tess scratch his forehead. As she admired his dishy face, tight little tummy and sturdy legs, Van and Rhiannon darted up, tails wagging.

"You can get the palomino, Dr. Tess. His name is Butterscotch. My dad got him for my mom a long time ago, but she doesn't really like horses. You could ride Butterscotch if you wanted. We could take a trail ride together."

Tess clipped the lead shank on Butterscotch and followed Cassie through the gate and up to the barn. "We'd have to ask your dad first, but I hope we can Cass, that sounds like fun."

"Sometimes Pony Club meets here, and we all ride out to the creek for a picnic. My dad comes along. We'll do that in the spring, again, I'll bet. Most days my dad doesn't have time for a trail ride, so I just ride here in the ring and around the barn. Butterscotch's stall is on the left," Cassie said, expertly turning Sparky into a grooming stall and clipping him in cross ties.

She came out of the tack room with a carryall filled with brushes, currycomb, and a hoof pick. "You can visit with me, or groom Butterscotch, whatever you'd like, Dr. Tess," Cassie offered politely.

"Oh, you know I like visiting with you. I'll groom Butterscotch later."

Tess watched Cassie move around the pony, currying and brushing his coat then picking his hooves. She chattered the whole time about her friends, school, Aunt Olivia's dollhouse, the soccer team she'd played on over the summer, and the books they'd get from the library. When she was finished grooming, she turned to Tess. "My dad usually helps with my saddle. It's kind of heavy," she said, wrinkling her nose.

Tess followed her to the tack room, which was spotless. Saddle racks lined the back and side walls, and bridles hung on hooks in a neat row. Shelves and cubbies above held liniments and incidentals. Cassie found her saddle pad and took Sparky's bridle off a low hook while Tess grabbed the small western saddle and cinch that Cassie pointed out.

Jake came striding through the big barn door then, the late afternoon sun shining brightly behind his broad shoulders. "Look at the two of you!" he exclaimed, pressing a big, muscular hand against the tack room door jamb. He shot Tess a broad smile, and she felt her heart lurch. *Why does he have to be so darn good looking?*

Cassie put the saddle pad on Sparky, and Tess helped with the saddle and cinch. Jake stood back, watching with appreciative eyes. "Dr. Tess helped with Butterscotch, too, Dad. She's real good around horses. I'm going to do the bridle myself, unless he acts up," Cassie said determinedly.

"Okay," her dad nodded. "Have you guys seen the dogs?"

"They followed us over here. I guess they're around somewhere," Tess told him.

"Van was sniffing Rhiannon, Daddy, then they were dancing down by the pasture when we brought the horses in," Cassie said.

"Dancing?" Jake glanced at Tess. Shrugging, she walked out to the pasture, calling for Rhiannon.

*****

Jake followed Tess out of the barn, whistling for the dogs. The sun was a blazing ball of orange now, dropping into the western sky. It was getting dark earlier, but tonight, the air was still warm. Standing next to her, he asked, "Do you have plans for dinner, Tess?"

"Not tonight," she smiled.

"I take Cassie back to her mom's at seven. Want to grab a burger at Green Forks with me afterward?"

"Sure, Jake, thanks." She flashed him an easy smile. The dogs ran up then, panting.

"Thanks for all your help here today," he said, as Tess walked with him back to the barn.

"Sure thing. It was a great experience. I learned a lot."

"You ready to take off?"

"I think Cassie wants me to watch her ride."

"She does likes an audience," he admitted. "I really appreciate the interest you've taken in her, Tess. She mentioned that she stops by your place sometimes. I hope that's okay. You'd let me know if it was an imposition, right?"

"Cassie's good company, Jake. I enjoy spending time with her, and she's really something with animals. I've never seen a kid handle a pony as naturally as she does. Nothing fazes her."

"Wait until you see her ride," he grinned.

Carrying two folding chairs from the tack room, he followed as Cassie led Sparky into the corral, brushing dust from the chair seats before Tess sat down then giving Cassie a leg up.

After she put the pony on the rail at a brisk walk, he took the chair next to Tess. Quietly, he said, "I don't let on to Cassie, but Sparky behaves better when I'm in the ring. He was pretty frisky last time she rode." He watched as Cassie picked up a jog. "Lookin' good, Cass," he called, "Keep a leg on him so he doesn't scoot sideways." Turning to Tess, he asked, "Do you ride?"

Tess kept her eyes on Cassie as she jogged across the diagonal. "As a kid, I bugged my parents for a pony relentlessly. They finally let me start lessons in fourth grade. When I was twelve, I talked them into leasing a hunter for me, a thoroughbred gelding, fifteen-and-a-half hands. I showed in my teens—not the A circuit, just with a group of kids at the local hunter shows in Chester County. I was on the equine team in college and did some eventing throughout vet school."

"So you are an equestrian," he said approvingly.

"I guess you could say that," Tess answered, shrugging. "It's a loaded term. You always want to be a better rider, wish you had more experience. I didn't come from a horsey family, so that was a disadvantage."

Cassie legged Sparky nicely into the corner, picked up a little lope, and made an even, tight circle. "Wow, Cassie, you are amazing!" Tess called, her face radiant. She turned to him. "What about you and horses, Jake?"

"Well, you could say my family was horsey, though I wasn't coddled. I grew up handling horses of all kinds, the mean ones, the ugly ones, and the sweet-tempered ones. By the time I was fourteen, I'd saved enough for a good broodmare, and my dad let me start breeding Quarter Horses. I rodeoed as a kid and broke two-year olds through high school and college for extra cash. I got my business degree from Colorado State but came right back here after college. My heart has always been on the ranch, and I've never really strayed."

"I can see why," Tess said. "This is a great place. I'd have killed to spend summers here when I was Cassie's age."

He had no trouble imagining Tess at McGreer Ranch during summertime. "We have a pool out behind the house. You can bring your suit and swim whenever you want next summer, if you're still around. Alice does. We like the company. And you must miss riding. You can hop on my horses anytime. They're all sound and safe. Just let me know you're here."

"I do miss it, so thank you. I figured once I got settled, I might start riding for real again."

"Sherri Tarleton has some nice hunters, and a big indoor arena. She rides all winter. We get a lot of snow up here, but it doesn't usually stay that cold. Mine are all Quarter Horses, so they don't mind a trail ride in the snow. In fact, it suits them. I can teach you how run barrels or to rope and cut, if you want."

"That would be a blast," Tess nodded, her eyes still on Cassie and the pony. Cassie switched directions at the lope. "Sparky does flying lead changes?"

"I'm a sucker for horses in general, but my kid brings out the worst in me," Jake admitted under his breath. "Sherri Tarleton found him. He cost a bundle, but he's worth it. Sparky jumps, too. Did you see the little English saddle in the tack room?"

"I did. I'm super jealous. Cassie is going to be some rider, if she sticks with it."

Cassie brought Sparky back to a jog, circling in front of them, then stopped. "Daddy, I'm getting tired of all this ring stuff. Why don't you and Dr. Tess tack up, and we can take a trail ride? Dr. Tess should ride Butterscotch. He's lonely. Nobody ever rides him. I bet she'd like to see the ranch and the view from the ridge."

Cassie was persuasive, and she sure knew how to charm him. It was hard to be practical now that he saw so little of her. "That's a nice idea, Cassie. Maybe we'll plan that for another time. It's going to be dark soon. You have homework, right?"

"Yes, unfortunately," Cassie said, with great emphasis.

"Ah, watch it. Dr. Tess is here. Don't you remember hearing how hard she worked in school? That meant homework, too. Didn't it, Dr. Tess?"

"It did. You've got to balance work and play, Cassie. It's tough sometimes," Tess said, giving her an encouraging smile.

"I'll set up a few barrels. You can run them while I get the horses in and fed then it's time to get over to the house and buckle down," Jake said, turning to Tess. "You still want to stick around?"

"I can't miss the barrel race," she smiled, her blue eyes dancing. He handed Tess a stopwatch, paced off and set up three barrels, and then went for the horses.

Tess stayed with Cassie as she ran the barrels. Leading the horses in, he watched them whooping and carrying on. While he was haying, Cassie groomed Sparky and Tess groomed Butterscotch, and they chatted the entire time.

He couldn't help smiling as he hosed the dogs down in the heated wash stall and started Tess's truck. When Tess said goodbye, Cassie hugged her slim waist and looked up at her beseechingly. "Thanks, Dr. Tess. We've got to ride together soon, okay?"

"Sure, Cass," she said, touching his daughter's head. Their faces glowed. *They sure have some connection.*

"Thanks for keeping an eye on Cassie," he said intently, walking her to her truck.

"It was fun, Jake. I like kids, and kids and ponies are even better. Cassie's a real gem."

"Well, I think so, and she's got a real soft spot for you. I'm just sorry we're only having burgers for dinner. You want Mamma Boccini's instead?"

"I like Green Fork's burgers, and it will be fun to see Alice and Lotts."

68

"I'll cook next time. After our trail ride," he said, feeling a slow smile spread across his face. "We'll have a fire then, too."

She smiled back at him, shy now. "I'd like that."

Two hours later, showered and shaved, he ambled into Green Forks to have a beer with Lotts and wait on Tess.

"Hey, stranger, how are things?" Lotts asked, tying his apron on. "Alice might bring Tess over later. You sticking around?"

"I'll be here."

Lotts raised his eyebrows, watching for his reaction. "Like I said before, Tess is a nice girl."

Jake grinned at the sales pitch. "You think so? She is a nice girl. But Tess would not be a good rebound woman," he said definitively, doffing his hat and running his hand through his hair.

"Why not?" Lotts asked.

"Too east coast and way too pretty. Every time I see her, I promise myself I'll be able to resist her, next time."

"Hah. How's that working for you?" Lotts asked, rubbing down the bar with a rag.

"Not so good."

"Sounds like a catch to me. Rebound women can be smart and pretty."

"When they are as smart and pretty as Tess, they aren't rebound women—they're keepers. And although I like the idea of Tess as a keeper, she's in a class by herself. She's young, and I don't think she's big on serious relationships. Plus, she's a tenderfoot. She won't be around here for long. Even so, I'm buying her dinner," he admitted sheepishly.

"Hah. Sounds like a rebound to me."

"Doc sent Tess out to the ranch today to see our branding operation. She pitched in like a ranch hand. I'm just being neighborly is all," Jake said, knowing nothing escaped Lotts.

"Chickenshit." Lotts grinned.

"Better a chickenshit stallion than a gelded bronco, I always say," he replied evenly.

Lotts set a draft in front of him. "If she's so inclined, she'll be paired off in no time, I imagine. Plenty of hot-blooded stallions around here eyeing up the pretty girls."

"No doubt about that. Ron was glaring at me the night of the accident and again last Monday at the Grange, acting real macho. I think he'd like to date her."

"Ron Karachek, the cop?"

"He works for the Ag Department, deals with her through work."

"So it's open season, then," Lotts said, grinning. "New girl in town has all the bucks fired up."

"Like I said, too high stakes for me," Jake said determinedly. "She's only here until spring, and she might not stick around that long. Winters are tough around here."

"Only when you don't have a sweetie to cuddle with," Lotts fired back, grinning like a devil. "Alice is from down south where it's warm. She never minded cold winters 'cause I never gave her the chance to."

Jake sucked the foam off his beer, tempted by the thought of cuddling Tess in front of his fireplace. A few minutes later, she came through the door with Alice, a white down vest over her fairisle turtleneck sweater, her skinny legs in pale blue cords, and sporting buff shearling snow boots on her feet. Her hair hung loose and curly over her shoulders. *Damn, she's a knockout, and she's not even trying.*

Tess spied him and smiled shyly, happy to see him. Despite what he'd said to Lotts, he felt a familiar tug of inevitability as he strode across the bar to greet her.

*****

Tess saw Jake walk towards her, wearing dark jeans and a flannel shirt. Resting his hand lightly on her back, he kissed her cheek and offered her a drink. *He's just a complete gentleman and so damn hot.* After Lotts took their dinner order, Jake led her to a booth, hanging her vest on the post next to his hat and suede jacket. She wasn't sure if this was a date, but it felt great to be with him again.

By eight-thirty, they'd eaten burgers and sweet potato fries, talked about their day and a little about Cassie, and finished their second drinks. The bar was packed and getting louder, and the games at both pool tables were four deep.

She liked sitting across from Jake, watching the line of his jaw as he spoke, taking in the corded muscles on his forearms, wrists and neck, his wide, broad shoulders, and the wavy dark hair that fell across his forehead. "Big turnout for the tournament tonight," he commented, pulling his glance away from her briefly to look towards the pool tables.

"I don't think I've been here on Thursday night, yet," she answered, playing with a coaster. Gazing at him for too long made her want to crawl into his lap and nibble his lips.

"You want another drink?"

"Sure, one more," she smiled. Jake got himself a beer, set an Alabama Slammer in front of her, and eased back into the booth. She wanted desperately to flirt, but she had something to tell him. *I better see how he takes my news before I make a giant fool of myself.* Sipping her drink, she glanced at him, toying with her straw. "Um, Jake, I have a kind of weighty topic to discuss."

Crossing his arms over his chest, he gave her a lazy-eyed smile of approval and leaned back in the booth. "A weighty topic? We've already done an auto crash and a trip to the ER. Then there was your move and meeting my daughter. Today we permanently disfigured two hundred calves. What else could there be?" he teased, tapping her ankle gently with his foot.

She smiled nervously, distracted by the bulk of his arms and shoulders and chest. "Van is neutered, right?"

"No, I use him for stud," Jake said, raising his eyebrows.

Tess felt heat rising in her face. *Oh, just shoot me now.* Biting her lower lip, she stared at the worn Formica tabletop then up at him. "I didn't realize Rhiannon was in heat until I got her home tonight, Jake. I'd booked the surgery to spay her next week."

His deep brown eyes flickered with amusement. "You are saying that what Cassie referred to as Van and Rhiannon 'dancing' this afternoon means there will probably be a litter of pups sometime around Thanksgiving?"

"That's what I'm saying." Red-faced, she put her hands to her burning face, still biting her lip. "The new vet gets a personal fail for canine population control, on top of her abysmal driving record. Please don't tell anyone," she whispered. "I am so completely embarrassed."

"You're always bringing me trouble, aren't you?" he teased. "How did I ever get mixed up with you, Crash?"

"Hey, Rhiannon and I have to bear the responsibilities, here," she said with a little pout.

"But I suggested you let Rhiannon out of your truck this morning, remember?" he said smoothly. "And Rhiannon was with me all day. I didn't notice she was in heat, either."

"That's true." She perked up.

"I'll take my share of responsibility," he said evenly. "Australian shepherds are always in demand around here. Rhiannon's part collie, she has a good temperament, and she showed herding instinct today."

"Good," Tess said, cheered considerably. "It'll be a shotgun wedding, then."

"Van's family won't shirk their duties, Crash," he assured her. "I'll mention it to Aunt Olivia, and Alice and Bea and Doc will help spread the word, too. It'll be just after Christmas when the pups are weaned, we won't have any trouble finding them homes."

"Thank you. I'm paying an extra fifty bucks a month to keep Rhiannon at my apartment, and I don't even want to think about what Ernie's going charge to let me keep a litter of puppies there."

"Aw, we've got you covered. I can set up a whelping box at the ranch so the pups don't bother your neighbors," he offered. "Cassie will have a blast with the puppies, and Tilda won't mind pitching in."

"Thank you, Jake," Tess smiled appreciatively, eyeing him shyly. "Bailing me out again."

He leaned forward, his brown eyes on her, serious now. The heat in them made her toes curl. In a low voice, he said, "You can count on me, Tess. I hope you know that."

She shivered, wishing she could dive onto him but glad when he leaned back in the booth, out of reach. "Everyone's talking about the new vet in town. It's a very popular topic. They're all impressed with what a great job you're doing, Crash."

"Really?" she asked, pleased.

"Yup. Sherri Tarleton is in your cheering section. She's a hard sell, so that's got the ranchers convinced. Here in town, Bea is talking you up, and Gertie and my Aunt Olivia are both raving about you to the church ladies."

"I met your Aunt Olivia on Tuesday. She brought Buxie and Susie in."

"Did she?" Jake grinned. "I'm sure I'll get an earful of praise for you Saturday night at dinner, then. Was it worth it, coming all this way for a vet job?"

"I wanted to use my skills where they seemed worthwhile, and Doc said I was needed here. It's nice to feel needed, so yes, it's been worthwhile. This still feels like an adventure, and I'm learning so much. In the suburbs, animals are mostly company, but here they're an integral part of people's livelihoods."

"So an auto crash, a hick town, a ton of hard work branding, de-horning and castrating calves, and a stray dog that might be pregnant qualifies as an adventure?" he asked fondly.

"Sure it does," Tess said decisively, flashing him her flirtiest smile. "I like it here. The work is interesting, and I lucked out with the people I've met. Alice and Bea and Doc. And you and Cassie."

He smiled at this. Catching his sober, intent gaze, she let her lashes flutter, brushing her leg against his under the table with a slow, inviting smile, determined to wear him down.

*****

Jake could pretend to Lotts he was just being neighborly, but he couldn't take his eyes off Tess. When he felt her leg against his under the table, blood surged everywhere but his brain. He'd committed her to memory—her rosebud lips, which she bit nervously from time to time, and the strong, thin, sensitive fingers that had handled the branding tools with such precision earlier at the ranch.

The heat between them was affecting her, too, he could tell, and he remembered how she clutched his back when they'd kissed. *I'm getting in deeper and deeper here. Maybe I should just give in. She's damn-near perfect. But she'll be gone after spring, and by then, I'll be head-over-heels. . .*

A dark shadow loomed across their table, blocking the overhead light. "Tess!" Aaron said enthusiastically.

"Hi, Aaron," Tess answered, flashing him one of her high-wattage smiles.

"How's the truck running?" Aaron asked, ignoring Jake. He motioned to the spot next to her, and Tess scooted over to let him in. Jealous, Jake turned to the game on the television over the bar. Noise escalated around the pool tables then loud cheers erupted. Alice turned the jukebox up. The bar was packed three-deep. Jake pretended to watch the game, hearing less and less of what Aaron and Tess were saying. *Might as well bide my time.*

Lotts caught Jake's eye and grinned. *A chickenshit stallion would get up politely and leave Tess with Aaron,* his expression said. Jake stayed put, nursing his beer and ignoring Lotts' I-told-you-so grin. *He's just sorry he didn't put money on this.*

Aaron stood up a few minutes later and spoke to Jake. "I'm going to get Tess a drink—you want a beer, man?"

Jake looked down at the inch of beer still left in his glass. "I'm fine, thanks." When Aaron left, he slid around the table into the booth next to Tess and caught her eye. "You shoot pool?"

"Not while anyone is watching," she answered, crinkling her nose.

He touched one of her curls. "Having fun?"

"It's okay," she shrugged, gazing at him with big blue eyes, which asked a question he wanted to answer.

Alice had turned the jukebox up, and the first strains of a Dave Matthews tune broke through the honky-tonk. She smiled at him from the bar, and when he recognized the song she'd chosen, he grinned back. Jake grabbed Tess's hand. "C'mon, Crash."

As he led her to the open area in front of the jukebox. she recognized the familiar melody, and her eyes flashed with laughter.

"Let's dance," he murmured, pulling her close. His hands strayed to her waist. She giggled but stayed with him, lithe and fine, golden liquid in his arms. He spun her around, and she broke into a self-conscious grin as he caught her. Putting her arms around his neck, she leaned close and whispered, "Jake, in case you haven't noticed, we're the only people dancing here."

"We're doing just fine, Crash. This is our song," he answered. As Dave Matthews crooned, he whispered the words to "Crash" near her ear. She rested her head on his shoulder, and her hair brushed his cheek. The thread of desire that had pulsed all day unfurled, warm and insistent. He grabbed a chunk of the curls cascading down her back, closed his eyes and gently kissed her lips, her forehead, her eyelids. *She's got me.* When the song ended, he held her waist and whispered, "You want to get out of here?"

"Maybe," she nodded, her smile a definite 'yes'. Aaron had disappeared into a crowd at the pool table.

"Wanna catch a movie?"

"What's playing?"

"We can find out. Headlight's fixed in the truck. C'mon, let's go." Jake grabbed her vest from the pole above the booth and helped her into it then shrugged into his suede jacket and led her out the door. *Lotts won this time, and he's sure to let me know about it.*

*****

To: Sam.Bam@vmailcom
From: Tess.Bam@gmailcom
Date: Thursday, October 4 11:46 PM

Subject: First Base.

Sammi~

    Icebreaker!! At Last! I learned a ton at Jake's ranch today and got to see Cassie ride, too. She is SO amazing on her little pony! Jake bought me a burger for dinner at Green Forks, Alice put Dave Matthews on the juke box, and after we danced....yes, the ONLY couple dancing in the bar... to CRASH! Then, he took me to the movies and fed me popcorn. Have no idea what the movie was about but YUM, his lips tasted great butter-flavored! Sammi, Green Junction is the scariest thing I've ever done. I'm finally on my own here, and now it's starting to feel like I might even belong! YES!

Love, Love, Love Happiest Tessiest.

    Tess pressed "Send" and climbed into her pajamas. Snuggling under her down comforter and quilt, she could still feel Jake's soft flannel shirt on her cheek. The day at the ranch had been amazingly special. When Jake pulled her against him to dance, she'd felt something connect between them, something concrete and irrefutable.

    He was so careful and measured with her, contained—like he was holding back—but safe, too, and solid, his liquid eyes so affectionate and tender. It scared her, but she wanted more. Hugging the covers around her, she tried to sleep.

*****

To: Tess.Bam@vmailcom
From: Sam.Bam@vmailcom
Date: Friday, October 5, 1: 26 am

Subject: ONLY YOU!

Tess,

******

Early Saturday morning, Tess's cell rang.

"Hey, Tess. I just finished feeding horses. What are your plans for the day?" Jake's voice was as warm and gentle as it had been Thursday night, and she felt her pulse quicken. *Calm down, silly.*

"I'm just about to take Rhiannon for a run in the park. Alice and I are at the clinic 'til noon, but after that, no plans," she said.

"The Green Junction pass up to the Sawatches will only be open another week or so before it's snowed in for winter. There are some real pretty views up there. I wondered if you and Rhiannon would like to ride up there to take a look at it with Van and I this afternoon?"

"Sounds great. I'll be finished at the clinic around noon."

"Okay, I'll meet you there. We can grab lunch at the diner then head up to the mountains."

Tess arrived early to the clinic, but there were already three cars in the parking lot; two emergencies and her first appointment. She sutured and bandaged an Irish Setter with a deep splinter and torn front pad while Alice tranquilized a barn cat, a large unneutered male that had tangled with a raccoon. Bea came in as Tess and Alice were inoculating a new litter of eight Saint Bernard puppies. By the time Vicki dropped Cassie off at nine, things were really humming.

"So, Dr. Tess, we are really busy today," Cassie announced importantly as she lead an older, balding man with a cat carrier into the examining room.

"I don't know what we'd do without you this morning, Cass," Tess said, giving the little girl a gentle squeeze before lifting the cat carrier onto the high stainless-steel table.

"Now, then, Mr. Zweigstich, let's see to Harris." The man's brow was furrowed with concern; his bushy eyebrows almost met in the middle. She glanced at the chart Alice handed her. The cat had been vomiting, but the diagnosis, hair balls, was an easy one. "He's a long haired indoor cat, Mr. Zweigstich, have you tried wheat grass?"

"Wha-ell, the Doc suggested it, but ah forgot t' tell the Missus about it. Seems strange, but we'll have t' givvit a try."

The morning was a whirlwind, but somehow the four of them managed to keep up. At ten-thirty, the tomcat caged in the back room started to howl. "Did you weigh him before you sedated him?" she asked Alice, alarmed.

"I did my best, Tess. He's close to eighteen pounds. The dose of sedative should have knocked him out for four hours."

"Yikes. Well, maybe he'll settle down. Let's give him a few minutes."

By eleven, the tomcat was on a screaming for vengeance concert tour. "Okay, he's a one-cat-Judas-Priest-show back there," Tess said. "It'll back up the rest of our appointments, but we don't have much choice. It sounds like we're running a torture chamber back there. Let's book a room and sedate him again, Alice."

"Do you want to do the castration now, too?"

"Did his owners feed him this morning?"

"They said just a bit of fish to bribe him into the carrier."

"We might as well. Can Bea handle the desk? I'll need an extra set of hands."

Tess and Alice worked quickly, but stitching and castrating the tom took the better part of an hour. The waiting room was standing room only when they'd finished, and all the examining rooms were filled.

"I'll ask Bea to stay at the front desk so I can help you get caught up back here," Alice offered. She disinfected tables, dispensed medication, and drew blood while Cassie ferried patients to the examining rooms. At ten minutes past noon, they had almost caught up. Tess saw Jake's truck pull in behind the clinic. When she led her patient out, he was standing in front of Alice's desk.

"Daddy, what are you doing here?" Cassie asked, clearly pleased.

"Ah, I needed to grab some wormer for the horses. We're out at the farm," Jake said smoothly, pulling his daughter up into his arms.

Her hands wrapping his neck, and she kissed his cheek. "What a nice surprise. And you shaved. Your cheeks are smooth, and you smell good."

"Let me get that wormer for you Jake. Ivermectin, 5-dose pack?" Alice asked, glancing towards the parking lot nervously. Vicki's car pulled in. Heavily made up, she slammed her car door and marched up the ramp, sky high heels clacking.

Tess guided a little boy and his mother with their guinea pig into the closest examining room. "So this is Sylvester?" she asked the little boy, taking the brown and white spotted cavy from his carrier and nestling him in her palm.

"Uh-huh," the little boy replied shyly. "He needs his teeth clipped, we think."

Flashing an encouraging smile, she stroked the little rodent's back and said, "Hmm, well, let's just have a look. Could you hold Sylvester, Jimmy?"

Setting the guinea pig on the table, she pulled up gently on the skin around its incisors, trying to ignore the commotion in the reception area.

"Just what is going on here?" she heard Vicki screech and wished she'd left the tom cat until last. *He'd drown out Vicki's squalls, anyway.*

"See, those are the little pouches where he holds his food," she said to the little boy.

"He has chubby cheeks," Jimmy agreed.

"His teeth could use a bit of attention," Tess agreed, "Does Sylvester mind having them filed?"

"Doc's done it before," Jimmy's mom smiled.

Tess heard Bea's low, calming voice pass the examining room door as she walked Vicki to the back. "Mom, what are you so upset about?" Cassie asked tentatively. They were right outside the door now, and Tess heard Vicki snap, "You wouldn't understand, Cassie. Please, get your things and wait for me out front."

"I'll just grab a small file and clippers for his toes, then, okay?" Tess asked, and Jimmy and his mom nodded.   Darting into the dispensary, she was surprised to find Vicki seated at the table, a big purple leather purse open at her feet. Vicki glared at her. Flashing a quick smile, Tess rooted nervously through the drawers until she found her tools. Back in the examining room, she nipped the little rodent's nails and hit his teeth ever so gently with an emery board. After she'd finished, she gently tucked the little guinea pig back in his carrier.

"Thank you, Doctor Tess," Jimmy smiled, picking up Sylvester's carrier.

"You bet, Jimmy." She walked Jimmy and his mother out to the reception area where Cassie waited in her coat and hat. Holding her backpack, she looked upset and anxious.

Tess disinfected her tools and stepped back into the dispensary, surprised to find Vicki still there. Startled to see Tess, Vicki snapped her big leather bag shut and brushed past her rudely, face averted. Once in the hall, Vicki called sharply, "Come on, Cassie, we're leaving!"

Why was Vicki still back here? Feeling unnerved, Tess tucked her tools into the drawer and moved to where Vicki had been standing. The glass cabinet door was unlocked and partially open. When she saw what was behind the glass, her breath caught. *Tranquilizers and barbiturates.* Disturbed, Tess slid the door shut, locked it, and walked briskly down the hall.

Vicki stood in the reception area, fumbling with the buttons on her fancy long coat. Jimmy's mom was finishing with their bill, and she and Jimmy moved towards the door, waving goodbye to Cassie. Cassie waved back then crossed her arms and pouted, clearly unhappy. *She's been waiting for her mother for some time.* Purse over her shoulder, Vicki tossed her hair. "Okay, let's go, squirt."

Flinging herself forward, Cassie wrapped her arms around Tess. Tess touched her woolen cap, meeting the little girl's troubled eyes. "Thanks for your help, today, Cass," she said.

Vicki grimaced and rolled her eyes impatiently. Bea hurried out from the back, a bill folded in her hand. "Here, Cassie, Doc wouldn't forgive me if I forgot to give you this. See you during the week?"

Vicki's eyes flashed. "I'm not so sure she'll be by this week, Aunt Bea." Her lipsticked mouth twitched, and she motioned towards Tess. "We better just see you and Doc at the house for a while. I'm not sure the clinic is the best place for her to visit."

Cassie, her arms still tangled around Tess's waist, looked crestfallen. Tess saw regret in Bea's eyes. "Whatever you think best, dear. Doc and I are always glad to see you." Hastily tying her coat belt, Bea continued smoothly, "I'll walk you out. Good-bye, girls, thanks for your help today." As she waved to Alice and Tess, Bea's eyes flashed apology. Tess felt terrible as she watched a dejected Cassie walk to her mother's car.

After the door had closed, Alice exhaled. "Whoa. I don't remember twenty minutes that tense around here, ever. It was a crazy morning to begin with. Count on Vicki to ratchet things up to a full boil. Poor Cass."

"Cassie was stuck square in the middle," Tess said uncomfortably. "I can't believe her mother won't let her come by anymore. I can probably kiss visits at my apartment good-bye, too. Maybe dating Jake isn't such a good idea. I never wanted to cause trouble for Cassie."

Alice eyed her sympathetically. "Tess, Vicki will always be a handful. It's no fun for Cassie, but remember, you're a bright spot for her. That little kid adores you, and Jake needs a life, too. I saw the way he looked at you when you two were dancing Thursday night. You'll just have to decide if putting up with Vicki is worth it. I wish I could say something more hopeful, but honestly, I doubt it will get much better."

Chagrined, Tess tidied up the lab and checked on the tom cat, thinking hard about what had happened. She felt terrible about how callous Vicki had been to Cassie and the hurt she'd seen on the little girl's face. *Is any of it worth it if Vicki hurts Cassie and Jake because of me?* She wanted to tell Alice about Vicki's strange behavior in the dispensary. *But what did I see, really? If I say something, it might seem to Alice or Bea that I'm making trouble for Vicki.*

The sound of Jake's truck engine cutting out and the front door opening and closing made her stomach clutch. *It will be hard enough to see Cassie from now on. It's probably not worth the fuss.*

She threw her lab coat into the laundry bag. Alice bustled back, handing Tess her jacket and knapsack. "I'll finish here; you get going."

"Um, Alice? I noticed the medication doors were open in back today. I know we were really busy, but let's make sure we keep those cabinet doors locked, okay?"

"Odd," Alice replied, "I'm pretty sure I locked them."

"Maybe we shouldn't keep the key in the drawer below."

"You're right, that isn't safe. I'll get wrist holders tomorrow. We can wear the keys from now on."

"That would make me feel better, Alice, thanks."

Still feeling tense, Tess walked into the reception area, shrugging into her jacket. With a quick, apologetic smile, Jake took her knapsack and grabbed her hand. Tess saw Van in the back of the truck, smiling and wagging his tail.

"I sure didn't mean to cause a commotion in there," Jake said as he opened the truck door for her.

"It was unfortunate, especially for Cassie," Tess answered, tossing her bag on the seat and climbing in.

Holding the door, Jake met her eyes. "Was Vicki really hard on her?"

"I'd say so."

"Vicki was tearing for a fight from the second she arrived, that's for sure," Jake said, shaking his head. He shut Tess's door, walked around the front of the truck and climbed into the driver's seat.

"Vicki won't let Cassie come back to the clinic this week," she said quietly as he put the key in the ignition. She wanted to be diplomatic, but she couldn't hide anything, either.

"What?" he looked stunned.

"Vicki told Bea that Cassie wouldn't be back for a while. Maybe we should skip the diner, Jake. The way Vicki looked at me, it was clear that I was the problem. I don't want to cause any more trouble for Cassie. She's devastated already."

"Tess, I am so sorry." He thrummed his hands on the steering wheel, eyes somber. "Look, I know you're upset. I am too, but let's not let Vicki ruin the rest of our day. It's beautiful out. Do you want to head up to the mountains? We won't have too many more of these days before the road closes for winter."

Remembering the almost desperate way Cassie had hugged her good-bye, Tess couldn't forget what she'd seen in the dispensary. *Should I say something to him about it? He's trying to make the best of all of this. I don't want to open another can of worms for him. I wish I was clearer about what happened.*

"I'll call over for a pizza. Shall we go get Rhiannon, grab it on our way out of town and picnic in the truck?"

"Sure."

The road into the Sawatch Mountains doubled back and around, climbing higher and higher. Tess's ears popped as she balanced the warm pizza box on her knees. Close to the tree line, Jake pulled into the lookout. *It's mesmerizing.* They were surrounded by deep, white snow, shimmering sunlight, and the bluest of skies.

Sitting in the warm truck munching pizza, looking at the wide, picturesque valley spread far below, Tess put the stress of the morning aside.

Leaning over, Jake wiped a bit of tomato off her chin with his napkin. "I've got snowshoes in the back, Crash, when you're ready to go. There's another lookout just above us, less than a mile up the trail."

"Wow, there's more? There's already so much to see from right here."

"You'll see lots more from up above. C'mon, you ready?" He helped her adjust the snowshoes to her boots and handed her poles, and they started up the switchback to the first lookout. "It'll be avalanche season up here before too long." Jake looked towards the steep inclines above them. "There won't be too many more hikes, but you'll be fine shoeing in the park for the winter, if you like it. There are trails at the ranch I can show you, too."

The dogs stayed nearby, barking and playing in chest-deep fresh powder. When they'd reached the lookout, he handed her binoculars and stood behind her, pointing out landmarks in the foothills and the different ranches she knew in the valley. "See the old rail line below the interstate over there, where it cuts through the mountain?"

She adjusted the focus. "Wow, I see it!" He pointed out other spots in the village. She saw the spires of the churches in town and the cupola of borough hall, the diner and even the tall white Victorian where she lived, all in miniature so far below.

"When I'm walking downtown, I can see so much above me, but I never thought about what town would look like from up here. This is fantastic!" Still holding the binoculars, she turned to Jake. "Thanks for thinking of this. It's something I'll always remember."

"I'm glad you like it," he smiled.

*****

As terrible as Jake felt about the run-in with Vicki, Tess was too close to resist. As she stood in front of him, binoculars in hand, he wrapped his arms around her waist and touched his lips to the top of her head above the spill of curls. She smiled and turned to face him. Tucking his hands under her jacket, he slid his hands up under the hem of her turtleneck, touching the skin on the small of her back. Smiling, she tilted her head up, drowsy-eyed in the sunshine. Touching his tongue to hers, his pulse raced with desire. They kissed until they were breathless with cold then hiked back to the truck and kissed some more while the engine warmed the cab.

"I'm so glad you crashed into me," she smiled into the spot where Jake's jaw joined his neck.

"We lucked out, huh?" he murmured, running his fingertips along her cold, pink cheek.

"Do you think I would have met you, otherwise?" she asked.

"It's a small town. I wouldn't have let you stay away for very long," he whispered, pressing his lips to her forehead.

"Let's go back to my apartment," she offered.

"After this morning, maybe we should just take it easy for a while." He was glad when she tightened her hands on his back in response.

"We can't undo this morning, even though we'd both like to. The best we can do is play it cool and stay out of Vicki's way. You can leave your truck at the clinic, if you want," she suggested, her lips close to his ear.

Too tempted to refuse, he kissed her nose, which was still cold. "Let's try to avoid a scene like this morning."

"We can't let that happen again," Tess agreed.

He pulled into the clinic parking lot and left the engine running while the dogs whined and jumped around in the back. He wanted her so badly. *If you leap now, you're a goner for sure. You're probably a goner already.*

"You and Van coming over?" she asked, her hand on the door latch. She leaned over and kissed him, and he clasped the sides of her face, searching her eyes. He saw her desire, and it made him cautious for them both.

"I'll be honest. If you want to keep this just to kissing, I shouldn't come. I pride myself on self-control, but you have a powerful effect on me."

She kissed him again, grabbing his lip gently between her teeth. His groin tightened reflexively, and he sighed against her lips. *Does this girl have any idea what she's doing to me?* "Tess, I mean it. I've wanted to be close to you since I watched you come out of Dave's garage that first day, as nuts as that is."

"So why wouldn't you have lunch with me when I asked at the doctor's office?" she asked curiously.

"I was fooling myself. I had to play it cool, for my own sanity," he admitted. "And I wanted to give you a chance to get settled in."

"Come on, I know how to play it cool, too," she said, slugging his shoulder and opening the truck door. "We'll just talk. I promise to keep my hands to myself."

"Who are you fooling?" he grinned, letting the dogs out of the back of his truck. She tossed him her keys.

At her place, the dogs bounded onto the porch in front of Tess. He parked her truck and walked in, smiling every bit of the way.

Boots and snow pants were kicked off on the living room floor, and Rhiannon and Van wrestled with a rope toy. He found Tess sitting on the bed, her back against a pillow, thin, fleece-clad legs crossed on top of the blanket. He leaned against the door jamb and grinned down at her. "Is this where you entertain?"

She eyed him mischievously and clasped her knees to her chest. "Only when it's you. If my parents knew about this, though, they'd have a sofa air-dropped. Alice's table and chairs in the kitchen are all I have to sit on. My bed's really cozy, and it's this or the floor. Are you hungry? Do you want something to eat?"

"Oh, I'm hungry. Like a wolf. But what I want is right here." He leaned over and kissed her, then licked her pink lips, sliding his tongue between her teeth. She sighed and put her hands around his neck.

"Do that some more," she whispered, her eyes dark with desire.

"Let me get the fire stoked, first, get rid of the chill in here. I'll be right back."

In her living room, the dogs had settled, curling together on the rug in front of the hearth. He opened the damper of the wood stove and added wood to the fire. When it was roaring, he pulled his fleece off, walked down the hall, and sat on the bed next to her, taking her in his arms. She studied him solemnly, tracing a finger down the length of his jaw. "You take really good care of me," she said, "I like it. I've never met a man like you."

He grinned at her, raising an eyebrow wickedly. "I hope not. So tell me about the men you've met."

She wrinkled her nose. "Do I have to?"

86

"Well, I don't need gory details. You did say you've never been in a serious relationship."

"Does that mean you don't trust me?" she asked, brow furrowed.

"I trust you, but you may not know how it feels to have your life turned inside out by someone you care about," he answered, settling her close against his chest. "It's not an easy thing to bear. I know you're only planning to be here until spring, but you're terrific with my daughter and I'd like to see more of you," he whispered, nuzzling her hair and kissing her forehead. "I haven't dated in close to eight years. I'm trying to get some sense of where you're at."

"I had casual flings in vet school," Tess confessed, taking a deep breath. "With lame guys. My mother says I have a knack for unsuitable men, but Alice assures me that you're okay."

"She's right, I am. I'm very okay. Why lame guys?"

"I'm not sure. They were older, mostly. I didn't really have time for a relationship."

"But you do now. And I'm an older man," he said, gently pressing her back and pinning her under him.

"That's right, you are," she said, twining her legs around his. She put her hand on his ribs, under his T-shirt and her touch made him blaze with longing. "Jake, you are part of what makes my life here so fantastic. I like this little town, but it wouldn't be half as much fun if it weren't for you. You make me feel safe, safer than any guy I've known," she whispered. "It's a little scary."

He kissed her mouth, tasting her, full and ripe and sweet. "I'm glad you feel safe with me. You're very special, y'know that?"

"It was awesome being with you and Cassie the other day."

"You fit right in on the ranch. I liked having you there with us, Tess." He gazed down at her, his elbow pressing into the pillow, touching her hair while her fingers stroked his back. "Cassie really liked having you all to herself the other day. She doesn't get that kind of attention from her mom. She's had it kind of rough lately." He buried his nose in her hair. "Vicki's really self-centered, as you may have noticed. It's always all about her. You know how to handle kids."

"You think so?" Tess asked, looking at him with curious intensity.

"Sure, you made Cassie feel supported; you encouraged her, but you set some boundaries, too." He slid his hand to her hip.

"I did? In that short time?"

"Well, you reminded her about balancing work and play, you joked with her, made her feel special. You were very tuned in. It felt like I could trust you with Cassie, and that's really important to me."

"Hmm, so you're emotionally astute, too, aren't you? You read into things, like a shrink." She wrinkled her nose at him again.

He wasn't sure it was a compliment, but he grinned at the idea. "No one has ever put it quite like that, but yeah, I guess I am emotionally astute, besides being hyper-responsible and a total sucker for you. Vicki was always a mess, so to stay one step ahead of her, I sort of got that way."

Having her in his arms like this, talking and touching, was as close as they'd been together. "You made me feel special, too. Will you come back to visit us at the ranch?" he asked, squeezing her waist.

A bright smile spread across her face. "Of course I will. I don't think I could ever get too much of that."

His heart surged with appreciation. "Thanks. It means a lot to me that you feel that way."

After he left Tess's apartment, Jake tried to get his head around what he was feeling. His marriage had been on the rocks for years before his divorce, and he'd lived through a long, lonely dry spell. *I'm really lucky to be with Tess now, but she'll leave in spring.*

He didn't want to get hurt, and there was Cassie to consider. *Cassie and I could both be really attached by then, and if I let us get too close, it will just hurt all of us when she leaves. I better take it easy, for all of our sakes. I can't afford another disaster.*

*****

To: Sam.Bam@vmailcom
From: Tess.Bam@vmailcom
Date: Saturday October 6, 8:14 PM

Subject: Rocky Mountain High

Deariest Sammi Bambergiest,
    Jake took me for a hike today....Our date ended exactly two minutes ago. Call me tomorrow morning and I'll tell you all~

Loviest, Happiest Tessiest

*****

Tess and Alice handled Monday morning clinic work. Doc and Bea were taking Mondays off now, staying close to town in case they were needed. Tess did the afternoon ranch calls. It was a busy day, and she didn't get home until after eight. For dinner, she dumped a can of organic mushroom soup into a pot and made a salad and garlic bread.

Jake called at bedtime. "Hey, gorgeous, how was your day?" His voice was gentle, soft and familiar, and a wave of heat coiled deep inside her.

"Busy. Doc and Bea had off today. Ranch calls were crazy. One of the Carson's sows delivered a litter of fourteen piglets, and wound up with a prolapsed uterus. Sherri Tarleton had a three year old stallion prospect with a punctured foot. He was an awful lot of fun to play with. Even sedated, he kept trying to bite me."

"Ouch. Sounds pretty intense. I want to keep you busy here with me at the ranch, but I promise not to bite," he said, chuckling deep and low. "At least, not too hard."

"Hmm, if you are thinking of keeping me 'busy' the way you did Saturday, can you hold that thought 'til the weekend?"

"Ah, but I have Cassie this weekend, and I want to keep you 'busy' sooner. I can cook us dinner tomorrow night if you're free.

Tuesday is Tilda's night off. We'd have this whole place to ourselves."

"Very tempting. What's on the menu?" she asked, warmed at the thought of being with him again.

"I'm breaking out the McGreer spaghetti and meatball recipe. It's world-class."

"Irish spaghetti usually is," she joked.

"Hah, I'm only Irish on my dad's side. My mom was one hundred percent Italiano. Her parents came from the old country before the Second World War. Wait 'til you taste my meatballs."

"Hmm, I think I'm looking forward to tasting your meatballs, somehow," she said. Jake laughed. "I'm impressed that you're cooking."

"Oh, I'll be cooking alright. And there will be a fire in the fireplace, too. Plenty of heat here at McGreer Ranch."

"Heat as in licking flames?"

"Lots of licking flames."

*****

Tuesday night, the last glimmer of light settled over the frosty snowpack and into the western sky over the Sawatch Mountains when Tess pulled into McGreer Ranch. Jake was waiting on the porch. He pulled her into his arms, and they kissed deeply. He led her through the mudroom. Once she'd wrestled out of her work clothes, she followed him into the kitchen in wool socks and fleece leggings. He poured an uncorked bottle of Barolo, twirled the glass and handed it to her. "Bet you're hungry," he said, tugging on one of her curls.

"I am." She suddenly felt shy. He stuck a tray of garlic bread under the broiler to toast. Smiling at him, she peered into the pot of spaghetti sauce bubbling on the stove. "Yum, smells delicious, Jake."

He put the pasta into boiling water, grabbed his wineglass, and led her to the leather sofa. Wrapping her in his arms, he buried his nose in her hair. "Mmm, I'm really glad you're here."

90

"Me, too," she told him, snuggling inyo his chest. The fire crackled on the hearth, and *Don Giovanni* was on the stereo. "You were right; it's plenty warm here."

He pulled her close and kissed her, letting his lips and tongue tangle with hers. "Yup, I'll keep you warm. You're drinking a wine that is older than I am, you know."

"Really? McGreer Ranch is full of surprises."

"Ah, that it is," Jake grinned mischievously. "You stay and warm up. I'll go pull dinner together."

*****

Jake congratulated himself on pulling together a practically perfect dinner. As she finished eating, Tess flashed him her biggest, flirtiest smile. "So, I'm impressed. You were right, your meatballs definitely rank, and I'm Italian. Perfect balance of oregano and garlic, nothing Irish about them at all."

He cocked an eyebrow, smiling as he took her plate. "Glad they pass muster."

She grabbed the bowls of pasta and the salad and followed him into the kitchen. He stacked dishes in the dishwasher, purposely bumping her as she covered bowls and stuck them in the fridge. He poured them coffee and led her back to the living room. He threw a log on the fire, stoked it until it's snapping heat filled the big vaulted room, and then sat next to her. Coffee cup in hand, Tess pressed her back against a pillow on the arm rest, tucking her wool socks under his thigh. *She belongs here, right next to me, all cute and angelic.*

She was still smiling, her blue eyes clear. "Mmm, this is cosy. I could get used to this, I think," she said, sipping her coffee. "Thanks for dinner, Jake."

"It's fun to cook for you. Too bad you're only here until spring."

She wiggled her toes under his leg. "It's not like my departure date is anything certain. Apparently, Doc would like me to consider taking over the practice. I guess he doesn't want to say anything official until I'm more settled."

"Really?" Jake felt his eyebrows shoot up. "Well, that fits in with his retirement plans, then, doesn't it?"

"It seems to." Tess agreed. "Alice told me about it right after I started, and Bea's mentioned it since then, too. She's hoping I'll decide to stay. Bea wants to start spending time in Florida next winter."

"But you wouldn't consider it? I mean, a commitment like that would be a huge career stall for you, right?" he asked skeptically.

Brow furrowed, she looked at him, her eyes a little hurt. "How do you mean?"

He touched her cheek but held eye contact, feeling protective of her. "Tess, ranch work is grueling. It's a dirty, difficult, tedious life. It's commendable that you came out here for the experience, but don't you see yourself at New Bolton or another top clinic, teaching or doing specialty surgery in a more sterile, professional environment?"

"Is this some version of your 'city girl' impression of me?" She was smiling, but he sensed he'd hurt her feelings.

Pulling her against him, he threw an afghan over her legs and tucked her head to his chest, fingering her curls with his fingers. "I guess I see this a little differently than you do. I recognize your talent, your ambition, and the income potential of a real career. This has nothing to do with how you fit in here. I love having you here, as does everyone who's had you work on their animals, but you'd never get any kind of professional recognition from a practice here in Green Junction. I want what is best for you—out of real and sincere respect for you. I'm not sure Green Junction has what it takes to satisfy your long-term ambitions or give you the life you deserve."

"I haven't given much thought to my long-term career goals," she acknowledged soberly. "Having the majority of my work on a ranch, out-of-doors might get old as a lifestyle... I see that, but right now I'm completely fascinated by it. And really, very happy. I guess time will tell, right?"

The fire crackled in the hearth. "I guess it will." June was months away, and he had no intention of leaving Tess to visit in front of any man's fireplace but his. Pushing away the last nagging doubts, Jake turned off the lamp. Tilting her chin up, he gently kissed her sweet, pink lips. "The next time we do this, I want you to spend all day with me here at the ranch. We can take that trail ride."

"Deal," she said softly. When he kissed her again, she sighed. Touching his tongue to hers, he shivered with desire, feeling his heart melt. An hour later, they were on the rug in front of the fireplace. Her hands were under his shirt, shooting fire through his bare skin. As he caressed her warm, flat belly, she wiggled her hips under him.

"I want you, Tess, so very much," he murmured, gasping as her fingers slipped into his waistband. "But I want this to be right—for both of us."

"How can this be wrong? It feels so great to be with you," she said.

"It does feel pretty terrific, doesn't it? I want you with me tonight. But as much as I want to make love, I think we should wait."

"You do?" she asked, kissing him and sliding her hands into the small of his back.

It took everything he had to resist grinding his hips into her. "Girl, you're killing me."

"I want you, too," she replied, brushing her fingertips up his back, whispering, "but there's plenty of time."

"We both had an early morning and tomorrow will be another long day." he murmured., "It's getting late, and it'll be snowing again soon, if it isn't already. The roads get slick after dark. I hope you'll stay here. The guest room is made up."

He kissed her, holding on. The firelight glowed against the silhouette of her cheekbones, sparkling off her irises. "God, Crash, you are gorgeous. Will you stay?"

"Alice walked Rhiannon earlier and fed her. She'll be fine."

"There's a new toothbrush in the guest bath. I can't wait to feed you breakfast," Jake murmured as he untangled himself. Still flaming with desire, he stoked the fire and showed her to the guest room.

At the guest room door, Tess gave him a chaste kiss. "This is really thoughtful, Jake. I'm glad to be here, thank you."

"Mmmm, you can't imagine how much I like having you."

Well after midnight, a waxing moon glowed through the big picture window in his bedroom, rousing him. He heard soft footfalls in the carpeted hallway. "Tess?" His bedroom door squeaked, and she padded across the wide hardwood planking and stood next to the bed, moonlight dancing in her curls. He smiled at the sight of her. "Hey. Can't you sleep?" he asked gently.

"I woke up and wanted to be next to you. Is that okay?" Her voice was soft, a little timid.

"Is it okay? It's much better than okay. C'mon in here; there's plenty of room." He threw his wool blanket and down comforter back, and she slipped in next to him. Snuggling her close, he slipped his nose against her curls. The feel of her, smooth and warm next to him made his groin ache. "I promised to keep you warm, didn't I?" he whispered.

"Uh-huh," she murmured, shifting her face against his chest.

He slept later than usual Wednesday morning, cuddling Tess close, unwilling to rouse her. While she showered, he scrambled eggs and broiled bacon for them. After they'd eaten breakfast, he warmed her truck and walked her to it, handing her a piece of buttered toast and a travel mug of coffee. Standing on the front porch, he watched her truck pull away, catching the wave and last smile she flashed him.

Walking into the house, Jake felt the turmoil and disappointment he'd carried for the past few years seeping away, replaced by a buoyancy and satisfaction he hadn't felt in a long while. *If Tess were staying in Green Junction past June, this would be really perfect. But I'll never ask her to make a sacrifice like that.*

*****

To: Sam.Bam@vmailcom
From: Tess.Bam@vmailcom
Date: Wednesday, October 10, 8:56 AM
Subject: Petticoat Green Junction Just keeps getting better!

Sammi~

Jake made me dinner last night. There is a wine cellar at the ranch, stocked with, among other things, Jake's great-uncle Carlo's wine from Italy. If this is love, Sammi, I'll have another helping please!

Jake's parents, Maria and Billy, were teenage sweethearts here in Green Junction. His mom left for New York City with her mother after her dad, a train man, passed away from a heart attack. But Maria and Billy couldn't bear to be apart, so Billy came to New York, to propose. Uncle Carlo traveled by train from NYC with Maria and her mother to Green Junction for their wedding, bringing cases of specially selected Italian wines: Barollo, Chianti, Valpolicello, and Barbaresco. Cousin Carlo oversaw the wine import business while Uncle Carlo spent that summer at the ranch, building the wine cellar.

Super romantic, right?? (Even better, the wine import business is still going, on West Broadway, you can stop by!) Needless to say, we drank un fantastico Barollo (Grandma Angliotti will be so pleased) AND got molto vicino al grande sesso (shh, don't tell her that!) Jake's so great to snuggle with, Sammi, it feels so right!

Love,
Barely Dressied-Tessie

*****

To: Tess.Bam@vmailcom
From: Sam.Bam@vmailcom
Date: Wednesday, October 10, 7:49 PM

Subject: RE: It just keeps getting better!

Stay Dressied-Tessie: You poor thing, sampling vintage Italian wines from the family cellar ~ Keep up the good work! Ciao, Bella!!

Love, Sister Sammi

6

"Mother Superior Jumps the Gun"

To: Sam.Bam@vmailcom
From: Tess.Bam@vmailcom
Date: Thursday, October 11, 6:56 PM

Subject: Holy Smokes, Batman!

Jake's Aunt Olivia left a message at the office, inviting me to lunch at her house on Saturday.......Yikes! Can you believe it? Thank goodness Mom shipped my dress clothes. I got them from the post office today, just in time.

Love, Better be Dressied Tessie

*****

To: Tess.Bam@vmailcom
From: Sam.Bam@vmailcom
10:49 AM Friday, October 12

Subject: Definitely No Joker!

Dear Better Be Dressied Tessie:....maybe split a magnum of champagne with Auntie O tomorrow, to get the party started? Mark my words, darling, she's vetting you, but as a vet, no doubt you'll pass muster! My heart bleeds for you, darling~ Enjoy Lunch!

Love, Sister Sammi

Saturday, Tess was the first to arrive at the clinic. She left before noon to dress at the apartment. Feeling anxious, she chose a simple black turtleneck sweater, tall black boots and an ankle-length pleated skirt her mother had sent. It didn't take long to dress, but her fingers faltered as she secured her hair with a barrette and pulled her long coat on. "You stay here, Rhiannon, and take care of the house," she whispered, feeling very, very subdued.

Ten minutes later, she was pressing the doorbell of the imposing brick Georgian on Talbot Street, trying to ignore the loop-the-loops in her stomach. *I hope I can eat!*

Olivia McGreer opened the door, wearing a ruffled blouse and flowered silk skirt, a fancy gold and pearl pin at her neck. "Doctor Bamberger," she said, in a pleasant, distinguished voice, her smile warm and sincere as she clasped Tess's hand. "Welcome."

"Please, call me Tess. It's lovely to see you again."

"I'm delighted as well. Thank you for coming." She graciously motioned Tess into the formal entry, a large, marble-tiled hallway with a crystal chandelier hanging overhead. Her silver hair was pulled back tightly in a bun, she wore freshly- applied lipstick, and she really did seem pleased to see Tess. Despite the formal setting, Tess relaxed as a uniformed maid helped her out of her coat.

"We'll just sit in the library, and Stella will bring tea," Olivia said, indicating a door on her right. In the room lined with bookshelves, a pair of wing chairs flanked a small marble hearth where a crackling fire was laid. The heavy, expensive drapes were open, and autumn sunshine filtered through shuttered windows. Tess sat in one of the wing chairs while Stella carried a silver tea service in, setting it on the table in front of the hearth.

"I hope you are finding Green Junction to your liking, Tess," Olivia said, pouring tea into a bone china cup and handing it to her. "You've been very well received here, dear. Every rancher you've visited is singing your praises, and Doc and Bea are thrilled." Olivia offered her a sugar cube from silver tongs.

"That is so kind of you to say, thank you." Tess held her cup to Olivia.

"It's the absolute truth, dear. My praise is well-deserved. Ranch veterinary work is a very tough job. Few women would do it, and I mean that as a compliment. Your dedication is admirable." Olivia held the pitcher of cream. "You've captured my grandniece Cassie's imagination as well."

"She is a bright, talented little girl," Tess agreed.

"That she is. And her father has made himself no stranger, I understand." Olivia smiled as she plopped cream into Tess's cup and then her own.

Tess blushed furiously as the image of the bare, muscular chest she'd woken up next to Wednesday morning flashed in her mind. Stirring her tea to gain time, she tried to recover. "He's a wonderful person," she stammered.

They visited amicably for a few more minutes before Olivia said, "Shall we go to the dining room? Stella has prepared Lobster Newburgh. I hope seafood is to your liking."

Throughout the elegant lunch, in a dining room as polished and formal as the rest of the house, Olivia continued her skillful gleaning of information, covering Tess's education and parents and upbringing and touching ever-so-slightly on her political inclinations. The Lobster Newburgh was delicious. She managed to enjoy it while successfully deflecting Olivia's questions, answering cheerfully, elaborating on some, playing down others. *Samantha was right. She's vetting me.*

Just in time, Stella cleared their lunch dishes. She set a silver coffee service on the sideboard and plates of chocolate raspberry torte in front of Tess and Olivia. Olivia poured coffee, continuing in a lowered voice. "I do want to bring up my nephew again, Tess, since it's clear to me that Jake has singled you out."

Tess blushed, unsure of what to say. "Jake was very kind to me when I first arrived. He's been a thoughtful and generous friend. I'm grateful to know him, and I always enjoy the time we spend together."

"I'm glad to hear that chivalry is not dead in the McGreer family. Even though his marriage was difficult, he was a devoted husband and father, I can assure you. His father doted on his mother until her death, so in his early years, he had an excellent role model. You've seen him yourself with Cassie?"

"I have. He's obviously a dedicated parent, very patient and loving," she confirmed with a smile, unnerved by Olivia's intensity.

"I'm not going to mince words, dear. Jake is my brother's only son. I have no children of my own, and I've taken a strong interest in his welfare since he lost his mother as a little boy. My brother misses his wife dreadfully and has never remarried. The disagreeableness of Jake's marriage took a very heavy toll on him, and I've been afraid he would follow his father's path of solitude. It is encouraging to me that he's shown an interest in you."

Astonished by Olivia's candor, Tess was unsure how to respond. Thankfully, she didn't have to because Olivia continued.

"I say this because I was uncertain if Jake would recover, in light of the loss of his mother. It's very important to me that he finds a woman able to be the companion he deserves. I can say that upon first impressions, you seem to me to be that woman. I've been delighted by the prospect since I heard of his 'friendship' with you," she finished enthusiastically.

Tess had been sipping her coffee somewhat nervously, and at Olivia's last words, she coughed into her napkin to hide her surprise. "Well, I'm certainly aware of the compliment you are paying me, but I have no idea that Jake's feelings for me are that serious. As it currently stands, I'm only here until spring."

"But that might change. Bea and Doc hope it will. Jake is quite taken with you, and Cassie's affection for you is clear."

"It's very kind of you to say. But if I were to be in her father's life, Cassie might feel differently, especially if her mother is unhappy," Tess said quietly, acknowledging her fears aloud for the first time.

"You do understand the complications inherent in step-parenting, then," Olivia said sympathetically. "Tess, I wonder, would you be willing to accept a stepdaughter? And how would your parents feel about your involvement with a divorced man, especially one with an ex-wife as difficult as Victoria? I realize I'm putting you on the spot, but I do believe that Jake's feelings for you would likely become quite serious in short order if your involvement continues. I suppose I'm trying to prevent any misunderstandings, as much as I can. He is a devoted father, has a gentle and trusting heart, and considerable wealth. He has so much to offer the right woman."

Tess was unsure of how to answer Olivia's questions tactfully. She met Olivia's eye, and she could see, underneath her prim words and formal demeanor, a very devoted, cautious concern for Jake and Cassie. However unorthodox her methods were, Olivia was well intended. "Jake and Cassie are fortunate to have someone who cares about them the way you do," she said quietly.

Olivia reached across the table and took her hand. "Thank you for understanding, Tess. I do so appreciate your visit. Please forgive me if I've been overbearing. It's not my intention to interfere."

"I appreciate your position. I'd want to protect Jake and Cassie if they were mine. Though I haven't given it much thought, I'm sure I'd be thrilled to be a stepmother to a child as special as Cassie. I really adore her. And my parents are certain to spoil any grandchild absolutely rotten, no matter the circumstance." She smiled at Olivia. "Of course, it's much too soon to think seriously about this, anyway, right?"

Olivia returned the smile, and they made small talk for the remainder of her stay. Once in the hall, the maid brought Tess's coat.

"Well, Tess, I'm glad you accepted my lunch invitation, and I hope we can do this again soon. It's wonderful to have a new face in town, especially one as interesting as yours."

"Thank you." Tess smiled graciously, pleased to have survived the meeting.

*****

Subject: YOU CALLED IT!

Dearest Sam Bam,

Aunt Olivia serves a rockin' lobster newburgh, is the essence of doting aunt, and a mad skilled interrogator to boot. NO one has elicited my thoughts on career, family, education, parenting, marriage and YES the latest presidential election with such adroitly tactful skill and elegance. I've "met the parents" before, but Olivia takes the cake. That said, she truly is a gem, while making it clear I'd best not cross her boy! Sammie, thanks for being the terrific sister that you are!

Love ya, Tessie

*****

Before he left the ranch Saturday afternoon, Jake called Tess. *It's been all of three days, and I'm crazy to see her.* His heart snagged at the sound of her voice. "Cassie and I are headed to Olivia's for dinner. I'm just checking to make sure you survived," he said cautiously.

"Of course I did. We had a *delicious* lunch," Tess said emphatically.

"Sure you did; Stella cooked. Great food is not the problem at Olivia's—it's whether or not you can enjoy it while she's fishing. Did she pull her overprotective headmistress routine on you?"

"Jake," Tess giggled.

"So she did," he grumbled. "What did she say? I'll never get it out of her."

"I'll tell you later," Tess said coyly.

"That bad, huh? I'm just glad you made it out of there alive. I can swing over after dinner, shortly after seven, if you'll join me for a drink. We won't be able to stay too long, though, I'll have to get back to Cassie."

"Let's grab a quick drink, then. I'd like that. You're dressed up, right?"

"Wool trousers, a dress shirt, sweater, tie and my grey overcoat. Olivia wouldn't have it any other way."

"Great. I'll wear my Olivia clothes, too. We'll both be stylin' for Green Forks."

Jake walked into Green Forks three hours later, his hand at the back of Tess's white wool coat. She looked gorgeous, elegant and very together. He found them a booth, and Lotts brought drinks over, a beer for him and an applejack and cider for Tess.

"Lotts, what'd we do to deserve table service? Nobody else gets that around here," Jake baited, taking Tess's coat and hanging it on the pole next to his.

"Anybody caught dancin' in the bar gets a free next round," Lotts grinned wickedly. "And two free rounds for table dancing. It's good for publicity."

Tess flashed Lotts a smile. "Announce that to the entire bar, turn up the jukebox, and I'm in."

"So where are the two of you coming from, all dressed up?" Lotts inquired.

"Dinner with Aunt Olivia, of course." Jake answered, sliding into the booth across from Tess.

"Both of you?" Lotts asked with significance, eyebrows climbing his forehead.

"Tess had lunch with Olivia today," Jake corrected. "Cassie and I had dinner."

"Ah, divide and conquer with coq au vin," Lotts teased good-naturedly.

"Lobster Newburgh and braised short ribs, okay? Now get out of here. You ask too many questions. If this is the cost of table service, I'll ferry my own drinks," Jake grinned, taking a draught of his beer.

"You and Lotts are an entertaining pair," Tess said, sipping her drink.

"It's a problem we've had for years, and there's no cure for it. Want to dance?" Jake asked, touching her fingertips and smiling into her blue eyes.

"Hah. Not tonight. Angling for those free drinks, I see. Think I'm a cheap date?" She squeezed his fingers, teasing him with a flirty smile.

"Not on your life. And I think whatever you said to Aunt Olivia made a very strong impression. She's singing your praises. As I knew she would." He pulled her fingers to his lips, brushing them with a kiss.

Tess blushed. "Thank you. She thinks the world of you and Cassie."

"And expresses it as only the very formidable Olivia McGreer can, I'm sure. So she pulled out the stops, huh?" Jake asked, eyebrows raised.

"I don't kiss and tell. Or in the case of Olivia, lunch and tell," Tess said primly.

"Well, it was a lunch and learn, right? I'm sure she was digging." *How badly did she put you on the spot, Tess, and how much damage control do I need to do?*

"In a polite way," Tess conceded.

"Tess, my aunt is the proverbial wolf in sheep's clothing. She and her cronies in the Ladies Brigade are the intelligence unit of Green Junction. Nothing escapes them. My father and I have gotten many laughs out of the old dame's attempts to orchestrate. It's become a family tradition. But it's less funny when it's my life she's trying to engineer, especially with regard to you. At least give me a hint."

Tess took a deep breath. "She seems to think things are serious between us. Or soon to be serious." She bit her lower lip. Her look was questioning, like the look Cassie gave him when she wanted the truth, straight. "Are they?"

Jake hesitated, trying to hedge. "Look, Tess, Olivia's tried to pair me off since the divorce papers were signed, and she's raving over you. She thinks Cassie needs a suitable stepmother sooner rather than later, something she's mentioned more than once since she realized we were dating."

Tess swallowed and looked at him with wide eyes. He tugged at his shirt collar uncomfortably, loosening his tie and watching her face as the weight of his words sunk in. Finally, her voice tight, she asked, "And what do you think?"

"Do you really want to discuss this now?" he asked, draining half his beer.

"It's as good a time as any," she answered, shrugging her shoulders and looking down, toying with her straw.

He took her hand again and squeezed it, and her eyes met his shyly. "I'm really glad you came by Tuesday night, Tessie, and I'm glad you stayed. I liked making you breakfast Wednesday morning. I hope we can do that again."

"Me, too," she agreed, all cute and glowy.

He took a deep breath and blew it out. Trying to answer the question her curious eyes posed, he said. "As for the rest of it, Cassie is lacking in the mothering department, as you well know. She'd certainly benefit from the right stepmother. But you know how I feel about your career prospects here."

Tess nodded.

"I'd like to be married again, very much," he said, still clasping her hand. Their eyes locked for a long moment, until she blinked. He smiled, a little red-faced. "As much as we here in Green Junction appreciate you, Doctor Tess Bamberger, I think you at least need to get through a winter and spring before we have any version of this discussion again, okay?"

*****

The phone rang at six on Monday morning, snapping Officer Ron from his morning nap. His boots thumped off the Formica desk, taking pens and papers to the floor with them. Rubbing the ache at the back of his neck with a chubby hand, he picked up the receiver.

"Green Junction Po-lice," he mumbled.

"Good Morning. I'd like information about an auto incident that occurred on Friday, September 23, at 12:36 a.m.," a crisp female voice said. "According to the information my insurance company provided, the police report is 10-00623."

A grin spread across Ron's sleepy face. "I can help you with that, Ma'am. Just give me a second to pull the file."

"Thank you. I didn't realize I'd get such prompt service. It's nine a.m. here in Philadelphia. I know it's much earlier, there."

"Oh, we're a twenty-four hour station," Ron answered, setting the phone down and pulling the report he'd filed weeks ago from the filing cabinet. "Yes, Ma'm, what can I do for you?"

"Well, by the hour of the incident, I couldn't help but wonder what exactly the circumstances were?"

"According to the report, visibility was poor. A female driver lost control of her car and was unable to stop at the signed intersection. The driver of the truck, a thirty-two year old male, had a .038 blood alcohol level. Skid marks indicate he may have been traveling at a speed higher than the posted thirty-five miles per hour. Frozen precipitation covered the roads, and it was raining, a freezing rain. The air temperature was twenty-two degrees, in gusty winds."

Ron heard a sharp intake of breath. His smile widened.

"This is Noelle Bamberger. I'm an attorney, and my daughter Tess was driving that car. You are saying the driver of the truck that hit her was drunk?"

"Well, Ma'am, he was darn close to the legal limit. That's all I'm saying. Shall I fax you a copy of the report?"

"Please do."

He flipped the fax machine on, punching in Noelle Bamberger's Philadelphia number. *And Vicki's already given her lawyer a copy of this, too,* he thought with satisfaction.

*****

Wednesday night, Jake was in his office going through mail. He picked up an envelope with his insurance company's return address and frowned. Tensing, he tore it open. As he read the letter inside, the breath rushed from his chest. Stunned, he read through it again. A sharp pain stabbed his gut, as if he'd been knifed. He sat down heavily on his leather desk chair.

Why would Tess have gotten involved with me, when she clearly had doubts? As growing rage at Tess's duplicity welled inside him, he felt humiliation turn to white-hot fury. *Has she just been playing me, all along? And I thought things were going so well between us. Christ, I even mentioned marriage!* He spun his chair and stood up, pressing his hands to the wall behind him. *I've let my guard down and been made a fool of again. Tess isn't who she pretended to be. What is my problem with women, anyway?* There was no relief from the torment. Once again, he'd fallen for the wrong girl.

*****

Thursday afternoon, Tess treated a six-hundred pound sow for mild mastitis, vaccinated her dozen four-week old piglets, said goodbye to the Carsons, and climbed into the Tacoma. Her cell buzzed as she pulled away from Carson Ranch.

"Hey, Tess. How'd it go with the pig?" Alice asked.

"She's a mean sucker. She was uncomfortable when I got here, and it took plenty of sedative before she'd let me mess with her. I hope the Carsons see a big improvement by tomorrow afternoon. The infection should have cleared out by then. I told them to call and let us know how she's doing."

"Good. Listen, I just heard from Jake. His favorite gelding tangled with barbed wire; he's all torn up and needs stitches. Do you know how to get to McGreer Ranch from the Carsons?"

"Not exactly."

"It's about twelve miles. At least you're on the right side of town." Alice gave her the directions, and Tess pulled up Jake's address in her GPS. "Take your time, Tess, and drive slowly."

Twenty minutes later, Tess pulled into the gates of McGreer Ranch, drove over a knoll and around to the horse barn, glad for the lingering daylight. She was going through her supplies, assembling a suture kit, putting hypodermics, antibiotics, and a sedative in her bag, when Jake came out of the barn. His glare was chilling, and his eyes blazed with anger.

*****

When Jake saw Tess's maroon Tacoma roll up near the horse barn, he set his jaw. *Might as well get this over with.*

"Hey, Jake," Tess said with a smile, laying out her supplies. "Alice called. She said your big red Quarter Horse tangled with some barbed wire, and I should come right over from the Carsons." She glanced at him worriedly. "Weren't you expecting me?"

"I requested Doc Harnes," he managed to say, his voice tight.

"Doc's been booked at the clinic all day, I'm doing ranch rounds this afternoon. I'm certain I can handle this," she said, eyeing him curiously.

"I'm sure you can, but considering all the nonsense with my insurance company, I'd hoped Doc would come out."

"Insurance company? What are you talking about?" She looked puzzled.

"Tess, I got a letter yesterday." He was trying to keep his tone calm with little success. "My carrier has received notice from your insurance company, stating that I'm at fault for our accident due to my blood alcohol level and rate of speed. My insurer suggested I retain an attorney since you're now planning to sue me."

"Jake, what are you talking about? Blood alcohol level?" She stared at him aghast. "Were you drunk?"

"No, Tess, I was not drunk," he said, biting off each word. "In fact, I hadn't consumed a drop of alcohol. I drank ginger ale and water all night, and Alice will vouch for me. But there seems to be a problem with the police report—something else I need to look into," he snapped. "Why didn't you at least tell me what was going on? And why would you spend the night with a guy you you planned to sue?" His voice lashed out, his anger rising.

Her tender face flinched, but he continued, venting his fury. "You know, Vicki will be thrilled to use this stuff in her next custody suit. She's made no secret of her intent to move Cassie to California, and I haven't even started on what it'll do to my insurance rates. Why would you pull something like this on me?"

"Wait, Jake. There must be some misunderstanding," Tess said, looking like she'd been struck. "I don't know anything about this lawsuit or the police report. I haven't spoken to my insurance company about anything other than medical bills, I swear it." Tears of humiliation glistened in her eyes. She wiped her face, shaking her head. "Look, this is silly. I can't do this right now. Why don't you show me your horse?"

Impatient and frustrated, he led Tess down the center aisle of the barn, sliding open Alchemy's stall door. Inside, his prize chestnut gelding stood eating hay. Blood seeped from wounds on the animal's copper-colored chest and numerous gashes on his front legs and belly. Tess inhaled sharply.

Turning to him, her eyes pleading, Tess said, "Your horse is suffering. He needs immediate care."

"Fine," Jake nodded stonily. He left to carry her things in, angry with himself. No matter what happened, he prided himself on staying calm, especially with visitors to the ranch. But her betrayal was so like what he'd felt through his marriage—so very unexpected from what he'd believed her to be—he'd just lost it. *As angry as I am with Tess, I'm even angrier at myself for being led in, for being a sucker again. I'm a fool, for trusting so easily.*

Setting the suture kit and medications down outside the stall, he rigged her an adjustable light, flooding a hospital-bright arc on Alchemy's belly and legs. Tess approached the horse slowly, gingerly touching his shoulder. "Easy, fellow, just let me take a look at you," she whispered, squatting next to Alchemy. Looking closely at the cuts near the bone on his knees, pasterns and fetlocks, she made certain there was no damage to the tendons and nerves.

"Alchemy was limping when I brought him in. It's been about an hour and a half. I didn't see anything that suggested permanent injury or lameness. I gave him some Dormosedan I keep for emergencies, three-quarter cc's," Jake offered stonily, clipping a lead rope on the gelding's halter.

"That should keep him for a while, then. I'll give him more, a little later." Speaking soothingly to the horse, Tess injected a local anesthetic. Jake saw her hands shake as she threaded a needle with dissolving suture. He held the big chestnut steady, and she began stitching. "How did he get into barbed wire?"

"We brush-hogged some brambles last spring below the paddocks. I'm wondering if the tractor didn't kick up some old barbed wire that had been lying in there and no one spotted it. He has a bad habit of jumping out of his paddock. Somehow, he got tangled in the barbed wire. By the time Ralph cut it off his legs, he'd already been thrashing around in it for who knows how long."

Tess nodded. Despite the circumstances, she'd managed to gain Alchemy's trust immediately. *This must be nerve wracking for her, too. But what had she expected?* As aggravated as Jake was, he had to admire her resolve.

For over an hour, she worked silently, completely focused. As his fury subsided, he couldn't help admiring her, hair pulled back in a ponytail, cheeks fresh and smooth, and trim, even in her baggy coveralls. He knew she was talented, but he'd never seen sutures so careful and pretty. After layering two sets of suture in the deepest wounds, she said, almost to herself, "I'm trying to keep this really neat to minimize scarring."

"I can see that. Alchemy was a conformation champion as a two and three year old. I'm grateful for whatever you can do for him appearance-wise."

"You got it," she said, glancing away quickly when he tried to meet her eye. He remembered how passionate she'd been with him, how close they'd been to making love, and his heart wrenched. *Why in the hell would she complain to her insurance and ruin everything for us?*

*****

Shocked by Jake's manner, Tess focused on connecting with Alchemy. "You're going to be okay, guy," she soothed, giving him another shot of Dormosedan. The copper-colored quarter horse flinched and shifted his weight. "You're a real trooper."

Her nervousness and tension had dissipated as she worked, and she was pleased with the results. An hour and a half after she'd begun, Tess heard a child's voice call into the barn.

"Daddy?"

"In Alchemy's stall, Cass."

"Hi, Daddy. Is Dr. Tess here for a trail ride?" Tess's heart sank at the eager anticipation in Cassie's voice. Two familiar amber eyes peeped over the stall wall. "Hi, Dr. Tess!" Cassie called cheerfully.

Tess took a deep breath, smiling bravely, "Hi, Cassie."

Jake's voice was clipped. "Cass, Alchemy and Dr. Tess need more time here in the quiet, and Van is probably still cooped up in the house. Can you go get him and bring him down here? I'll help you with Sparky when Dr. Tess finishes up."

Tess's insides twisted at the coolness in his voice. *Does Jake want to keep Cassie away from me now, too?* There was just one gash left under Alchemy's belly. "I think this is the last one that needs sutures, Jake," she said quietly, her face burning with humiliation. "I'll use Furazine and tape the rest."

A half hour later, she pulled her surgical gloves off and packed up her suture kit. Jake carried the lamp to the truck, and she followed with her bag. Cassie was leading her pony Sparky from the paddock. "Sparky looks great, Cassie," Tess called, infusing her voice with as much warmth and encouragement as she could muster as she opened the cab door to let Rhiannon run.

Jake helped Cassie tie her pony in the grooming stall, saying, "You start grooming Sparky, Cass. I have to talk to Dr. Bamberger a minute. I'll be back to help you tack up."

Jake approached her truck, handing her a letter with a grim look. "I made a copy for you."

While he brought the rest of her things to the truck's tailgate, Tess read the letter. *This is for real.* The knot in her stomach tightened worse than before, and she began to feel nauseous.

Looking straight at him, she said, "I wish you'd called me right away. I wondered why I hadn't heard from you, Jake. I knew nothing about the breathalyzer, and I absolutely have not spoken to my insurance company about a lawsuit."

Flashing an annoyed glare, he stood stiff and unyielding. She touched his arm, searching his face for some kind of reprieve. "I know it seems unlikely and I don't have an explanation for this right now, but I'll do what it takes to clear this thing up. I'm sure Alice can vouch for you as far as that night at the bar."

Jake exhaled. His face softened, and some of the tension left his shoulders. "Look, Tess, you know I've had my fill of lawyers."

If you've had your fill of lawyers, you won't want to meet my parents. Tess's throat closed as the realization hit her. *I was still on Mom and Dad's policy when the accident happened. They must have found out about it and started digging.*

"Jake, tell me about this police report," Tess choked out.

"Ron gave me a breathalyzer test after the ambulance showed up. He told me it was inconclusive, but he had a real smirk on his face when he said it. Ron doesn't like me. I hate to think he'd lie about something like this, but he does like to push his weight around. A .038 is below the legal limit, but the way the report reads, alcohol impairment was a factor in our collision. It's insane. I wasn't drinking."

"Alice served me ginger ale and water all night. She'll tell you." Jake continued. "You know how badly I feel about the accident, but this complaint makes me look irresponsible and willfully negligent." He shook his head, eyes tormented. "Are you sure you didn't tell anyone you suspected I'd been drinking?"

"Jake, I swear it. I had a concussion that night, but I could still testify that you showed no signs of intoxication, if it comes to that. Remember, you checked my pupils? And there wasn't alcohol on your breath, so that's something. The ambulance crew was there, too. You have plenty of witnesses," Tess said, keeping her voice down so Cassie couldn't hear.

"Maybe, but the stink Vicki could cause over the report is the last thing Cassie needs. My attorney will have it on his desk first thing tomorrow. I have to challenge it legally."

"Look, I'll go to bat for you, Jake, I promise. We'll get this straightened out, okay?"

"Thanks for that, Tess. Let cooler heads prevail, huh?" he asked sheepishly, shooting her an appreciative look.

"As far as Alchemy, I've given him a tetanus and IV antibiotics. He'll need to be checked on later tonight and first thing tomorrow morning. Call right away if any sutures pop. Here are some oral antibiotics. Give them twice a day, until he's healed. I'll be out to remove the sutures early next week, unless you'd rather have Doc do it."

Cassie called out from the grooming stall. "Hey, Dr. Tess, can you stay and watch me ride?"

Tess walked towards the barn, her heart locked in her throat. "I'd love to, Cassie, but I better not today. Have fun with Sparky and your dad, okay?"

"Don't forget our trail ride next time!" Cassie called out, smiling.

"Okay!" Tess waved, forcing the most pleasant smile she could muster and backing towards the truck. "I've got root beer and vanilla ice cream at the apartment, any time you want to stop by!"

"I missed working at the vet office this week, Dr. Tess. I'll try to stop by soon," Cassie promised.

"I'm always happy to see you, Cass," Tess smiled, ignoring the hot tears that threatened to well and trying to feel brave.

Jake stood by Tess's truck. "Thanks for your help with Alchemy today," he said tightly. "Look, you do great work, and it was really fortunate for us all that you were here today. I'll make sure Cassie gets to the clinic on your shift in the next week or so, okay?"

"Uh-huh," Tess nodded, "That sounds good." Tired of faking it and anxious to get off McGreer Ranch, Tess climbed into her truck. Tears blurred her vision as she drove towards town. The knowledge that Vicki could interfere with Jake's relationship with

Cassie over the accident was like a kick in the gut. *And Jake doesn't trust me, not even enough to call to talk, which makes it even worse.* Her thoughts turned to anger. *How dare he think the worst of me!*

*****

As soon as she had cell reception, Tess pulled off the road and dialed her mother. "Mom, I'm looking at a copy of a letter Jake McGreer received from his insurer based on a complaint about a police auto accident report. You or dad don't know anything about this, do you?"

"Your father and I received copies of medical statements, so naturally we looked into it, dear. The police report says the driver had been drinking and was presumed speeding. As you know, you were insured on our policy. We took action to protect you."

Her voice burst with fury, "Mom, you seriously did this without even consulting me?"

"Tess, please calm down. We knew you had a lot going on with your new job, and we didn't want to trouble you. We did what any good attorney would have advised in your situation."

"But, Mom, I didn't ask for an attorney's advice!" Tess was barely able to conceal her anger. "This is my life, and your interference has really messed things up for me here."

"Be that as it may, you were hit, and the driver was near drunk. Were you hurt?"

"I'm not discussing the accident with you, Mom. I can't trust that you and Dad will respect my privacy."

"Tess, that's nonsense. What were you doing out at that time of night, anyway, in a strange place? I wish you'd stayed in the hotel room in Colorado Springs where you said you'd been," her mother answered frostily.

"Mom, this accident was most definitely not Jake McGreer's fault. His insurance company is under the impression I'm gearing up for a lawsuit, which couldn't be further from the truth."

"Well, dear, facts speak for themselves. Of course you should recover a settlement if you can."

"Mom, you are completely unaware of the facts, I assure you."

Her mother sighed. "Oh, Tess, why do you have a blind spot for such inappropriate men?"

Her mother might as well have slapped her. "What is that supposed to mean?" she asked, astonished. "Look, Mom, you spent all last summer humiliating me with snide comments, and you're still at it. I know you don't want me here. You've made no secret of your disdain for this place and my choices. But this is my life and these are my dreams, so please, can you stop insulting me? I've tried to be patient, but it really feels like you don't respect me at all."

"Tess, your father and I will call later from home," her mother said quickly, ending the discussion.

Great, and I was just finally letting her know how I've felt. Angry and upset, Tess picked up a pizza at Mamma Boccini's and took it back to her apartment. Sitting at Alice's little bistro table, she ate two bites of the first slice and put it down, sickened with despair. *How could they do this to me?*

After she'd spent an hour crying to Samantha on the phone, Tess opened her Endocrinology textbook, trying to distract herself with the lymphatic system of *Suidae Suinae Sus. At least I'll be prepared if the Carson's sow doesn't improve. I can't do much for my own life, but I can still fix a pig in a pickle.*

Her cell buzzed at eight. "Tess," her dad said gruffly, "Mom's on the other extension. I need to start off by saying that your mother and I have reviewed your legal position, and we agree that you should sue the driver of the truck, despite the fact that he's now a friend."

"Dad, would you two please knock it off? Receipts for medical payments were mailed to your house while I was on your insurance policy, but they're mine to deal with. I'm an adult," she protested, her voice straining with anger, "I'm the expert in my life. I can't even believe you or mom would make inquiries without discussing your concerns with me. Now you are making legal recommendations? There is absolutely no way this will turn into a lawsuit."

"Why would you take that position, Tess?" Noelle admonished.

"Because the accident was unavoidable, Mom. I slid on an icy road and ran a stop sign."

"Tess, this man sounds like a yahoo cowboy. He's dangerous. He was drunk and speeding," her father interjected.

"Dad, I was almost completely in this 'yahoo cowboy's' lane when he hit me, and if he'd not been paying attention, it could have been much, much worse. Jake helped me. He insisted I go to the hospital for a CAT scan, and he took care of my dog. He's a very decent guy."

"Tess, you didn't tell us about a dog," her mother's voice quavered.

"No, I didn't, Mom. If I had, you would have harassed me with the details of every disease and parasite the dog could possibly expose me to my entire trip cross-country in an attempt to convince me that picking up a stray dog on the highway is a bad idea. I picked up an abandoned dog, I moved to a place you don't like, and I survived a car crash. I'm a vet, an actual professional, with an advanced degree. I'm not just your little girl anymore, and it's high time I get to make decisions about my life. I have to tell you, too, Mom, that the snotty, hurtful comments you've been making non-stop since June are most unwelcome."

"Now, just a minute, Contessa," her father berated. "I will not have you speaking to your mother this way."

"Dad, I will try to forgive you both for sticking your noses into my affairs if you consider that had someone other than Jake hit me, I would not have gotten to the hospital. In the off-chance I was hemorrhaging, I'd be dead right now."

"You don't know that, Tess," her mother said scornfully, "And it's no reason to give this man a free pass on drinking and speeding."

"I do know it, Mom. Jake wasn't drinking. He's got witnesses, including me. The cop gave him a breathalyzer test and then lied about his blood alcohol level. The police report is false, and it's being used to hurt Jake."

"That sounds like nonsense. Honey, we are trying to protect you."

"You're not protected me, Mom, not at all. You're not even listening. Please, at least have the courtesy to hear what I am saying. You've caused me serious problems. I'm tired of your second-guessing. It might just have been a bad habit while I was home, but now your meddling has undermined everything I've worked for here. This is a small town and word travels fast. If this thing ever turned into a lawsuit, no rancher in town would let me step foot on their property for fear of being sued. The last thing I need is a reputation as a litigious, arrogant east-coast brat. People around here know Jake McGreer, and they know Officer Ron. That police report will not hold up in court, believe me."

"Your mother and I have been worried about you, Tess," her dad said, a warning note in his tone.

"Well, I'm worried, too, Dad. About you," she said. "You assume that I can't take care of myself, but how well are you taking care of yourself? Have you taken the advice your cardiologist gave you? Cutting out red meat? Starting an exercise program to lower your cholesterol and blood pressure? Are you still smoking cigars? This works both ways, Dad. You get to make your own life choices, so why can't I?"

"Tess, I'm shocked," her dad said, his voice muted.

"So was I when Jake showed me the letter from his insurance carrier, Dad!" She burst into tears. "Please, I'm very upset now. Try to understand how terrible this is for me. I have my own auto and health insurance now, I've taken a loan for my own vehicle, and I really, really need to be in charge of my own life. Thank you for all you have done for me in the past, but please, please, let me take care of the yahoo cowboys in Green Junction."

"I've got it under control, I promise you," Tess said, trying not to hiccup into the phone. "I'll call when I'm ready to talk, but, please, don't count on it being very soon. I'm ready to say goodnight."

"All right, Tess. Good night, then," her father answered gravely.

Tears running down her cheeks, Tess clicked off her cell. She had a lot to try to explain to Jake.

*****

"Well, you're here early," Lotts said when Jake walked into Green Forks that night. "Pool Tournament doesn't start 'til after eight. What'll it be?"

"Bourbon, scotch, beer," Jake answered tonelessly.

"That bad, huh?"

"I just dropped Cassie off. Vicki came out, waving a copy of a police report right in front of Cass, screaming about a modification of custody. She's still trying to find a way to get to California with Cassie, after all this time."

"What's this about a police report?"

"Officer Ron falsified his report of my accident with Tess, to make it look like I'd been drinking. Alice warned me, but I wrote it off. Someone complained to Tess's insurance."

"Tess complained that you were drinking?" Jake saw shock and surprise on Lotts' face, and he felt the anger he'd felt on Monday all over again. *That's just about how I feel buddy, times ten. I almost made love to her the other night.*

"Hard to believe, but what other explanation could there be?" he asked, still tormented.

Lotts slid a beer in front of Jake. "Here, guy. Start with the easy stuff."

Jake held up a hand. "No way. Ron will be scouting for my truck tonight. Vicki's sure to be looking for more ammunition."

"Jake, you sound like a hunted man. Vicki's riding you hard, and Tess let you down. Possum's the only way to call their bluff. You gotta just roll over and play dead, and things will settle down. Drink that beer, you'll feel better," Lotts coached.

"How the hell did I get in stuff this deep, Lotts?" he asked, sipping the foam from the top then pushing it away.

"I don't think it was any one particular thing, Jake. Murphy's Law, more like. Couple little snowballs, and you wind up under an avalanche." Lotts set a ginger ale in front of him, looking Jake in the eye. "This one is on the house, my friend. Pretend it's forty year old, barrel-cured scotch. And keep thinking...possum. You just play it cool. The lawyers won't get blood from a stone. I'm not at all surprised about Vicki, but this just doesn't sound like Tess. What a shame."

"Alchemy tangled with barbed wire today. While Tess was at the ranch to suture him, I blew up at her," Jake said morosely. "She insists she didn't contact her insurer about anything more than medical bills. I'd like to believe her, but what other explanation could there be?" he asked bitterly, trying to keep the hurt out of his voice.

"You think Tess is lying? I don't see why she'd lie, man. She's got to establish a professional reputation around here. Seems like she's damn sweet. Maybe a little 'high-octane' for Green Junction."

"She's 'high-octane' all right, and my truck runs on diesel. I fell hook, line, and sinker into a whole lot of east-coast, ivy-educated trouble, with no idea how it's going to affect my time with Cassie..." His voice trailed off. He drained the ginger ale, and Lotts poured him another. When Jake's cell buzzed, Lotts moved to the end of the bar.

Jake ended the call after a few minutes, and turned to Lotts. Resigned, he said, "Tess didn't tell her parents about the accident. They got insurance receipts and started asking questions, so Ron faxed them a police report with a false blood alcohol reading. Tess offered to file an objection to the police report with Sergeant Fuller first thing tomorrow and have it sent to both insurers. I guess it might help."

"Her parents?" Lotts asked quizzically.

"Lawyers, Lotts, more lawyers. The ivy-educated tenderfoot's parents are overprotective, east-coast lawyers. Doesn't it just figure?" Jake said, shaking his head.

"Aw, man, they think they're looking out for her. They're lawyers—that's just what they do. Alice says Tess moved all the way out here to get some space, and feels like she needs to prove herself. She must be pretty shaken up right now."

"She is." Jake winced at the pain he'd heard in Tess's voice, remembering the cruel way he'd lashed into her at the ranch. He took a deep breath. "Tess did a damn good job with Alchemy, I'll give her that. I'll bet he'll only have a light scar or two; she got the sutures that neat and pretty."

Lotts gave him the once over, shuffling a stack of coasters. "Aw, give her more than that. She's got a crush on you, and she's got to be embarrassed as hell. It's not going to make her new job any easier if the ranchers around town hear about any of this," he said, his words a question as much as a statement.

"You think I would rat her out because her parents are sharks? Never. I won't mention this to anyone. Vicki might, though."

"Ah, everybody knows Vicki's trouble. They'll take what she has to say with a grain of salt."

7

"Don't Go Breakin' My Heart"

Saturday morning Tess got up early and took Rhiannon for a run. The sunshine was bright but a chilly breeze gusted, taking her breath. In the park, she found an upland trail that looped around town. Sheltered by aspen and pine, the wind was bearable, and Tess logged five miles, catching scenic glimpses of the valley.

She hadn't spoken to Jake since Thursday, but she'd managed a long talk with Sergeant Fuller at the police station the day before, telling him everything that happened the night of her accident. He'd been open-minded, helping her fill out a rebuttal to the report, faxing it to the insurance companies, and somehow, she trusted him. *He doesn't seem like the kind of guy to let Jake take the fall for this.*

After her run, Tess showered and dressed. Bea and Doc were at the clinic for the morning, Alice was doing lab work, and Tess was on call. Unless a ranch call came in, Tess had the entire day to herself. *The entire day to think about the bomb my parents have dropped on my life.*

She'd heard nothing from Jake and had not seen Cassie. *When will I ever see Cassie after all of this?*

She wished she could tell someone about Vicki and the medicine chest, too. *But I'm really not sure what I saw, and why would I want to make more trouble for anyone right now, especially when my reputation is on the line, too?*

Still, it worried her, thinking of Cassie. *And now both of her parents hate me. I sure wish I could do more for that kid.*

*****

To: NBamberger@SNLLawcom, RBamberger@RSTBLawcom
From: Tess.Bam@vmailcom

Date: Saturday, October 20, 8:38 AM
Subject:

Dear Mom and Dad,

I'm just writing to tell you that, other than being very upset about your interference in my life, I am doing well. Alice and I are going to the Hallowe'en Dance tonight at the Elks Club. It will be a good chance to meet the ranchers and people from town.
I love you both, and I know you care (too much!), but it's going to take me a while to forgive you. I really need to be on my own with a chance to make my own decisions and, if necessary, my own mistakes. I hope you can appreciate that.

Love, Tess.

*****

To: Sam.Bam@vmailcom
From. Tess.Bam@vmailcom
Subject: You are awesome.
8:41 am, Saturday, October 20

Sister,
Thanks for the calls this week. You've made me feel a million times better. I seriously appreciate your understanding and support.
Hope this all blows over. Alice thinks it will. Trick-or-Treat tonight will be tough. After so many treats, it feels like I've been tricked.

Luvvya, Tess.

*****

Tess tidied her apartment, unable to stop thinking about the fun she'd had with Cassie, playing with Rhiannon and making root beer floats. Recalling the million questions Cassie always had for her, her eyes started to tear. *Okay, I'm officially a complete wreck now.*

Unwilling to be alone, Tess headed for the clinic.

"So what's the story with this blood-alcohol report?" she whispered to Alice in the lab.

"Ron gave Jake a breathalyzer test after the accident," Alice said, eye-dropping a slide and peering into the microscope. "You didn't know?"

"Uh, no, I'd passed out, and the ambulance people were working on me, so I didn't see that part. Jake didn't smell like alcohol when he was helping me, though."

"Jake was at Green Forks for the pool tournament. He stayed late then spent twenty minutes helping me clean up. He didn't touch a drop of anything alcoholic all night, Tess, I swear it. He drank two ginger ales then water. I've already told Sergeant Fuller. He called to ask the day after the accident.

"I spoke with Sergeant Fuller yesterday. Do you think Ron lied about the test results?"

"Ron's despised Jake for a long time, it seems. When they were in high school, it was over sports and girls, Lotts said, and now Ron's jealous of Jake's ranches and of how everyone around town looks up to him. It seems like Ron's always wanted to stick it to Jake. He finally found a way to do it."

"I'm so angry with my parents for interfering, Alice. My mother still refuses to understand why I didn't stay in Philadelphia to join a suburban practice on the Main Line and marry Starchy Archie."

"Starchy Archie?"

"My intended, as far as my parents are concerned." Tess sighed. It felt so good to unload on Alice. "He's a junior partner at my father's firm. Six foot four, one hundred and eighty pounds, red hair, freckles—not a bad guy but basically a total dork. My father is his mentor. Archie will make full partner next year."

Alice smiled sympathetically but said nothing. "You know what my dad always says about Archie?" Alice shook her head. "He spends eight or ten hours with the guy at work every day and thinks I should marry him, but all he can say," Tess pretended to take a club in her hands, took a backswing, then swiped her arms in a wide arc, "is 'That Archie! He's got a heckuva golf swing'!"

"Tess, that's not so bad," Alice admonished. "That's how fathers are. Your dad probably really likes him."

"It's repulsive, Alice, and it gets worse. After I joined some fancy vet practice in the suburbs, Archie and I were supposed to book a wedding at the Four Seasons, buy a McMansion in Paoli, choose china, crystal and silverware patterns, fill a classroom at the Friend's Select school with freckle-faced, red-haired kids, and divide summers between a country house in the Poconos and a beach house at the Jersey Shore. Can you see me in that life, Alice?"

Alice only smiled.

"My parents have built it up so much, Archie is paralyzed by me. They kept inviting him to dinner at our house, until he started freezing when I came in the room, like a jackrabbit with halting speech. How can they have bred me, born me and raised me, but have so little idea of who I really am?" Tess wailed.

"Well, from what you've told me of your conversation Thursday night, you've set some clear boundaries," Alice soothed, sticking another slide under the microscope. "They'll get it, I promise you. They may not like it, but they'll get it. Have you spoken to Jake?"

"I called him yesterday, to see how Alchemy is doing. It was tense, but it wasn't as bad as Thursday. Thursday was brutal. I was so humiliated, Alice. It hurts that Jake didn't trust me. He thinks Vicki will use the police report to start some custody thing again."

Alice put a finger to her lips and said quietly, "I think she already has from what Jake told Lotts."

"Seriously? Ugh." Tess put her head in her hands, groaning with dismay. "Can't Vicki see how much Jake cares about Cassie? He must have been at least decent to her, when they were married. I can't imagine otherwise; he's a reasonable guy."

"Vicki moved to Green Junction to live with her father after her parent's divorce, and Jake started dating her right away. When she got pregnant with Cassie, he asked her to marry him. They had this big wedding, but soon after Cassie was born, Vicki decided that she hated her life in Green Junction. She left Cassie with Jake and went to California to stay with her mother. He had to jump the moon to get her back here, but as soon as he did, she filed for divorce and tried to get full custody of Cassie so she could leave again."

"Sounds brutal," Tess said, her eyes wide. "But I guess I had some idea that it must have been."

Alice continued, keeping her voice low. "He didn't have a prenup, and she took him to the cleaners, fighting over every last thing. The divorce took forever. It was only final last May, and the custody agreement requires them to both live close by. Honestly, Tess, Jake was devastated until you showed up, and Vicki's still furious that she can't leave town."

"And now my parents blew it for us," Tess said morosely. "Jake will never give it another shot, Alice, will he?"

"It's done, sweetie. Don't blame your parents. Let things calm down a bit, and I bet he'll come around," Alice reassured her. "Jake's no fool."

"I hope so. Thanks, Al." Tess gave her a hug. "I left pizza for you. I'll see you later, right?"

"Yup, Hallowe'en party tonight!" Alice chimed. "I'll bring lasagna over and your headband with bunny ears. Any last-minute cold feet?"

"Are you kidding me?" Tess assured her, faking enthusiasm as best she could. "My feet are white like a rabbit and ready to hop, Wonderland Alice."

*****

To:Tess.Bam@vmailcom
From: Sam.Bam@vmailcom
Date: Saturday, October 27, 4:43 PM
Subject: Parental Bomb Drop

Tessie,

It's Hallowe'en, so shake it out, babycakes, and try to have fun tonight. ~I'll be roaming the streets of the Big Apple as Pebbles, with no eligible lion, tiger or bear in sight. If you see Bam-Bam, send him my way! (Can sabertooth loincloths be dry cleaned..??)

Love, Sam Bam-Bam...Bam-Bam!

*****

To: <u>Sam.Bam@vmailcom</u>
From: <u>Tess.Bam@vmailcom</u>
Date: Saturday, October 27 3:55 PM
Subject: Bam-Bam goes my heart

Pebbles,
Will be playing White Rabbit to Alice's Wonderland...Hope your drunken mayhem is Yabba Dabba Do, and you find all the Bam-Bam you can manage....loincloth optional!!

Love You, Tess Bam-Bam...Bam...Bam...

*****

At six-thirty, Alice bustled into Tess's apartment with takeout from Mamma Boccini's, wearing the full skirted blue dress that Tess had found for her at the thrift store, white tights, and black-buckled shoes. On a hanger in Tess's closet was a white ruffly pinafore Alice had borrowed from Bea.

They ate and tidied up quickly. While Alice pulled on a blonde wig in front of her dresser, Tess climbed into a one-piece white flannel pajama she'd ordered. Buttoning up the front, she said, "Hah, I can wear this next year, too, Alice. You can be Ahab, and I'll be the whale!"

"Oh, you look cute, Tess! I hope you're here, next year."

Standing in front of the bathroom mirror, Tess positioned the headband with bunny ears, put lipstick on her nose, and drew whiskers with eyeliner. "

Ready to go, White Rabbit?" Alice asked, shrugging into her coat and picking up the huge cardboard playing cards Tess had painted.

"Yup, let's go face the mob," Tess said, feeling cheery. As she pulled on her white ruffled coat, the cell in Tess's pocket buzzed. *What's Sammi doing calling me? She's supposed to be out looking for Bam-Bam.*

"Tess?" Her sister's voice was frantic. "Tess, Mom just called. Dad's been taken to the hospital in an ambulance. She thinks he's had a heart attack. It'll be two hours before I can get there. Oh, Tess, what if he doesn't make it?"

A wave of panic surged over Tess as, blindly, she stammered, "I'll be there as soon as I can, Sammi. I'll text you when I have a flight."

"Okay. I'm still in New York in this crazy Pebbles dress, but there was no time to change. I don't even have an overnight bag. I have to go, I'm at the train station, and I have to pay the cabbie. See you in Philadelphia."

"I love you, Sammi."

"Me, too, Tess."

Feeling the tears welling in her eyes, Tess ended the call, struggling to catch her breath. "Tess, what's wrong?" Alice asked.

"That was my sister. It seems my dad had a heart attack. My mom is at the hospital with him now. It sounds really serious. I need a flight out of Denver as soon as possible."

"I'll drive you to the airport. Oh, honey, I'm so sorry."

As Alice spoke, Tess flipped her laptop open and searched flights online. Hurriedly, Alice changed. Within five minutes, Tess had a flight booked. "I'm just taking a carry on; I still have clothes at home. But what am I going to do with Rhiannon?" she asked, an edge of desperation creeping into her voice.

"Jake and Cassie will be happy to help, you know that," Alice soothed, following her into the bedroom. In the middle of her cheeks were still two circles of lipstick, barely rubbed off.

Tess went to the bathroom to rub the color off her nose, handing Alice some tissues and cold cream. "My flight's just before midnight. We have time to leave my apartment key with Lotts and tell him what's going on."

For the next eight hours, Tess was tortured by the memory of the last two conversations she'd had with her parents. She'd been so angry, burnt with resentment from all the undermining they'd done. *I let it build up instead of dealing with it, thinking that once I got out here, it wouldn't matter.. I was foolish—and childish, really.* The words she'd last spoken to her father echoed in her head, haunting her the entire flight. *What if that was the last thing I ever get to say to my dad?*

Arriving in Philadelphia, she sprinted from the gate towards the airport exit, texting Sam. *3:36 am "Any word?"*

3:38 am "Still waiting. He's in surgery. There's hope."

Flailing her arms, Tess hailed the nearest cab. The yellow sedan sped north on 76 in pitch black darkness, slowing as it wound through the labyrinthine construction around Thirty-Fourth and Spruce Street. Finally at the curb, she grabbed her carry-on and ran towards the brightly lit University of Pennsylvania Hospital sign, shoving through the doors and into the glass vestibule. Gasping to the receptionist, she raced to the elevator, following signs to the floor ominously marked "Cardiac Unit."

Standing in its brightly lit hallway, Tess saw the shadowy forms of her mother and sister, seated in the hushed waiting room. She stood stock still. *I'm too scared to go forward, and I can't go back.*

They moved towards her. Under the bright florescent lights, Tess saw Sammi's short fake fur coat, pulled over grey tights, her raggedy-hemmed haltered mini dress slashed with grey paint, but it was the appearance of her indomitable mother that was most startling. Her chignon in loose disarray at her collar, Noelle Bamberger looked frail and uncertain, her eyes tired and shaken.

Then she heard Sam's voice and saw her eyes. "Tessie? Daddy's had a blocked artery. They were able to stabilize him. The surgery was a success."

"Thank God," Tess exhaled, almost collapsing to the floor. Her mother and sister surrounded her, their hugs offering comfort and assurance.

"We can see Daddy in an hour or so when he's out of recovery," Sam said.

"And now we can make sure some real experts see to that neck and head of yours, after that terrible auto accident," her mother sniffed.

Mom may be down, but she's not out. Tess put her arm around her mother's tight shoulders as she met Sam's steady gaze. Once Richard was out of recovery, Tess, Samantha and Noelle took turns sitting by his bed, holding his hand for fifteen or twenty minutes at a time. He was pasty-faced and fragile-looking in his blue hospital garb, surrounded by tubes, bags, needles, and monitors. The tense morning passed slowly. By Sunday evening, he'd improved markedly and insisted that the girls and Noelle return home for a good night's rest.

"Well, he's back to being himself, calling the shots again, looking out for us," Sam remarked with an impish grin.

Noelle nodded, visibly relieved by her husband's recovery. "He's out of danger, it seems."

Tess said nothing. She'd been awake for thirty-six hours, wracked with guilt over her own careless words. *It almost feels like I jinxed him.*

"He's got the best medical care in the world, Tessie. He'll be okay. The doctors said he'll be fine, better than before, even," Sam said with as much enthusiasm as she could muster, giving Tess a squeeze. "And now there's a chance he'll follow the doctor's orders."

"Oh, he won't have a choice about that," Noelle said with conviction. *At least mom sounds like her old self.*

"C'mon, it's been a long night. Let's find the car and get a good night's sleep," Sammy said.

As Sam maneuvered her mother's Volvo north on Lancaster Avenue, Tess felt dazed and disoriented. *It wasn't too long ago that Mom and Dad had all the answers, but now it almost feels like I'm the parent. It's all too crazy. Everything is happening too quickly.*

It was dark when they arrived at the house. The neighbor's Hallowe'en decorations cast an eerie, surreal gloom, but Buster was waiting at the door, so happy to see Tess his whole body wiggled. Even so, it was strange to be home. Tess tried to eat the takeout her mother ordered, but it tasted like cardboard. She brushed her teeth and crawled into the white canopy bed in her old room, too tired and numb to think. *I hope Mom won't notice how much weight I've lost. She doesn't need anything else to worry about.* When Buster poked the door open to lie on the carpet beside the bed, she let her hand trail down his back. She'd almost drifted off to sleep when her cell buzzed.

"Hi, Tess. How are things?" Jake's voice was calm and concerned.

"Okay. My dad is out of danger. The surgery was a success," she heard her voice waver and tried to steady it.

"That's good news. Cassie and I grabbed Rhiannon this morning, first thing. She's here at the ranch with us. We've been thinking of you."

"Have you? I appreciate that."

"Cassie wants to say 'hi'. Can I put her on?"

"Sure."

"Hi, Dr. Tess." Cassie's voice was quiet and shy on the telephone.

"Hi, Cassie. Thank you for taking care of Rhiannon for me."

"We didn't get a chance to ultrasound her belly to see the puppies before you left."

"I know, honey, but I'll be back soon. How is Sparky?"

"He's fine. I took a trail ride with Daddy today. It was cold and Sparky was frisky, but I didn't let him get away from me."

"You're a good little rider, Cassie. Did you have homework this weekend?"

"Nope, we had a bunch of tests on Friday so Ms. Roper gave us the weekend off. In math we are adding double digits. I got a ninety-five on my test and ninety on spelling."

"That's the way, Cassie. Take your time with homework, and you'll ace the test."

"I'm going to look through those puppy books we got at the library."

"That's a great idea. We'll see what others we can find, when I get back, okay?"

"Yup. I want to learn all about puppies. My dad said I could keep one of Rhiannon's."

"That will be fun."

"I know—my own puppy! I'm so excited."

They chatted for a few more minutes. When Cassie wound down, Tess said, "It's great to talk to you, Cassie. Thanks very much for taking care of Rhiannon. I'll bet she really likes being at the ranch with you and Van and your dad. You have a good week in school, and work hard, okay?"

"Okay, here's my Daddy. Hope your daddy is feeling better and I can see you soon, Dr. Tess."

"Thank you, sweetie. I hope to see you soon, too."

"You two sure are good friends." Jake's approving words comforted her. "I'll give the good news to Alice so she can let Doc know. We're all pulling for your dad, Tess."

"Thanks, Jake," she said, emotion choking her voice. "That's nice to hear."

"Just take it easy, Crash, okay?"

"Bye, Jake."

*****

Jake hung up the phone and reached for Cassie.

"Gosh, Daddy, what happens when someone's heart breaks?" Cassie asked, her face full of alarm.

He pulled her into his arms. "You've heard me talk about heartbreak, haven't you?" he asked soberly. "Heartbreak is a term that means emotional pain. It's not like a heart attack. A heart attack is physical; something malfunctions in your body. C'mon, let's look it up on the Internet, and I'll try to explain it better."

Jake and Cassie spent the next hour online until Jake was satisfied that Cassie understood what had happened to Tess' father. Before they clicked off the computer, Cassie made him promise to make an appointment for a stress test. He put his arms around her. *She has too much to worry about, this little girl of mine.*

"I love you endless miles, Cassie," he said, tucking her head under his chin.

"I love you buckets and buckets, Daddy." Cassie put her strong little arms around his neck and squeezed.

He couldn't imagine life without his daughter. *It hadn't taken Tess very long to grow attached to Cassie, either.* He felt a wave of guilt for what he'd put Tess through. "C'mon, let's make some meatballs, and we'll have spaghetti for dinner," he said.

While the meatballs were cooking, he and Cassie bundled up, and traipsed to the barn in the day's new snowfall, the dogs at their heels. He fed and watered the horses while she groomed Sparky. After dinner, a bath and bedtime story, he switched the nightlight on and left the door open a crack, just the way Cassie liked it.

Quarterly reports were down on his desk, and he had plenty of other work in his office, but he went to his room to read. The ranch house was big, and Cassie felt safer if he was nearby. He liked to stay close until she fell asleep.

Closing his eyes, he nodded off, remembering how Tess felt in his arms. Despite all the confusion, he ached to be close again. *But Tess is in Philadelphia now. She'll be reminded of her old life, and all its opportunities, and she'll leave in June, for her own good. It will hurt, but I'll bear it, and so will Cassie because that is what's best for Tess. Her talents would be squandered in Green Junction. In the meantime, we all better play it cool.*

*****

Monday morning, Tess waded past tubes and machines to visit her father, who'd been transferred to a private room. "Hi, Daddy," she said, kissing his nose.

"You showed some presence of mind, warning me about this, Tessie," he said weakly.

"Daddy, stop, please. I've felt horrible about it since Sam called. Will you forgive me?"

"There's nothing to forgive, darling. You were right, obviously. I've learned my lesson. I ignored advice I should have heeded and showed a great deal of hubris with my health. Your mother and I were very presumptive with our behavior. It took me a while to accept it, but I'm proud of you for insisting that we let you fend for yourself," he smiled feebly, patting her hand, "And here you are, taking care of me. I'm so glad to see you, daughter."

"Thank you, Dad." Tess hugged him. "I love you so much. I've felt terrible, all this time, for what I said. I hope it didn't upset you too much?"

"No, darling, you didn't upset me. Your mother and I were concerned for what you were going through, and it didn't take much for me to realize the part I'd played in complicating things for you. But don't for a minute think that discussion had anything to do with this heart attack. How's your mother been?"

Tess saw the twinkle in his eye. As she squeezed his hand, the tears welled. *He loves us all, so much.* "Mom and I haven't really talked, but things are okay. She seems to be holding up."

"Well, that's your mother," he nodded, "She's a force of nature… never ceases to amaze me. How are things going with that young man?"

"What young man?"

Her father's eyes crinkled, and a look of amusement crossed his ashen face. "Your yahoo cowboy, of course."

"Kind of a disaster, still, but he did call yesterday to see how you were," she admitted, shrugging her shoulders. "He's keeping my dog, and his daughter likes me, so that's something. Thanks for asking."

"I'm sorry for interfering, Tessie, and I'll tell him so if I get the chance. Even a cranky old legal beagle like me won't scare him away if he really loves you."

"Thanks, Dad. We were sort of dating, and now we're not. I don't think Jake loves me. We're just friends, really."

"Good friends is the best way. Your mother and I were friends in law school, both dating other people, until I realized she was the one for me, and look at us now. Listen, Tessie, this is your sister's last day home. There's been enough commotion, and I won't have you stuck here worrying about me. Go have some fun with her."

"Give us one more day here with you, Dad. Sam will be back next Friday, and Mom wants us to go shopping."

"Well, today you and Sam are having lunch at the White Dog on me. This all might have been prevented, if I'd humbled myself and taken my doctor's advice, just like my daughter suggested."

"You don't know that, Dad," Tess insisted.

*****

Tuesday morning after Tess dropped Sam at the train station, she went downtown to visit Grandma Angliotti.

On her way home, she put in a call to her advisor at New Bolton, equine surgeon Marguerite Sanders. In her late-sixties, wiry and focused, Dr. Sanders had broken into veterinary science at a time when few women entered the field. She was a pioneer, responsible for significant improvements in many large animal surgical techniques, and had taken a special interest in Tess. Dr. Sanders had a gap in her schedule, and they arranged to meet.

"Have you had your fill of the demanding physical labor of a large animal, field-based practice yet?" Dr. Sanders asked with a smile when Tess arrived in her office late Wednesday morning.

"Not yet," she smiled back, thinking of the enthusiasm the ranchers around Green Junction seemed to have for her presence there.

"Tess, our surgical teaching fellowship posts will open again in June. They are one year assignments, but Dr. Drake is retiring next spring, and we'll be seeking a permanent replacement. We were all really impressed by your performance here. I know what you are capable of, both as a surgeon and a teacher. I'd be happy to recommend you for the fellowship if you are interested. Our fellows will receive strong consideration for Doc Drake's position."

Dr. Sanders was serious, Tess realized, and the offer caught her off guard.

"You don't need to give me an answer now, but think about it, okay?" Dr. Sanders asked, eyeing Tess kindly.

She sat in on Dr. Marguerite's practicum lecture at noon, and at one-thirty left for the hospital to visit her father, thinking the entire time about a career move back to Philadelphia. *Who could have imagined Dr. Sanders would consider me for such a prestigious post? And why would I ever turn it down?*

That evening at dinner, after a phone call with Alice, Tess told her mother. "Alice got an envelope at the office today with tickets to the VFW Christmas Dinner Dance the Saturday before Thanksgiving. There's a Tree Lighting in Green Junction's town square beforehand."

"Is it a formal?" her mother asked, stars in her eyes.

"Semi-formal," Tess replied dolefully. The sender of the tickets was a mystery. When Alice regretfully admitted she'd had no news from Jake, Tess reminded her that Ron had offered to send them the tickets. *Can I withstand an entire evening with Officer Ron, especially after what he's done to Jake?* The sinking feeling in her gut intensified. *At least Mom is excited. Maybe she'd like to dance with Ron.*

"We can go dress shopping tomorrow night, dear, before Daddy comes home. And we'll buy those wonderful little gold sandals we saw Monday night with Sam. Remember, you said you didn't have any place to wear them?"

Tess stifled a groan at the prospect of yet another evening with her mother at the King of Prussia Mall. Noelle thrived on the bustle of the suburbs, but the crowds and traffic reminded Tess of the quiet peacefulness she loved in Green Junction.

She let her mother choose her dress and shoes for the dance, and Noelle only smiled when Tess selected cotton and wool turtlenecks instead of silk blouses and more sports bras than lacy ones. Tess managed to hold her mother to two cashmere sweaters and asked her to help select one for Alice. *God forbid I'm the only woman in Green Junction wearing cashmere. Thankfully, Aunt Olivia can balance the score.*

"Alice is a good friend, isn't she?" Noelle asked. Tess felt her mother gently take her arm as they made their way across the darkened parking lot, Tess carrying all the bags.

Smiling, she said, "She is, Mom. Alice gave me the courage to try Green Junction. Really, she's so good to me out there. I picked the job because of her and Doc. Doc knows so much, and Alice always backs me up, no matter what. I hope you can try to understand what working there means to me. And it's so, so beautiful there. I hope you and Dad and Grandma will all come visit before I leave."

"Tess, I am sorry for jumping to conclusions about that young man. I was anxious after you'd left, and I missed you. You were so far away. It wasn't fair for me to channel my anxiety the way I did, though. I created distance between us and then overreacted at the insurance receipts, which set your father off. The police report seemed to validate all my concerns, but I should have spoken to you first, I see that now."

"I hid the accident because I didn't want it to turn into some kind of huge production, Mom. All summer, you made no secret of your disapproval of my move. It just seemed like a hassle to compound that with anything else."

"I know I'm responsible for the communication breakdown, dear, and I'm sorry. I am. I'm still mystified by it all, though. What is the attraction to Green Junction?"

"I just feel stifled when I'm here, Mom. It's hard to explain, really, but out there, the spaces are so big. It's a small town, and people really pitch in and help each other out in a very cool, old fashioned way. It's a good change for me. And the work is fascinating. The animals aren't just pets, they're vital to the economy. The ranchers I work with have given their lives to raising animals. It's a round-the-clock commitment, and it makes them different people—better people, in some ways. At least, that's what it seems to me."

Tess felt her mother's arm slip around her waist. Quietly, Noelle said, "I wish I'd given you a chance to try to explain that, Contessa, before you left. Honestly, dear, I was selfish. I couldn't get past the feeling that you were abandoning me by leaving and choosing a path I didn't understand. But I made one snap judgment after another. I didn't even try to understand, did I?"

"It didn't seem so, Mom."

"Promise to make me understand, next time, no matter how hard-headed I am, okay?" Her mom kissed her cheek, handing Tess the keys.

*****

"Well, sister, you've been a major trooper, staying with Mom and Dad all week," Sam said Friday afternoon when Tess picked her up at Penn Station. She pitched her bags in the back of their father's Volvo and took the pale leather passenger seat next to Tess. "Thankfully, my crunch project is over, and my family medical leave was approved for the next two weeks. I'm glad I can be around while Dad adjusts back to his normal life and give you a break."

"The docs are really pleased with Dad's progress, but he won't be cleared to drive for a while, and he'll need to get to rehab every day after his release on Monday. One of us needs to be here. Mom won't be able to handle it on her own."

"I can cover, Tess. Mom and I will manage, and Dad will be on his feet soon enough. I'm just a train ride away if the office needs me. You should probably get back, right? Have you heard from Jake?'

"Not since Sunday night. Flowers arrived Tuesday. I left a message to thank him, and he hasn't called back. I really miss him, Sammi."

"Flowers are nice."

"They are, but it's hard to know what they mean. He hasn't tried to stay in touch, so flowers feel like a funeral arrangement," Tess sighed. "We never really worked things out after the insurance thing. Anyway, tomorrow Mom wants to get a jump on our annual coat shopping. Dad has rehab in the morning, so I guess we'll visit him after we find coats. You'll be on your own with Mom and Dad on Sunday, though. I'm invited to Courtney Morris-Blaise's baby shower."

"Wow, Courtney Morris is having a baby? Isn't her husband good friends with Archie what's-his-name, from Dad's firm?"

"You mean Archibald Lawson—Starchy Archie? We were both in their wedding."

"You think you'll see him?"

"I won't have a choice. Mom will finagle it, somehow."

"Good golly, Tess, she's relentless. I'm glad she hasn't tried to find dates for me."

"You didn't move seven states away, Sam. New York is just a train ride; she knows her grandchildren will be close. Your turn is coming, I'm sure."

"Oh, that's consolation. Maybe I should meet this Archie," Sam grinned playfully. "I could try to take some of the starch out of him."

"He's a nice enough guy. You can sure try," Tess smiled.

"How are Dad's spirits?"

"He's holding up okay; it's Mom I'm worried about. She's taking this hard."

"Dad is everything to her, you know? This is a taste of what it would be like if something really happened," Sam said.

"Something did happen, Sam."

After a stop at the hospital for a quick visit with their dad, Noelle drove them down to Grandma Angliotti's for dinner. Tess and Sam exchanged knowing glances when she suggested they meet Archie and a new junior partner from her firm, Mardon, for drinks later that night. "This is the time of your lives, girls, no need to hang around the house with me. I'll manage. I have Mardon's number for you, Sam."

Saturday morning, in the coat section of Lord & Taylor, Sam and her mother were immersed in the size-eight row, fascinated by the collar detail on a camel coat. Tess glanced at her watch. "I'm going to hit the ladies room, Mom," she called. Her mom nodded absently, so Tess snuck away, dialing Alice.

"Hi, Tess, I just got to the clinic. It's the usual dull roar around here. The only thing new is more snow. How's your dad?"

"Holding his own, thanks. The doctors are pleased with his rehab stats, so that's progress." *Just hearing her voice makes me homesick for Green Junction.*

"Have you heard from Jake?"

"Not since Sunday. I thought things might thaw a bit between us but apparently not."

"Oh, nuts. He's probably busy with Cassie and wants to give you some space while your dad's unwell. Are you having a little bit of fun, anyway, seeing friends or anything?" Alice asked hopefully.

"I have a baby shower tomorrow, and then a date with Starchy Archie," she said, not even trying to sound enthused.

"Hey, keep your options open," Alice said.

"I guess. My sister is here now, helping out. My mom is driving me crazy with this shopping. It's her stress release. I so wish you and I were the same size, I'd have a slew of new things for you."

"Oh, me, too!"

"I'll check back, Al, but let me know if you hear anything, okay?" It was hard to say good-bye, she felt disconnected from her new life, in limbo. *But with this offer from New Bolton, I'm not even sure what my real life is, anymore.*

"I sure will. Take it easy, okay, Tess?" She could hear the concern in Alice's voice.

Returning to the fitting room, she dutifully tried on the coats her mother had selected, doing her best to play along with this ritual. Looking at herself in a double-breasted navy wool coat almost identical to the red one she'd gotten three years before, she made a face in the triple mirror.

"What's the matter, honey?" her mom asked, smoothing her hair.

"I love that we always do this, Mom, but honestly, I can't help thinking that what I really need is a puffy, full-length down coat, something to walk the dog in on a chilly night or keep in my truck to warm up after a farm call."

Her mom swallowed hard, clearly dismayed that another vestige of the life she'd envisioned for Tess was being renegotiated. "Oh, dear, has it come to all that?"

"Green Junction isn't a fashionable town, Mom, and I'm sensitive about looking like a fussy easterner as it is. Let's pick out a really great coat for Sam, something very New York," she suggested, putting an arm around her mother's shoulder. "Then I'll treat you both to lunch."

"Lunch on coat day is my treat, Contessa," her mother said tightly. Then she sighed. Resignedly, Noelle conceded, "I suppose we can stop at Patagonia on our way to the hospital."

Tess gave her mother a hug. *This is huge, coming from Mom.*

*****

Sunday night, Buster snored gently on the floor as Tess lay in bed, watching the digital clock on her nightstand roll over. *10:28 p.m. in Philadelphia, 8:28 Colorado time. Jake hasn't called this entire week!*

Staring up at the lace canopy, she was restless, unable to stop thinking of her afternoon at Courtney's baby shower. All of her friends were married now with homes of their own. *Real houses, beautifully furnished. They're becoming mothers, and I'm still scamming deals in thrift shops.*

At the party, the girlfriends she'd had her whole life had teased about her status as a 'ramblin' cowgirl', but deep down, Tess felt like an outsider. When Courtney discussed plans for her nursery, the other girls chimed in. Suddenly, it seemed like they were speaking in foreign tongues. *I don't know a binky from a boppie from a Bjorn. Bjorn what? It's a whole other world!*

She trailed her hand off the bed to stroke Buster's back willing herself to sleep. Summoning her courage, she tried Jake's cell. She was put into voicemail, and hung up, feeling humiliated. *Is he avoiding my calls?* The thought was chilling. Tess was annoyed, but worried, too. *Texting Alice would be pathetic. She promised to call if there was news. In the meantime, difficult as it is, I have to accept that not hearing from Jake is his choice.*

Now, lying in bed, she felt a pang of longing—jealousy, even, at how established and adult her girlfriends' lives were. *I've seriously never given a thought to being married. When Olivia McGreer spoke to me about Jake, it seemed so far-fetched. All those weddings were just fun parties while I was in vet school, but even Alice has Lotts.*

Archie had shown up near the end of the shower with Courtney's husband Tom, and Tess had been relieved to see his placid, familiar face, as an escape if nothing else. She agreed to grab a quick drink at a nearby pub, but once there, they'd fallen into comfortable conversation.

Archie was intelligent, with a dry sense of humor. They talked about her father's health and her work in Green Junction. After the tumult and confusion of the past few weeks, his mildness and careful tact had been reassuring.

He'd ordered a second round and asked her to choose appetizers, while their friendly conversation continued to flow. When she confessed how out-of-place she'd felt at the baby shower, he'd nodded with understanding. *It had been reassuring to spend time with him.*

For the first time, she felt like a practice on the Main Line and a life with someone like Archie had appeal. With small-town charm and friendly, down-to-earth people, Green Junction was surrounded by natural beauty but if she stayed to take over Doc's practice, she could wind up alone in the middle of nowhere, full of heartache. *Archie isn't Jake, but things might never work out with*

Jake. The life that had been so easy to fall into in Green Junction suddenly felt very, very elusive.

The life my parents want for me seems boring because it's sane and predictable. It doesn't involve crazy long hours in the cold or hiking across snowy pastures to tend to sick calves. I love that now, but will it feel like fun forever? Dr. Sanders has all but offered me a permanent, salaried teaching post at a top veterinary facility.

Her flight back was on Tuesday. *What will Green Junction be like without Jake and Cassie? I'm not even sure I want to know.*

*****

Tess's father was discharged on Monday morning. He was in good spirits, but his pallor and unsteadiness concerned her. When Richard spent the entire first day resting in his recliner with Buster at his feet, Tess wondered if her father would ever be restored to the vigorous person she'd known before his heart attack.

On Tuesday morning, Tess hugged her parents good-bye and Sam drove her to the airport. "Last night was my first and last date with Hard-on Mardon," Sam giggled. "I can't imagine why the promise of Starchie Archie wasn't enough to tempt you to join us last night, Tess. If Mom thought it would keep us around, I bet she'd have Dad stage another heart attack. She could try to hand-select our husbands the way she does our winter coats."

"Archie's actually kind of sweet, Sam. And it's funny to joke now that the worst has passed, but Dad might have another heart attack. Or something just as bad," Tess said soberly, unnerved by her return to Green Junction.

"Oh, posh. Mom won't let that happen. Didn't you see all the muesli in the cupboard? She's going to march him to every test right on schedule, wait and see. They'll both be around for a long time."

"I'm glad you're feeling so optimistic."

"Why so glum, chum?" Sam asked, nudging her.

"I keep thinking about the job at New Bolton. I might take it, Sam."

"I thought you loved your work in Colorado?"

"I do, but everything seems a lot different since Dad's heart attack. Honestly, I would love large animal work anywhere. Staying in Green Junction may only set me up for more heartbreak and disappointment. Maybe Mom's right: maybe I should be more focused on building a career."

"Wow, I thought you guys were talking again?"

"I haven't heard from him for over a week now, Sam. I've left two messages, and he hasn't returned my calls. It's unsettling. I don't even know how my dog is."

"Wait 'til you get back there, Tessie. Don't jump to conclusions. It's been crazy these past few weeks. Maybe Jake didn't want to crowd you, or feel like he was pushing his way in while Dad was sick. You know how guys can be."

"Maybe," Tess answered. "But maybe too much about being happy in Green Junction depends on Jake. This thing with Dad scared me, Sam. Since the baby shower, I've been thinking a lot about the future. Suddenly, I want to be settled. I want a family of my own."

"I know what you mean. I'm twenty-eight, with no prospects on the horizon. The clock is ticking."

"Well, don't tell Mom that, unless you want her to start lining up dates for you."

"Yeah, after Hard-on Mardon, if I can't find someone on my own, she sure can't help," Sam giggled.

At the airport, Sam helped get her bags checked and gave Tess a big hug. "You can fly home for Thanksgiving, you know. We can't get enough of you here. No matter what, your biggest fan base will always be on the East Coast," Sam said.

Tess nodded, trying to keep the mournful out of her voice. "Good luck with Mom and Dad this week, Sam."

After buying a novel and two magazines for the flight, she ordered a grande cappuccino, adding a giant chocolate-chip cookie and an apple. *I do novels, caffeine and chocolate the way my mother shops for cashmere. Desperate times call for desperate measures, I suppose.*

Once in Denver, Tess made her way to the baggage carousel. With her mother's shopping habits, she'd had to check two additional bags and wasn't quite sure how she'd manage to get her carry-on, a giant duffle and a new rollie out to the blue Subaru.

Alice was waiting at the curb with her flashers on and jumped from the driver's seat, engulfing Tess in a big hug. Grabbing Tess's roll-behind suitcase, she flashed her peppy smile and asked "New coat?"

"I was so relieved when my mother agreed to take me to Patagonia, I let her choose the color."

"That indigo is gorgeous with your eyes."

"Thanks. She thought so, too. I wanted something light colored, to be visible walking the dog at night, but this won't show as much dirt."

"Does your mom know what a practical, accommodating daughter she raised?" Alice asked cheerfully, helping her lift the bags into the car.

"My practical side isn't the one she most appreciates," Tess answered, wrinkling her nose. "And I'm quite sure she doesn't consider me accommodating. Strong-willed, inconsiderate and unrelenting have all been discussed."

"You have a lot of your mom in you, that's all. Ye gads, what do you have in these bags?" Alice asked, a curious look in her sparkly green eyes.

"Don't ask. Grandma Angliotti sent along a tin of her hazelnut biscotti for the office, and I got a cashmere twin set for you. I hope it's your color."

"Oh, so do I." Alice slammed the hatchback, Tess climbed in the passenger seat, and they headed for Green Junction.

8

"Angel Flyin' Too Close to the Ground"

Alice offered to stick around to help unpack. When Tess gave her the cashmere twin set, Alice exclaimed, "This is an absolutely gorgeous green!"

"Hey, you've been my anchor though all of this; it's the least I could do. I really appreciate it, Alice. I thought the bottle green color would look great with your eyes."

"Oh, it will. Thank you! Are you going back for Thanksgiving?"

"My sister is there with my dad this week, and after that my mom can manage. But I might go home for the holiday. I guess it depends on Jake."

The apartment felt empty without Rhiannon, so when Alice suggested they grab a burger at Green Forks, it was easy to say yes. "Why not call Jake and let him know you're back?" Alice suggested. Determined to be strong, Tess answered, "No way, he knows how to find me."

She'd brushed her teeth and climbed between cold sheets when her cell buzzed.

"Hey, Tess."

"How are you, Jake?"

Jake cleared his throat. "We're fine, here. How's your dad?"

"Doing well, considering. The heart attack slowed him down, but he's coming along."

"Tilda and I looked after Rhiannon. Cassie's really excited about these puppies."

She remembered how she'd been at Cassie's age, fascinated by tiny newborn animals and the miracle of birth. "Did she get the books on puppies I sent?"

"She loves them. They're in her backpack all the time. I can bring Rhiannon downtown tomorrow. Would you want to go with Cassie and I to the library after school?"

"Sure, I'd love to. And maybe we can pop over to the clinic to ultrasound Rhiannon. I promised Cassie we would."

"That would be great, Cassie's asking about you. She wants to see you. I've been thinking about you an awful lot, too, but I wanted to give you some space while you were home."

He'd left her hanging, and his casual excuse annoyed her. He'd disappointed her by not trusting her, by not believing in her, but she was looking forward to seeing them. *Just breathe, Tess, and don't obsess. Things will work out, somehow.*

*****

From: Richard.Bam@vmailcom
To: Tess.Bam@vmailcom
Date: Wednesday, November 7, 7:28 am

Subject: How's my little girl?

Dearest Tessie,

I know I've said this, but thank you again for all of your loving attention here, daughter. I appreciate that your mother and I can count on you when the chips are down. I'm sorry I caused such a stir. Let me know how things go with the cowboy.

Love you,
Your Dad

*****

To: Richard.Bam@vmailcom
From: Tess.Bam@vmailcom
Date: Thursday, November 8, 8:26 PM

Subject: Your Grown Up Big Girl

Daddy,

I'm glad you are feeling better. I've been wondering how your physical therapy is going. I hope you are not trying to do any legal work yet, but something tells me you might be???????

As far as the cowboy, it's very confusing. You and mom created such a safe world for Sam and I growing up, and I am only beginning to appreciate the wonder of that. Cassie is such a sweet little girl, but I can tell how much her parent's divorce confuses and upsets her.

I met her at the library today with her dad. We picked out books on puppies, and she helped me ultrasound Rhiannon here at the apartment. You should have seen her face when I showed her all those little puppies on the screen!

Cassie makes me feel like I can work miracles, Dad. That's how I felt about you when I was her age. There were so many years in my life when grown-ups could fix everything. That sure was nice.

When I came here, I wanted to be grown up and on my own. I never imagined how much it would change me. Thanks for teaching me so much about how to live, Dad. I do mean that.

Your devoted daughter, Tess

*****

Friday night after dinner, Alice opened the package of Mamma Boccini's mocha cheesecake while Tess brewed decaf. "So when is Rhiannon due to whelp?" Alice asked, putting two slices on dessert plates.

"Three weeks from yesterday, or thereabouts. Her ultrasound looks good. Cassie and I found six puppies. Crazy enough, Thanksgiving Day is her due date, eight weeks exactly."

"Wow, so you'll be in Philadelphia?"

Tess poured decaf in the little white cups and set a cup and saucer in front of Alice. "I can't decide. My dad's doing much better now, and I can always go home for Christmas. I think I'd like to be here for the puppies, especially since Cassie is so excited about it. Jake's got homes for two of them, and Cassie will keep one."

"And clients at the office have spoken for three more," Alice said, her fork cutting smoothly through the mocha cheesecake. "Yum, chocolate cookie crust."

"Yup, Doc said the Cramers want a male, to surprise their little boy for Christmas," Tess answered, before tasting her first bite.

"How are you going to pull that off?"

"They'll be four weeks old by then, started on solid food. They can have him for the day, and bring him back to the litter afterward."

"That's great. All of them are spoken for, right?"

"They are," Tess said, her voice a little lackluster. *This is it; I've got to get this off my chest.* She took a deep breath. *"Alice, Bea mentioned she and Doc will be in Florida for Thanksgiving next year. Doc hasn't said anything to me yet, though."*

"He doesn't want to pressure you, especially with your dad's health. And he knows how things are with Jake."

"I wish I knew how things were with Jake."

"Tomorrow night's the Jackalope. Guess you'll find out."

"Oh, right, Jackalope."

"Everybody from town will be there. You're sure to see him and Cassie, too. Doc and Bea are really excited about introducing you to everyone. I'll be in the back helping Bea with the food, but you get to stay out front with Doc. Rotary's hosting, and Doc and Bea are on the Leadership Council, so it's kind of a big deal for them."

Tess thought about the almost parental pride Doc seemed to take in her—his constant, approving support—and felt horribly guilty. *Still, Alice asked you to tell her, and you promised you would.*

"Alice, a Surgical Teaching Fellowship will be advertised at New Bolton soon, to start next fall," she offered in a rush, "My mentor there, Dr. Sanders, has invited me to apply."

"Really? That's impressive, Tess. You should do it, keep your options open." Alice finished the last bite of her cheesecake, not missing a beat.

"It could lead to a full time teaching position there, too. I promised not to leave you in the lurch at the clinic, Alice, and I won't. If I get it, you and Doc will have plenty of time to find a replacement for me. I'd have almost a year in with Doc by the time I'd leave."

"I hate to think of you leaving, Tess, but you have to do what's best for you."

"Everyone's been so awesome, and I love the practice—you know that. I was up for anything when I got here, but my friends from home are all having babies. They have settled lives. I need to be thinking long-term, too." Tess gulped her decaf. Her voice a little desperate, she said, "Truthfully, it felt so right when things were going well with Jake, but now they're not. Cassie and I had a blast together with Rhiannon and the ultrasound, but Jake didn't have much to say. He's not interested in me anymore. It kind of makes me crazy, and I'm not sure I should stick around. We'd be crossing paths all the time, and sucking it up would make me nuts. Doc needs someone he can count on to stay and take over the practice, and I'm not certain I can commit to that."

"Where could you find another Jake?" Alice asked gently.

"Probably nowhere," Tess conceded, setting her cup in its saucer. "But I couldn't stand the torment of being close by and doing without him.

"Well, I'm glad you're back, and the New Bolton thing sounds great, even though it would take you away from us," Alice said, quiet understanding in her voice. "Don't overlook Colorado State, either. There must be some great opportunities up in Fort Collins. I'm sure Doc has contacts there he can steer you toward, if you're interested. Just take your time and give it all some thought, Tess. There's no rush, we can start advertising for a new vet anytime.

And don't give up on Jake yet. Rustle up one of your knockout dresses for the Jackalope tomorrow and slay him with your amazing charms."

She mustered a smile. "Thanks, Alice."

*****

From: Richard.Bam@vmailcom
To: Tess.Bam@vmailcom
Date: Friday, November 9 8:37 PM

Subject: My, How you've grown!

Daughter Tess,

Your sister mentioned the New Bolton opportunity. Don't be angry with her, please dear, she's worried about you. I won't say anything to Mother. You don't need the added pressure. You know we'd love to have you back. I imagine that you are feeling torn. These choices are likely to shape the rest of your life, so take some time making up your mind. I'm thinking of you, and I'm here if you want to talk. Whatever you decide, know that I'll be behind you.

As far as me, rehab is going well, though I never expected to spend quite so much time on the treadmill. It makes me loopy.

Archibald Lawson has been dropping by afternoons to help me get caught up on my cases. Your sister has been a big help, too. She cooked dinner tonight, three courses, do you believe it?

I'm so proud of my girls. You and Samantha and your mother have always been the light of my life.

Love, Love, Love You Always, Dad.

*****

From: Tess.Bam@vmailcom
To: Sam.Bam@vmailcom
Date: Friday, November 9, 7:42 PM

Subject: What's cooking, hot stuff?

Sam,
You've spilled the New Bolton beans AND you're cooking dinner?
What has come over you?

Love, Tess

PS: Remember to take the brownies out of the box before you put
them in the oven.

*****

To: Tess.Bam@vmailcom
From: Sam.Bam@vmailcom
Date: Friday, November 10, 10:36 PM

Subject: HAH!

Tessie,
Not apologizing for New Bolton bean spill; I'm worried about you.
So is Dad. We want what's best for you. FYI: made heart-healthy
boneless chicken breasts broiled TO PERFECTION tonight, with
salad, rice AND steamed broccoli! Granted, boredom here has
driven me into the kitchen, but anything is possible when one puts
her mind to it, so watch out! Archie liked dinner, and I'm planning
Thanksgiving. Mom's got her hands full at the office, but Grandma
will help. Shall we expect you?

Love, Big Sister Sam

PS. Did you know you can substitute applesauce for the veg oil in
brownie recipes? I'm making new discoveries daily.

*****

Sam,

So Archie liked dinner . . . What about dessert?? Did you serve something "starchy"? Yesterday was spay and neuter day at the clinic . . . Don't let that put a damper on your after-dinner plans, though!

Love, Snip 'n Clip Tessie

*****

Tess went into the clinic extra early Saturday morning to start kennel work before Alice arrived. Alice bustled in at five to eight, circles under her eyes. "Lotts and I didn't leave the bar until three this morning. I was not looking forward to a room full of messy, hungry puppies and kitties. Thank you so much for covering, Dr. Bamberger."

Tess smiled at Alice. "It was the least I could do, Al."

After work, Tess took Rhiannon for a walk. Her sweet collie-retriever's belly was filling out, her tawny coat glossy and sleek from brushing. Rhiannon was eating more and slowing down now, happy to return to the apartment to curl up on her bed in front of the wood stove and snooze.

Feeling restless, Tess dropped by the thrift shop to help Gertrude sort and label new items. At the bottom of a big box, she found a pair of dusty brown cowgirl boots with a low heel and pointy toe, their tall shafts embossed with decorative stitched vines and tiny pink flowers. "What a find! They're just like the boots Meryl Streep wore in Silkwood, Gertrude!" Pulling them on, Tess stood in front of the mirror, admiring her reflection.

Gertrude peered out from behind the register. "That film with Kurt Russell and Cher, the sad one, where she didn't have her kids? You're right, they sure are," she agreed. "Do they fit?"

"They're a size too big, but I can wear socks with them."

"Yup. You'll clomp around, soundin' like a real cowgirl, Tess. $5.99, and they're all yours!" Gertrude smiled.

The new inventory kept them busy all afternoon, and Tess didn't leave the thrift store until closing time. Eager to get home to Rhiannon, she opened her truck door and tossed the boots on the seat. As she climbed in, a Green Junction Police cruiser slipped into the spot next to her. Ron's bulky stomach filled the driver's seat. *Uh-oh.*

The cruiser's door swung open. Ron stood up with authority, pulling his pants up over his belly. "Nice day, today."

"Sure is," Tess smiled, slightly creeped out. He eased his bulk around the back of cruiser, slipping his reflective aviator frames up on his head as he moved towards Tess. She saw a revolver under his unzipped black jacket in a holster strapped to his chest.

"How've you been, since the accident, Tess?" Ron asked, meeting her eyes.

He wasn't concerned at the Rancher's Alliance presentation, and that was weeks ago. "I was fine just a few days afterward, Ron. You know that. It was nothing, really."

"You got hit hard, Tess. You were knocked out for a while, lost plenty of blood. It was some gash on your head. You musta been out of it that night." Ron nodded, trying to catch her eye.

Tess met Ron's swarthy face dead on. "Not so out of it that I wouldn't have noticed if Jake had been drinking, Ron."

She saw his Adam's apple jump as he swallowed nervously. "Tess, you can't be certain Jake wasn't drinking. I know the facts," Ron said, putting the cheap frames back over his eyes.

"This isn't really something I want to discuss, Ron. I'll see you later, okay?"

"I'll see you girls at the Jackalope later," he said evenly, fat lips thinning into a wide smile.

"We'll be there!" Tess said brightly, completely revolted. *Doesn't he know when to give it up?*

"You have a nice day, Tess," Ron said, turning back to the cruiser.

"You, too, Ron." Relieved to be free of him, she climbed into her truck and slammed the door. *He didn't really send those dance tickets to the office, did he? How can I possibly spend a whole evening with him?*

At home, Tess polished her new boots and searched her closet. She found an apple-green, lambswool knit dress her mother had sent and took it to the mirror. Long-sleeved and empire waisted, its swingy skirt hit right above the knee. *Simple and friendly, like a first grade teacher, and it will work with my new boots. I might even kind of blend in.*

Pulling on dark green tights, Tess rehearsed the faces of all the people she'd met at the clinic, matching faces with pets and trying to remember names. *I don't want to forget anyone.* She put knee-socks on then the boots. *I'm going to flub names, and I'm starving. I could eat a whole antelope myself right now. At least the boots look like they belong in Green Junction. It sure feels like I don't.*

Waiting nervously for Alice, she curled her eyelashes, fired up her laptop, and slipped lipgloss, her driver's license, and some cash into a little hip purse.

*****

To: Tess.Bam@vmailcom
From: Sam.Bam@vmailcom
Date: Saturday, November 10, 8:26 am

Subject: You were right. He's a really nice guy . . .

Tess,

Archie likes "sinfully delicious" for dessert . . .with extra applesauce.

Love,
Sinfully Delicious Samantha

*****

To: <u>Sam.Bam@vmailcom</u>
From: <u>Tess.Bam@vmailcom</u>
Date; Saturday, November 10, 4:26 PM

Subject: The Archie's of the World are underrated

Sam,

   Tonight's the Jackalope. I'll meet the whole town. I'm nervous, Sammi. What if Jake's still acting like a Jerkalope?

Total Mess-Tess

*****

"Whoa, look at that coat!" Alice raved as Tess climbed into her car. "You look fabulous."

"Well, as you can imagine, my mother is obsessed with the Lord & Taylor President's Day coat sale. This was the one from two years ago," Tess said self-consciously, comparing the bell sleeves and streamlined bodice of her double-breasted magenta boucle to Alice's bright patchwork quilted coat and suede slouch boots. "Do I look too east coast for the Jackalope?"

"You look gorgeous, like spun gold and fine wine. I love those wide sleeves. It's a welcome change from muddy Carhartt's, no?" Alice smiled.

"Yes," Tess agreed emphatically.

"Ready for some fun?"

She sagged a bit. "As much fun as I can have, I guess. I'm really stressed about meeting everyone, and it's going to be awkward with Jake. I hate to admit it, but I have a really bad feeling about tonight, Alice."

Alice reached over and patted her hand. "Doc and Bea and I are all pulling for you, Tess. Doc is excited how well everything's been running at the clinic with you around. And lots of people around here already know and like you, including Jake and his Aunt Olivia. I'll mix you a special drink at Green Forks when the Jackalope's over, I promise."

The high school was just outside of town on a hill overlooking the park. As they parked, she saw a line of people on the sidewalk, waiting to get into the lobby. Her empty stomach clutched. "Looks like the whole town is here."

"Yup, the whole town and everybody from the ranches around town," Alice agreed cheerfully. "The Jackalope's a big deal. Didn't Sherri Tarleton want you to meet her sons? They'll be here tonight."

"Oh, great," Tess rolled her eyes.

"I promised to give Bea a hand in the kitchen before dinner. You just circulate and let Doc introduce you to everyone, okay?"

"Okay," she answered. "Sure, Alice."

In the lobby, they handed their coats to girls in band uniforms. Dropping a bill in the tip jar, she wished she could hide in the back with Alice. *I'm all thumbs in the kitchen, but I can take orders. Though, I don't know much about rattlesnake jerky.*

"You'll be fine. Keep smiling and try to remember names. There'll be a quiz later!" Alice teased, pushing the cafeteria door open.

The room was filled to bursting with men in jeans and boots and women in wide skirts, rich with the buzz of conversation and the heavy aroma of roasting meats. A long buffet was set across the front of the giant cafeteria, near the kitchen. Rows and rows of fold-out dining tables ran the length of the room, covered in red-checked plastic tablecloths and decked with silly giant centerpieces. The ladies had fitted large hares with small antlers, and they seemed to scamper along the middle of the tables amidst pineapples and fresh fruit. Something about the jackalopes made Tess's stomach even queasier. *No turning back now.*

The familiar shock of Doc's white hair rose in the midst of the crowd. "Let's head over there; maybe Bea is with him," Alice urged.

Not only was Bea with Doc, Cassie and Vicki were there as well. Vicki wore a lamé silver mini dress, fishnets and four inch platform heels and glared at Tess as she and Alice walked over.

Adorable in a red corduroy jumper, white tights and a white-ruffled turtleneck, Cassie looked anxious, bouncing next to her mother, hair in pigtails, feet in sturdy leather Mary Janes, carrying a little felt horse. *Where's Cassie's bubbly self-confidence? She's a different kid when she's with Vicki.* Thinking about what Vicki might have dropped in her purse, she worried for Cassie.

"Here's Dr. Bamberger," Doc said pleasantly.

"Dr. Tess!" Cassie threw her arms around Tess's waist. "I am SO glad to see you." She looked up, wrinkling her nose. "Are you going to try the antelope stew?"

"I will if you will!" Tess laughed as Doc handed her a glass of red wine.

Cassie grabbed her hand and twirled around. "My dad will be here later. I like your dress!"

"And I like yours!" she answered, squeezing Cassie's hand. Vicki smirked and rolled her eyes. Tess gulped her wine.

Looking between Vicki and Tess, Bea smoothed her hands over the front of her dress. "Good to see you, Tess. We're pleased you could come and meet everyone." Doc smiled, too, nodding amiably. Vicki tossed her head and the giant, hair-sprayed pouf at the front barely moved.

"You girls made it just in time, it's a full house, already," Bea said approvingly, still trying. Answering brightly, Alice chatted with Bea.

Wishing she could avoid Vicki's glare, Tess drank wine. Doc had just refilled her glass when she felt a tug at her sleeve. Officer Ron stood next to her, too close, in a polyester navy jacket, black cotton chinos, and his black cop shoes, grinning from ear to ear. *Will the disasters of this evening never cease?*

"Hi, Ronald," Bea said warmly, as Ron shook hands with Doc.

"How are you feeling, Dr. Bamberger?" Ron asked stiffly, smiling at Tess. Vicki's glare intensified.

"Fine, thank you," Tess answered, trying not be annoyed. *Haven't we been through this already once today?*

"So, I'll have the good fortune of seeing you at the Tree Lighting, weekend after next?" Ron asked, looking pointedly at Tess. Vicki's eyes narrowed even further. *Ugh!* Mortified, Tess raised her eyebrows, looking to Alice for help.

"Doc and I will be there, Ron," Bea smiled. "And I think the girls are planning to go, too, aren't you, Alice?" *Thank God for Bea.*

"I think we'll all be there, Ron," Alice nodded. *Thank God for Alice.*

"The dance afterward is a benefit for the police, fire, and ambulance corps," Ron explained, looking at Tess meaningfully. "You know about the tickets?"

"We got them at the office. Thanks for thinking of us, Ron," Alice said. Tess just smiled politely, repulsed by the prospect of wearing the fancy dress her mother had picked out to dance with tactless, deceptive, despicable Ron Karachek.

"I'm really looking forward to the Tree Lighting Dance!" Vicki stepped in front of Doc, grabbing Ron's arm and flashing him an inviting smile, heavy on the lipstick. "It's a great cause."

Ron's eyes roved over Vicki's low-necked lamé, and he moved her way. With Vicki at his elbow, Ron talked Ag Department news with Doc. Then, puffed with importance, he nodded to them all. "I'm headed down to the station for the night shift."

"We'll be on the lookout, Ron," Alice countered with an innocent smile. With an ingratiating smile for Tess, Ron stepped away and Vicki charged after him, hot on his trail.

Tess breathed a sigh of relief, but her eye caught Jake just coming through the door, and she tensed all over again.

Brow furrowed, he watched his ex-wife chase Ron into the lobby. Catching Tess's eye, Jake grinned, twisting an eyebrow sardonically. She couldn't help but laugh. His hair had gotten longer while she'd been away, and a dark curl fell over his forehead. In a chambray shirt, open-necked under a wool tweed sport jacket, jeans and brown dress boots, he was as appealing as ever. Cassie made a beeline for her dad. Tess turned back to her wine, trying not to drool. Shortly afterward, she heard Bea exclaim, "Well, hello, Jake!"

He was behind her now. She felt the electricity of his closeness torch up her spine. Touching her elbow, Jake murmured, "Nice to see you out on the town, Crash." Turning to Doc and Bea, he said, "Tess did a great job with Alchemy, Doc."

"How ever did he get into barbed wire?" Bea asked.

"Jumped out of the paddock. Best we can figure, the tractor churned some old wire up when we brush-hogged last spring. We didn't catch it, and that's what the horse got tangled in."

"I'll be darned," Doc said. "Alchemy's jumping the fence, again, is he?"

Jake smiled ruefully. "Usually he runs right to the barn, and we find him at dinnertime. I'm real glad Tess showed up when she did. She did such a great job with the sutures, the scars are barely visible." He met her eye, and his smile flashed gratitude.

"She's a quick hand with sutures. Did a neat job on Sherri Tarleton's gelding, too," Doc said. He and Jake were looking at her approvingly ans she smiled, getting lost in Jake's deep brown eyes. Catching herself, Tess pulled back, but he was still smiling. Nervously, she sucked down more wine.

Bea's eyes darted to Alice. "Ready for the kitchen, dear? I'll need to get my apron on; it's almost time to check the venison roast."

"I'm right behind you," Alice smiled, following Bea through the crowded room.

Escaping the Jake's heat, Tess ducked down, eye-level with Cassie. "Hey, Cassie, I like that horse."

Cassie held the brightly embroidered felt creature up. "My Aunt Olivia made him for me for Christmas last year. Do you want to go see Aunt Olivia? She said to bring you over."

"I'd like that." Tess offered Cassie her hand. Flashing an approving smile, Jake stayed to converse with Doc.

Cassie led Tess down the middle aisle to the table where Olivia was seated with her lady friends. Striking in black patent boots, long wool grey houndstooth skirt, and pale pink cashmere turtleneck, Olivia smiled a welcome, extending her hand graciously. "Well, here's Doctor Tess!"

"I brought her to see you, Auntie O. I knew your friends would want to meet her. Dr. Tess is a vet, everybody. She was in school for twenty years," Cassie explained in a conspiratorial tone, her eyes wide.

"It's a lot of work to become a vet," Gertrude offered with a smile. "Surely takes dedication."

"How are things, Tess?" Aunt Olivia asked, smoothing an errant hair into her smooth grey chignon, next to her giant pearl earrings.

"Great, very busy here tonight," Tess commented neutrally, holding her empty wine glass like an accessory. "Thank you for the lovely card; my father is doing much better, now."

"Oh, good," Olivia said. "I was worried for you, dear."

Gertrude smiled, her eyes black as onyx. "You look real pretty, Tess." Turning to Olivia, she said, "Tess came by today, helped tag some new things that came in to the thrift store. She's a big help. My days go quicker when she stops by," Gertrude said, "She really brightens a room."

"You must join our group for tea and Stella's chocolate cake, Tess," Olivia offered. "We meet every other Tuesday for lunch and bridge at my place. Bea often comes, and Alice is welcome. You'll be our guest of honor, next time."

"Thank you, I'm sure we'll enjoy that," she felt herself blushing with appreciation. As she visited with Olivia and Gertrude and the ladies from the Ecumenical Society, she couldn't help noticing Vicki, standing with a group of friends near the front of the room. They were whispering together, shooting her dirty looks. Nervously, Tess said, "Ladies, if you'll excuse me, I know Doc has some people he wants me to meet."

"Of course, dear. Delighted to see you again," Olivia answered. "I'll be after Bea to bring you and Alice by."

"Come back for dessert!" Cassie piped, and Tess squeezed her hand.

Moving towards Doc, Tess bumped into Sherri Tarleton, who nipped an open bottle of cabernet from the table and filled Tess's glass. While they talked horses, a pair of tall, lanky twenty-somethings approached, wearingi boots, jeans and fancy western shirts, grinning broadly. Sherri introduced them as her sons, Stuart and Brett. They had giant hands, freckled, tanned faces and wore their dark red curly hair identically: full in front but cut short over their ears and collars. *Western Starchy Archies! Wait 'til I tell Sammi!*

Vicki and her friends had moved to the side of the room now, standing closer to Tess. Tess saw Vicki mouth something to her. "What?" Tess asked, distracted from her chat with Sherri. Another girl squealed "Stewhair!" and the rest broke into peals of laughter. Self-consciously, Tess touched her hair, loose down her back and held at her crown with a barrette. *I haven't gotten stew in my hair!*

Doc was just across the table now, talking with Chris and Maybelle Carson. "You get on over to Doc, Tess, we could talk all day," Sherri motioned. "But don't forget to come out and ride my big hunter mare. I'm so busy starting three year olds, I'd welcome the company, and she needs exercise."

Feeling a glow from her third glass of wine, already gone, Tess said, "I'd like that, Sherri, thanks for thinking of me."

"Doc's got a full night planned for you, lots of people to meet," Sherri whispered, filling her glass again. "You'll need this."

Tess wobbled over to Doc and the Carsons, self-consciously tugging at the ends of her hair. *I really haven't eaten much today, and this "Stewhair" thing has me a little concerned. . . There isn't even any stew out yet, so it couldn't be in my hair!*

Bea and Alice and the other ladies were bustling from the kitchen, just filling buffet pans and soup crocks. Stuart and Brett had stayed at her elbows. Alarmed, she glanced over to Jake, seated with Olivia and Cassie. Jaw set, he looked away, pretending not to notice her. *Oh, great. He's ignored me for all this time, and now he's jealous?* Stung by Jake's rejection, Tess sucked down more wine.

Smiling a greeting, Maybelle stood next to Chris, holding a year-old baby. "Our big sow was firing from all cylinders within eight hours of your visit a few weeks back, Dr. Bamberger," Chris Carson told her approvingly. "We surely appreciate your help."

"Well, that's fantastic," she answered, catching her balance. "A touch of mastitis isn't uncommon after a sow's had a litter, as you know. I'm glad we treated it right away, though." Maybelle had another baby on the way, and Tess noticed dark circles under her eyes. *It has to be tough, caring for young children while running a pig and chicken farm. Maybelle and Chris aren't much older than me. There's a lot of work on their place.*

Thinking about her friends in Philadelphia, who seemed to have it so much easier, Tess held Maybelle's baby's hand, shaking it and cooing until her tiny, chubby face burst in a toothless grin.

Stuart and Brett spoke to Chris and Maybelle while Doc moved off towards an older man. Tess immediately recognized him as the man with the cat carrier, from the Saturday debacle with Vicki. *Is it Mr. Harris with Otis, or Mr. Otis with Harris?*

As Tess joined them, the man told Doc appreciatively, "Mah Harris had a hair ball, t'young lady took good care of him t'other week."

Mr. Otis! "Well, hello, Mr. O-" Tess started, but Doc was smiling, too, saying in his deep, approving voice, "Ah, Tess, you've met Mr. Zweigstich, then."

"Yes, hello, sir!" Tess said, taking his hand and shaking it enthusiastically. *How did I get Otis from Zweigstich?* "And how is Harrish?" *Harrish?* She glanced at her half empty glass. *Am I beginning to slur? Better not even try to pronounce Zweigstick, swigstitch . . .whatever.*

"Doin' quite well, ma'am, thanks for your concern. The missus planted some of that grass you suggested, and he's taken to that quite fine. Might be that'll take care o' th' hairballs."

"Yes, wheat grass usually does the trick, if they like it," Doc nodded with a smile for Tess. Mr. Swigstick... *Zweigstich!* moved off, and Tess faced a wall of strangers. *Or were they? Had she met them before?*

She was face-to-face with Vicki's girl posse. *Like a gang of alley cats.* All in lame and sequins, big hair teased in front, with too much makeup and high heels like ice-picks, they tried to stare her down.

Somewhat startled, she plastered a silly smile on her face and turned back to join Doc. He was chatting with Stuart and Brett, and she heard the smallest girl hiss loudly, "Does she think she'll monopolize all the testosterone in the room the entire night?"

"Just let her try," Vicki laughed. *Hissssss. Their claws look lethal.* Looking straight at Tess, she mouthed "Stewhair." "Stewhair!" another said, "Stewhair, stewhair!" All the girls broke into laughter and a chill went down Tess's spine. *What are they talking about? Stew Hair? Stewart, Stuart, like Stuart Tarleton?*

Doc was offering his standard introduction to more people she didn't know. "Here's Doctor Bamberger, you might be meeting her soon at your place. She's quite a veterinarian." Tess shook hands and smiled, greeting ranchers and townspeople.

Jimmy and his mom and dad came by, and Tess asked them about Sylve-essshhter. *Sylve-essshhter? Did someone fill my wine glass again?*

Aaron waved from across the room. "How's your truck running, Tess?"

"Great, thank you," she smiled politely, lifting her glass to him. "It's working out fine."

*****

A roast of venison was brought to the carving board and the crowd began to assemble. Stuart and Brett guided her to a place in line, and Tess feigned attention as they launched into yet another tale of their hunting and fishing exploits, sucking from her wine glass and letting her eyes roam the room. *This could be a very long night.*

Seated with Olivia and Cassie, Jake was steadfastly ignoring her, his jaw set. *I'm just batting a thousand, here. It's not like I can leave the line and just go sit with Jake. Even though I want to. Even though I really, really want to.*

Brett and Stuart were moving down the line. Tess thought of being next to Jake in bed and almost lost her balance. He glanced her way then furrowed his brow, tending to Cassie. *Just great. He's being very clear about how he feels about me. And his ex wife and her gal pals are pretty clear about it, too. They're making mincemeat—I mean "stewhair" —of me. .*

Loud conversation and the rich aroma of food washed over Tess in tangled waves. The room started to spin. A shadow hovered at her elbow. *Aaron, awesome, Jake will love this!* "Mind if I join you?" he buzzed, above the din.

"Not at all," Tess answered, stepping back, hoping at least for variety in the conversation. But the talk of caliber and range and sighting and tracking only turned to head gaskets and shocks and struts and transmissions and carburetors.

"That one I got with my twenty-two..." crowed Stuart.

"After the head gasket blew..." thundered Aaron.

"Turkey season, we use pellet shot..." squawked Brett.

Then, Stuart Tarleton asked Tess about his hunting dog's habit of marking trees to establish territory. She answered politely before draining her wine glass. *So this is the prize for the Testosterone Monopoly? The Pointer Pee Zone Award?*

Her wine was gone, just a tiny purple ring was left at the bottom of her glass. *And where is the wine fairy when I need her?* Ahead, Vicki was serving on the buffet, the only woman not wearing an apron. *Because an apron would defeat the effect of all that glitz stretched over her armored Wonder bra. She couldn't possibly cover all that cleavage!*

Vicki's girl posse filed through the buffet ahead of Tess, yakking and giggling and calling attention to themselves. The tiny girl who was after Stuart leaned over the buffet pan to purr a secret to Vicki. Vicki threw her head back with a peal of laughter, and both of them turned and looked at Tess with narrowed eyes.

I'd trade places in the Testosterone Monopoly game, to make some new girlll friendssshhh. But they're not very nice-sssh. Feeling doomed and miserable, Tess glanced towards Jake just as he turned away, pretending not to notice her. Aaron and the Tarleton boys filled their plates then headed for the carving boards.

"How is it out there?" Alice asked, perky as ever, as Tess took small portions of pan-roasted potatoes, pumpkin soup, and smoked trout.

"Social hour with Doc was fine, but since I've been acco*ssh*-ted by Brett and Stuart and Aaron, it's been non-stop talk of caliber and range and engine lube. I'm dodging bullet-*sh* out there, Ali*ssh*," Tess complained, rolling her eyes in bewilderment. "Vicki's friends keep shooting me look-*sh* to kill."

"Poor thing. The Tarleton boys are considered real catches around here. They're almost inseparable, and they can talk. Oh well, bet you made Sherri happy, and you've certainly gotten Jake's attention."

"Right, just the attention I want. He's barely said a thing to me all night long. Oh, Alice, pleas-*sh* let me come in back and help you clean up, afterwards," Tess begged.

"Sure, take cover with us married ladies as soon as you finish dinner, Tess. There's plenty to do in the back. I doubt Vicki will stick around for the real work. She's just serving to flirt with the men and make Bea happy," Alice whispered.

Tess tottered past the pan of rice right in front of Vicki, who pursed her red lips viciously, whispering "Stewhair" as she passed. Dipping into the crock of requisite antelope stew, Tess filled a dish and took just a single slice of venison roast at the carving board.

Doc was with a group of men standing near the kitchen door, a pitcher of beer between them, waiting for all the others to file through the line, and Stuart and Brett had disappeared. Tess finally saw them, taking seats across from Aaron at Vicki's girl-posse table. *Well, that's not an option.*

Despairing, her eyes scanned the room. Gertrude gave her a big smile and next to Gertrude was Jake, who glanced her way. When he realized she was alone, he stood up, giving her a big smile. Devastatingly handsome, he motioned for her to join them. Tess's breath caught, and she started down the crowded aisle, trying not to wobble. *He's waiting for me!*

She passed Stuart and Brett, ducking and chewing and gesturing enthusiastically, all elbows and angles. Then, a bowl of stew skittered off the table, landing on the floor in front of her. As it spattered her boots, Tess realized it had come from the little girl who'd made the testosterone comment, now seated beside Stuart.

Oh. Keeping her plate level, Tess started around the giant puddle, wondering if she should offer to help clean it up. An ice-pick heel shot out, tripping her. She slipped, losing her balance, sliding on the gravy.

Suddenly, there was too much room inside her new boots. A piece of cornbread skidded off her plate and bounced on the floor, and she was going down, she just knew it. She caught a glimpse of Jake's concerned face as she floundered, then fell, sliding face first through the puddle of stew.

The room had gone dead quiet by the time her plate clattered to the floor next to her. She heard titters from Vicki's girl posse as she lifted her head, hair dripping into the puddle of stew. *"Stewhair,"* someone whispered, but no one laughed.

Above her, Aaron asked, "Tess, you okay?"

Too mortified to be certain if the pain in her left arm was real or imagined, Tess stayed silent, very still, waiting for the floor to open up and swallow her.

Then Alice was there, wiping her off with a towel, wrapping a big white kitchen apron around her dress. A very real pain seared up her arm and shot into her armpit. "My arm," she whispered to Alice.

"What?" Alice asked, green eyes wide as she helped her up. They both looked at Tess's left hand, dangling at a weird angle.

Sick with pain, Tess pressed against Alice. *Don't dare cry, Stewhair! Just don't cry!*

"Oh, my god, Tess, is it broken?" Leaning on Alice, she hobbled towards the kitchen. Alice face wrenched at the sight of Tess's face. "It's broken, isn't it?" Bea and Doc and even Olivia came up, surrounding her with a protective cloud of concerned murmurs.

Once in back, Alice helped her to a chair, filled a wine glass and set it in front of her, while Doc tore into a cardboard box, quickly managing a makeshift splint with packing tape.

Stewhair! Shaking her head, Tess gulped wine, trying to forget the teased-hair, vicious red-lipped taunts, and finally, the ice pick heel that shot out just as the stew was being spilled. *They planned this.* Feeling her insides collapse, she reached up with her good hand and squeezed gravy from her hair, focusing on the ladies still bustling around like little hens—ferrying hot pans to the sink, cleaning out chafing dishes and wrapping food—to keep from crying.

Jake entered the kitchen through a side door. While he conferred with Bea and Olivia, Tess pretended to watch a woman carrying an urn of coffee out to the buffet, calling over her shoulder, "Let's get those cheesecakes sliced." Numbly, she remembered the look on Jake's face as she fell.

He was walking towards her now, dark eyes sober. Queasy with mortification, she was in too much pain to do anything about the stew dripping from her hair onto her dress, the crumbs of cornbread smashed into her chest.

"Pretty rough out there tonight, huh?" he asked quietly, shocked concern on his face.

Tess only nodded. *If I open my mouth, I'll start wailing.*

Under the din, Jake's voice was steady and comforting. "I'm taking you to the hospital, okay? I'll just go pull the truck around. You want Alice to ride along, too?"

"Just you," Tess managed, afraid to say any more.

Alice spread Tess's magenta coat around her shoulders, then helped her through the side door into the lobby while Doc held her splint, careful not to jiggle it.

The high school girls are all gone. "They had a pitcher full of tips, all for marching band," someone was saying, before they saw her and quieted.

Chris Carson held the door for her, looking concerned and solicitous. Then Jake opened the door from outside, and a rush of cold air blew in.

*****

Pushing down controlled fury at what he'd seen, Jake put his arm around Tess's ribs. "Just lean on me," he said quietly.

"Thanks." He saw tears in her eyes.

Alice hurried off, but Doc stayed with them, holding Tess's arm steady. Doc met Jake's eye, shaking his head but saying nothing. *He saw this happen, too.*

He helped Tess into the truck while Doc held her splint. Alice came running out with a mound of clean rags. "Oh, Tess, I'm so, so sorry about this, about all of it," he heard Alice say, as she propped the bundle under the splint to hold it steady. "It must hurt so badly. Is this okay?"

Tess's eyes were dilated by pain. "Uh-huh, thanks, Alice. Can you check on Rhiannon? I'll call you later."

"Of course, Tess," she answered. "I can take care of the dog and then come along right behind you, if you want. I'll be along in a flash."

"I'm alright with just Jake. He and I have done this hospital thing once already." Tess managed a wan smile. Kissing her cheek, Alice shut the door.

As he pulled away from the curb, Alice and Doc and Bea stood coatless, waving, gusts of cold night air mussing their hair. The parking lot was still jammed with cars. Heading for the highway, he asked, "You warm enough?"

"I'm okay," she whimpered. But her right hand went to her face, and she started crying for real, sobbing and shaking.

"Oh, Tess," Jake said miserably. "I can't even begin to tell you how badly I feel about what happened in there. Vicki and her friends were gunning for you all night, weren't they?"

"Yes," Tess gasped, choking and hiccupping. "It was terrible. She filed for custody, too, didn't she?"

Jake dug on the dash for the tissue pack he kept for Cassie. "Yeah, but I knew that was coming. We don't have to talk about this now; I know how upset you are. Your arm really hurts, doesn't it?"

"It does. I'm pretty sure the radius is fractured, and there's likely a hairline split in the ulna, too. I'm just hoping it's not a spiral fracture because then I'll need pins."

"You'd know," he smiled, sticking a wad of tissues in her right hand.

She blew her nose and swallowed hard. "Look, Jake, I think I need to tell you something. It's not because of what happened tonight, I swear it. I wanted to talk to you before I left for Philadelphia, but you were so upset about the insurance, I couldn't find the right time."

"What's up?" Jake asked, unable to miss a pothole.

Tess winced and caught her breath. "I'm worried about Cassie."

His eyes met Tess's, dark with concern. "You're worried about Cassie? What's going on?"

"Remember that day that you were at the clinic when it got crazy?" He nodded. "After you left, Bea took Vicki into the back, so she didn't make a bigger scene. I heard Vicki tell Cassie to get ready to go, but she stayed and hung around in the dispensary." Tess looked at him. "I think it was so that Cassie would stay out front, out of her way."

Jake nodded, brow furrowed, trying to figure out what Tess was getting at. She continued, gasping a little with pain. "I needed some tools from the dispensary. When I went back… When I went back, Jake, to put the tools away, Vicki stormed out past me. A door to one of the drug cases was open, the one with the tranquilizers."

"What are you saying, Tess?"

Facing him, she continued, "My worst fear is that Vicki might have been stealing some. . ."

"Some drugs?"

Stunned, he stared out the truck's windshield, squeezing the steering wheel as his mind worked. *Vicki's sure been erratic, and she's capable of it. She's capable of anything after what I saw tonight. What's been going on in my poor kid's life?*

Dimly, he heard Tess's pinched voice saying, "I hate to jump to conclusions, but it's been on my mind for a long time now, especially because Cassie seems so anxious when she's with her mother. I know it could have been some gum or lipstick or something, but I had to say something to somebody, and I thought it should be you."

He looked into Tess's pained, worried eyes, and swallowed hard. "You did the right thing, by telling me," he said. After a few silent minutes, he asked, "Is there anything else? I don't want to pressure you, but if anything is else worrying you, I'd really like to know about it."

"Ron showed up this afternoon outside the thrift store, asking about the accident, insinuating that I was too concussed to tell if you were drinking. I stuck up for you, though."

He touched her left knee. "Thanks, Tess. I'm really, really sorry about all of this."

After they'd wheeled her into x-ray, he called Alice.   "I'll have Doc inventory the meds first thing tomorrow, Jake. Whatever the outcome, it surely won't be held against Tess. You can't be too careful in this business, we all know that."

"Thanks, Alice. Cassie's with Olivia tonight. The doc's ordered a room for Tess. It'll be late by the time the bone is set and she's casted. I'll stay and bring her home in the morning. She's going to need company tomorrow, though, Alice. Cassie will need me, and Tess will need rest and quiet. I can't be in two places."

"No problem. Just text me when you leave the hospital. I'll grab some groceries and meet you at her place."

"Thanks, Al, I don't know what I'd do without you."

"You bet, Jake. I love you guys, you know that."

He stayed with Tess while the radiologist reviewed the x-rays. When they took her in to be casted, he called his attorney at home and then glanced at the clock on the wall. *Half-past eight here, eleven-thirty in Philadelphia. What's a good time to meet the parents?*

Ten minutes after they'd wheeled Tess away to be casted, he introduced himself to her father.

"Glad that you called, son. Tess explained to us what happened with that police report. I'm, er, very sorry for the confusion. Perhaps we owe you an apology," Richard said gruffly, after they'd discussed Tess's injury.

"I know how I would have felt, sir, in your shoes. I've got a little girl, too. You don't need to say any more."

"I don't have much background in criminal law or police misconduct, but I can, er, find some contacts in Denver, if you need them," Richard growled.

"I appreciate the thought. I'll let you know if I need any resources, sir." Jake didn't dare mention Tess's case against Vicki and her friends. *It was serious, but she'll have my head if I involve her parents.*

"You'll stay with her then, tonight?" Richard asked, trying to hide his concern.

"I will. Tess won't leave my sight until I'm certain she is okay. Alice has offered to stay at the apartment as long as Tess needs her."

"Very good. Perhaps Tess will call us, when the doctor's finish with her."

Jake didn't miss the worry in her father's voice. "She'll be in recovery in just a few minutes, sir," he said assuredly. "I'll pass on your request. If she's not up to it herself, I'll call to let you know how she's doing."

"I can't ask for more than that, Jake. She's lucky to have friends like you and Alice. She was very angry with us for getting in the middle of things, you know."

"You have a very special daughter, Richard, and I'm not only speaking for myself. Everyone here loves her, including my daughter Cassie. We were sorry to hear of your health condition."

"Oh, I'm on the mend, thankfully, just worried about Tess now. Thank you again for calling."

"Good night, sir."

Olivia picked up on the second ring. "I'm as concerned as you are, nephew," she said. "But Cassie's fine here, sleeping soundly. Judge Reilly may be willing to resolve things right away on Monday, if there's reason to believe Vicki is abusing medication. He's no stranger to your ex-wife's character, I'm afraid. Stella's coming in the morning, first thing, so don't worry about us. I want you to stay with Tess as long as she needs you, Jake. I mean that. You and Alice are all she has right now, and this must have come as a terrible shock. I still can't quite grasp what Vicki and friends put Tess through. "

"I've seen Vicki do some cruel and destructive things, but what happened with Tess tonight takes the cake."

"It certainly does. And it may have been criminal, as well. Tess's parents' are attorneys. She may press charges."

*****

Tess smiled drowsily as Jake entered her room, eyeing the fiberglass around the lower half of her left arm. "How much pain are you in?"

"I'm okay. It's going to be a real bitch tomorrow, though, if it swells. Speaking of that, Rhiannon's tummy is getting huge."

"Let Cassie and I take her to the ranch, then. One less thing for you to worry about with that arm."

"Rhiannon will like that," Tess sighed, closing her eyes.

Jake squeezed her toes. "Doc Powell said things went really well in there."

"Seems that way. Now I'll just need to keep it iced so the pain and swelling stay down. How were my parents?" she asked suddenly, her eyes open wide.

"I spoke to your dad. He was glad that I called. He apologized about the mix up."

"The mix up?" Her brow furrowed then she rolled her eyes. "Oh, you mean his yahoo assumptions?"

"The what? Has your anesthesia worn off, Tess?" he teased, smiling affectionately. "It was all very cordial, don't worry. They want you to call."

"Ugh. I guessed as much. Will you stay until it's over?"

"Sure, no sense going home now."

"No, I mean the phone call. I don't want them freaking out."

"Sure, I'm here for the duration, Crash. I'm taking you back tomorrow morning."

"What about Cassie?"

"She's with Aunt Olivia. She's fine."

"Can you really swing another night with me in the hospital?"

"Shhh-h," he soothed, taking the chair beside her and rubbing her good hand. "It's me or Alice, and I'm already here. Alice has nurse duty tomorrow. Here, drink your ice water." He held the capped cup and straw to her mouth. "Anything else?"

"I just want to sleep."

"Why don't I dial your parents, first?"

"Oh, okay," Tess grinned, rolling her eyes.

*****

Hours after Jake fell asleep on the bed near the window, he heard muffled sounds of crying coming from Tess's bed. "Hey," he whispered, padding over to her bed in his stocking feet. "Your pain okay?"

Tess wiped her cheeks with her good hand. "No, and it's two hours before I get another pill."

"More ice might help. I'll go get some." He paused. "What's the matter, Crash?"

"Nothing, really," she sniffed.

"Awww, it's not nothing. You must have a lot on your mind. I'll bring you some ice packs, and we can talk."

After he packed the lower part of her arm with six ice bags, he rearranged her pillows. "There, let me know if it gets too cold, but your pain should be better in a few minutes." He took the chair next to her, pulling it over so he was close to her face. "Now, what's going on?"

"Well, for starters, I've really missed you."

Jake sighed, and caught her pained blue eyes, feeling guilty. "I've missed you, too."

"No, I mean, I really missed you. Why did the insurance thing cause so much trouble for us?"

"It wasn't just the insurance thing, Tess. I haven't thanked you for all your understanding when I freaked out, I know that, and really, I'm over it. It's just... The insurance thing was a wake-up call. Things were really happening between us, and I realized it was probably too much, too fast," he admitted.

"It felt like you'd just forgotten about me," she said, biting her lower lip and wiping a tear from her cheek.

"To be honest, I keep thinking what your dad's perspective on all this must be. I've got these ranches in the middle of nowhere, and I'm here for the duration, stuck with my crazy ex-wife. Her friends just broke your arm. If I were him, I'd want to keep you far away from a guy like me. I'd want you out of this hick-mountain town and back in Philadelphia."

"Dad and I have talked about it. He wants what I decide is best for me. For awhile, it felt like that was Green Junction."

"You're a city girl, Tess. There won't be enough to keep you happy here."

"Maybe not," she said quietly. "I've been offered a Fellowship at New Bolton, Jake. It would likely lead to a teaching position there."

He felt something catch and twist in his chest. There was a long silence before he recovered enough to say, "Congratulations, Tess. It sounds like a very prestigious opportunity."

Her blue eyes were full of questions. "It seemed like things were working out for me here, but now maybe... " She hiccupped then sobbed, "Maybe they're not. You seem convinced that I don't belong in Green Junction, and maybe... maybe you're right. The fellowship starts next fall, so I'll be here through summer. There's still lots to learn from Doc." She looked at her casted arm packed with ice, and tears squeezed from her eyes.

Jake pulled his chair up close to the right side of the bed and took her good hand, squeezing it to his chest. "Tonight was rough, Tess. Your work matters a lot in this community, but New Bolton offers you so much more: prestige, an academic environment, and lots less stress, even excluding crazy ex-wives."

"I've had this weight of the Vicki thing on my mind, Jake, with no way to tell anyone about it. It's all just been so painful." Tears streamed down her cheeks. "I've felt lousy about the distance between us. Cassie is just so unappreciated when she's with her mother. When she's with you, she can be herself, but it's like she's on eggshells with Vicki. Her whole demeanor is different. I worry about her."

"You think I made a mistake, not fighting harder to have her live with me?"

"I think you did what you needed to do so things were settled in her life. But Cassie is happiest on the ranch with you—anybody can see that. She'd only benefit by spending more time with you, Jake."

He stood up for the tissue box, gently wiping her cheeks. "You've really been thinking about this, huh?"

"She's a great kid, and she doesn't belong with a mother who doesn't appreciate her when she has a father who worships the ground she walks on."

"I can't disagree with that," he said, squeezing her shoulder. "You are a great friend to both of us, Tess. I know its months away, but Cassie and I will really miss you when you leave."

"I'll really miss you guys, too," she sobbed, meeting his eyes with a look that tore him up. "An awful lot."

Tess was in her pajamas on Monday morning, just heating water for tea when Alice arrived. Rhiannon met her at the door, sniffing her boots for the scent of her dogs. "Wow, Rhi's tummy is really filling out, huh?" Alice asked, setting a bag of groceries on the counter.

Tess started a pot of coffee for Alice. "She's putting on a lot of weight, but she looks good, right? Jake said he and Cassie will get her settled in her whelping box up at the ranch this week before the puppies come."

"How are you feeling?" Alice asked, digging through the bags and putting groceries away.

"Better than expected, Al. There's still pain, but I'm getting used to the sling. I'm supposed to start using my fingers as soon as the swelling goes down, which means I could be back at clinic for work later this week. I'll need your help today, though."

"That's what I'm here for, honey." Alice said, too cheerfully. She poured herself a cup of coffee, set a plate of muffins on the table, and sat down. Her face looked anxious. *So the news isn't good.*

"Doc found medications missing yesterday, Tess. I've spoken with Jake. His lawyer thinks Judge Reilly will call an emergency hearing this afternoon."

Tess shook her head, angry with herself, feeling guilty for what Cassie had likely suffered. "Ugh. How sad for everybody, Vicki included. If there's a hearing this afternoon, how will it work? I mean, I need to be there, right?"

"I don't think Jake wanted to ask, but obviously, your testimony is critical. You witnessed Jake's condition at the accident scene, and Vicki's situation in the dispensary. It would be best for you to be there, Tess, if you're up to it. This time, Jake's lawyer told him the judge may speak with Cassie. Of course, that will be in chambers, not in front of a courtroom, thank God."

"This is a mess, isn't it?" Tess asked, rubbing her forehead with her good hand.

"It is. Doc is sending me over with our order records, and the inventory and the dispensary log. I'll have to testify as well. Doc and Bea will be there, but they don't want Vicki to feel they've chosen sides. She'll need their support, no matter what, though they're more concerned for Cassie." Sighing, Alice broke a warm muffin apart, handing a piece to Tess. "We just have to hope the outcome is for the best, that's all. Have a blueberry muffin, girl. They make even the worst news bearable."

Nodding, she took a bite. Swallowing, she said, "I'll need help figuring out what to wear. I don't know what I can fit over this cast, Alice."

"You're wearing your boots, right?"

"I don't think so." Tess shook her head wistfully. "The boots belong in Green Junction, but it sure feels like I don't."

"Oh, Tess, Green Junction adores you. I feel terrible about what happened Saturday night, but the boots are adorable. You know what they say about falling off a horse, right? We may only have you through spring calving, but there will be plenty of broken hearts when you leave. Wear those boots while you're here, and when you take them back to Philadelphia, they'll carry memories of all the people who recognize how special and wonderful you are."

*****

Late that afternoon, Tess's boot heels tapped down the marble tiled hallway of the courthouse as she hurried towards the massive exit door.

I am so glad my parents don't practice family law. From the witness stand, Vicki had used harsh words against Jake, disparaging him, criticizing his relationship with Cassie, and accusing him of alcohol abuse during their marriage. Jake's jaw had clenched as he bore it, a dull, trapped look on his face. *No wonder he's so afraid of getting too close, always looking for an out.*

A courthouse guard opened the heavy oak door for her. Cold air took her breath. The sun was dropping behind the Sawatch Range, the last of its brilliant orange glow struck furrowed clouds, melding with a cobalt sky.

Pulling her white coat close around her shoulders, Tess grasped the rail with her gloved right hand. Her left arm was in a sling. The cold breeze caught her coat and blew it open, as she made her way down the steps. In the charcoal suit he'd worn to court, Jake walked up the sloped ramp toward her, and pulled her coat closer around her shoulders, buttoning it for her. "Thank you," Tess smiled. "Where's Alice?"

Grabbing the fuzzy blue wool cap from her pocket, he pulled it over her tangle of curls. "She went over to the tavern to fill Lotts in." Eyes resigned, voice sober, Jake said, "I want to apologize again for what you've been through the past few days, Tess. It's been hell for you. I feel real bad about all of it."

"Jake, it's not your fault."

"Still, I hate the way you've been sucked into all this nonsense, especially the situation with your arm," he said, shaking his head miserably.

"It's not the greatest," she conceded, swallowing hard, meeting his eyes. "But we're all doing what we can for Cassie's sake. She's the one that really matters, here. And maybe the worst is over."

His eyes full of sadness and regret, Jake touched Tess's cheek with warm fingers. Then his eyes flashed pain, and he pulled back. Squeezing them closed, he cleared his throat. "Thank you for testifying, Tess. It would have been impossible for the judge to get a clear picture of what was going on without you."

"It wasn't any fun in there for any of us, but it had to be done," she said sadly. "How is Cassie?"

"She seems okay. She'll be with Olivia tonight, and her aunt will get her to school in the morning. With everything so tense, the judge wanted a cooling-off period to make sure neither parent could influence her until the drug test results are in. Both Vicki and I were tested. If they are both clear, my lawyer guesses we'll go on the way we've been. If Vicki's show drug use, Cassie will live with me at the ranch, and we'll renegotiate custody when Vicki finishes rehab. Doc took me aside. He admitted he's afraid she's been using. He's trying to find a good rehab program for her. I told him I would help with expenses if she'll go."

"Did Cassie meet the judge?"

"Yeah. My attorney said she was her perky self. She had her little horse along, and the judge asked about that. He asked what she did when she was with Vicki and then when she was with me. The lawyers weren't allowed to say anything. She talked about riding Sparky and making pancakes when she's at the ranch. At her mom's said she liked visiting the vet's office. He asked her to tell him what she didn't like. She said the ranch house was big, but I stayed with her at night so she wasn't scared. Then she said she gets nervous in the mornings before school when she's with Vicki, in case there's no milk for her cereal or she's late for school. He asked if her parents yelled at her. She said Vicki did but that I was patient."

"That's telling," Tess said gently.

"It is, isn't it? Much as I hope Vicki's not doing drugs, I don't want to have to stick to this order anymore, Tess," he said quietly. "You've been right about Cassie. She is tense when she's with Vicki, and her mother has only been getting nastier. I want Cassie with me from now on."

She could tell Jake felt guilty. She did, too. She said, "Sergeant Fuller pulled me aside and asked what happened at the Jackalope. That's where I just was. I think he'd like me to press charges."

"It's up to you, Tess. Vicki was the ringleader, but her two accomplices will likely take most of the heat. It'd be a shame if you let them off. They hurt you, and they should be punished. Aunt Olivia says their actions reflect poorly on the entire community, and I have to agree."

She sighed. "It was really ugly, wasn't it?"

"I can't ever remember feeling as powerless as I did watching you go down. I'd do anything to protect you from something like that happening again," he said quietly.

Including hiding your feelings for me, so nothing will stop me from taking that job at New Bolton? The thought snapped into Tess's brain and stuck there. She was as certain of it as she'd ever been about anything. *He's decided it's better for me to leave, so he keeps pulling back.* "What about Ron?"

"You heard Ron's testimony. The time on the breathalyzer printout was forty minutes after the 911 log says the ambulance left the scene. The judge is likely to strike down the results as irrelevant. Look, you must be tired and in pain with that arm. Shall I take you home?"

"I am tired, but I'd like to spend a few minutes with Alice and Lotts. I'll bet you could use some help unwinding."

"I sure could," he agreed. "I'd like the company if you want to head over to Green Forks."

As he made a right, heading for the tavern, she asked, "What will happen to Ron?"

"Judge Reilly wants an internal investigation. He subpoenaed Ron's cell phone records. Someone who'd had a lot to drink breathed into that tube twenty minutes after the ambulance left with you, and it wasn't me. The Sarge wants a confession from whoever it was so Ron can't just say the timer wasn't properly set as he did in court. Sergeant Fuller oversees the police department, but he has an advisory board for hiring and firing. The judge and district attorney sit on it, and neither of them have much patience for the stunt Ron pulled. He'll lose his job, if they can prove it was false evidence. Ron just better hope the Ag Department doesn't catch wind of his stupid tricks."

"Are you going to file a complaint with them?"

"I want Ron off the police force, I can tell you that, but I'm not too worried about his Ag job. Any rancher that has a problem with him can file a grievance. Ron can't do too much harm with goats and sheep and pigs and cattle."

At Green Forks, Jake opened Tess's door and helped her down, forcing a grin. "The lady vet in Green Junction is the best we've ever had. Once Ron's fired, we should probably hire a lady cop, too."

"Nothing wrong with that," Tess winked.
"I'll let Sergeant Fuller know you think so."

*****

To: *Sam.Bam@vmailcom*
From: *Tess.Bam@vmailcom*
Date: *Tuesday, November 13, 2:35 PM*

Subject: *Total Shakedown*

Sam,

   Vicki really did steal those drugs, some tranquilizers. She turned what she had left over to the judge. Doc won't press charges for theft, so the judge gave her court supervised visitation until she goes through rehab. I feel terrible about what Cassie has been through, but she'll have a full life with her dad at the ranch, and still see her mom every Saturday afternoon. Maybe it's best for everyone, at least for now. Vicki will have to pass her drug tests clean and get counseling before she gets to spend time with Cassie unsupervised.

   I can't drive yet, but my arm's getting better. Tomorrow I'll head over to the thrift shop. I can walk there, and Gertrude will keep me busy. I want to start using my fingers again, so that's a good way to do it. Jake's been sweet. There isn't much spark, but I know he's been preoccupied with all that's been going on. I've applied for the Fellowship at Penn, and I'll look at CSU. Since it looks like I'll be leaving, maybe it's best we're just friends.

   Love, Way-stressed Doctor Tess

*****

   Doc and Bea insisted that Tess not even step foot into the vet clinic. "You take a good rest, dear," Bea said. "You started back too quick last time, and I told Doc, we just can't have it again.

Alice and I are fine, and if we have emergencies, why, our regular patients can just wait until you're back on your feet."

Jake brought Cassie to the apartment on Wednesday after school.

"Hi, Dr. Tess! My dad said we can take Rhiannon home with us again! Her whelping box is all ready. How are you feeling?" Cassie asked, as she opened the door for them.

"In the mood for a root beer float, Cass, and then maybe another trip to the library. What do you think?"

"Yessss! That sounds great! And look how big Rhiannon's tummy is! Can I feel it, Dr. Tess?"

Jake held Rhiannon's collar and scratched her chest, while she showed Cassie how to gently palpitate her abdomen. Pulling out her stethoscope, Tess let Cassie listen to the tiny puppies' heartbeats. After root beer floats, Jake drove them to the library then back to her apartment. Tess clipped Rhiannon onto her leash, and handed it to Cassie.

"Thanks for sharing her with us, Dr. Tess," Cassie said as they left, tugging gently so Rhiannon padded hehind.

"Oh, it's the right thing for her. Rhiannon wants to get settled in front of that warm stove in your mudroom before her puppies come."

"Tilda will help. She likes puppies. I put a special blanket in the whelping box, last night. We'll take good care of her."

"I know you will, Cass," Tess said, hugging the little girl.

*****

Despite Bea's insistence that she take it easy, boredom drove Tess into the clinic on Thursday morning. Though her arm was still casted, she had no problem using her fingers. On Saturday, she and Alice took all the regular clinic appointments. The rest of the weekend was quiet.

Doc and Bea invited her for Sunday dinner, and she spoke at length to Doc afterward in his study. He was understanding—encouraging even—about the New Bolton opportunity. "You're much too young to stick with a practice if it's more study and research you crave. I'm glad you're taking a look at Colorado State, too," he advised. "If livestock management is where you're heart is, the microbiology and pathogens programs there are second to none."

When she returned to her apartment, Tess spent the rest of the evening on the Colorado State website, emailing to request more information about their research fellowship program.

When she arrived at the clinic Monday morning, Alice called hopefully, "Hey, Tess, looks like you have a farm call at McGreer Ranch Wednesday at noon."

"Jake and Cassie called last night. I'm invited to dinner, too."

"That's progress."

"It's only a farm call, Alice. What Jake's after is a bunch of healthy new stock."

"Well, Cassie will be there, and you'll see Rhiannon. It might be fun."

9

"Home On The Range"

Jake had close to two hundred heifers waiting in a temporary pen when Tess pulled up Wednesday afternoon. A thick blanket of fresh snow lay on the ground but the sun was bright overhead, and the temperature was above freezing.

He approached her truck, helping with her equipment. "We've selected these girls for breeding stock, so I thought we could get them all cultured and inoculated before we inseminate them," he said, scanning her face. "Is your arm okay?"

"I wouldn't be here if it wasn't," Tess smiled, all business. "These girls look good, nice size and weight. Do you have someone to help with record keeping? It will go a lot faster on my end."

"I thought I'd stick around," he said, trying to meet her eye. "Tilda is getting Cassie from school, later on."

"Okay, let's get started, then."

When they'd finished the twenty-ninth cow, he asked, "Tess, is everything okay?"

"Sure, Jake, everything's fine."

"You don't seem like yourself."

"No, this is me. I'm a one-armed vet, and we have hundreds of heifers here." Larry brought up the next cow. "30-JM345-12," Tess said, swinging her casted left hand his way. "Brucellosis swab."

He handed her the culture swab, disappointed. "Is this the way it is between us now?"

"I'm not sure what you mean," she said, concentrating on her work. "We've got to get this job done before dark, right?"

"C'mon, Tess," he cajoled, holding the container for her to drop the swab into. He wrote JM345-12 with a Sharpie, put it in a big Ziploc bag with the others, and waited for Larry to lead the cow away. "This isn't how we are," he whispered.

Standing on her stool, Tess tossed her head and turned to face him, not hiding her impatience. "Honestly, Jake, I'm still trying to figure out how we are. Things were great in the beginning, and I thought we were close. But you didn't call while I was in Philadelphia, and every time I've tried to talk about us since then, you've wanted to play it cool," she said. "So that's how I'm playing it. This is cool."

She motioned to Larry to bring the next cow, but Jake held his hand up, holding Larry off. Larry paused, shifting uncomfortably, looking away. Under his breath, Jake said, "Tess, I hope you don't feel that I've taken you for granted. You're completely incredible. I hope that you know that."

"Oh, so since I'm so completely incredible, we get to culture two hundred of your favorite cows together?" she laughed. Her indignation caught him off guard. "What about this suggests I'm 'completely incredible', Jake?" She tore open a swab packet with vigor, motioning for Larry to bring the next cow. "You just want your heifers bred."

Jake held his hand up. Larry circled the cow in tight quarters, pretending he couldn't hear. "Look, Tess, I'm sorry. I've wanted to see you in person so we could talk. I was a wreck after the hearing and I've been busy with Cassie since. I guess it wasn't fair to spring this on you on a veterinary call, but this is the first chance I've had," he admitted miserably. "Other times you've been here, I thought we had fun together."

Tess gave him a baleful stare before turning to Larry. "C'mon, Larry, we're ready for you here."

After she swabbed the cow, she handed the culture to Jake wordlessly, took the inoculation syringe in her right hand, and quickly thrust it into the bovine's back. "Okay, not only was it unfair, it was lame," Jake conceded, as Larry took the cow away. "You deserve a lot better than this, but I didn't think you'd mind. You've never been a hard sell before."

"Maybe that was a mistake." Tess said, her voice clipped.

"It wasn't a mistake, Crash. I like how easy-going and approachable you are. I like your exuberance." He put a hand on her arm to slow her incessant motion. Even the cast on her left arm hadn't slowed her down. "Tess, c'mon."

She flashed a look that pierced him. Swabbing the next cow, she hissed angrily, "You don't like my exuberance, Jake McGreer. My exuberance scares you." Larry looked away uncomfortably, whistling softly in the afternoon breeze. Staring at Jake resentfully, she popped the needle into the bovine's back. "It hasn't been right between us for weeks, Jake, not since the day I was here to suture Alchemy. And that was a long time ago." Their eyes locked for a long moment, and hers turned steely with the heat of her anger. "You've been certain all along you know what's best for me, Jake, but you're not at all concerned about what I might want."

Her words cut him. *Man, she can be tough.* Once Larry led the cow away, Jake stepped in front of Tess, who was still standing on the stool. Meeting her stormy blue eyes, he took her hands and said, "Tess, we've talked through this. You know how I feel about tying you down here. You and I could be close, probably very close, but how will Cassie take it, once you're gone?"

Tess pulled her hands away. "You don't get it, do you?" she hissed. "You don't want to get it. This is a lot more about Vicki than it is about me." Larry stayed yards away, circling the next cow. Jake gave Tess his full attention.

"What do you mean?"

"Vicki felt tied down, she made you miserable because she hates it here, so with me, it's like you're looking for an excuse—an out—to protect yourself. Whenever there is a misunderstanding, your first instinct is to bolt, and you do, every time. Instead of calling me when you got the insurance letter, you made unfair assumptions, certain that I'd turned you in... that I'd betrayed you. Instead of discussing it, you just waited, fuming, until I showed up. It was like you wanted there to be something wrong."

"Tess, I..." he began, but she continued.

"Then my dad has a heart attack, and you pretend not calling me is about giving me space, not crowding me while I'm home with my family. You sent flowers, but that was all. What was that all about, anyway, Jake? You can't really think that was 'making it right for me,' can you?"

"Probably not," he admitted sheepishly.

"The whole time I was in Philadelphia, you left me hanging. We could have stayed close, but you didn't really want that. You've treated me badly, Jake. You won't trust me, and you refuse to allow yourself to even give us a chance."

"Oh, Tess," he said wearily. "I trust you, I do. After the hearing, all you cared about was Cassie. My life is crazy right now, and honestly, I don't want you stuck with any part of it. You're incredibly generous, but I can't take advantage of that. I won't. It just doesn't feel fair to involve you—or worse, trap you. Look what happened with your arm. It's too much to ask."

"Too much to ask? Too much for me to ask, right? That I could actually know what is going on with you—between us? That you'd communicate with me, without holding back? Because then what we'd have would be real, as in a real relationship, real intimacy, real trust. You'd like to pretend you're doing me a big favor, making it easy for me to leave, but that's just an excuse. You refuse to take a chance and see if what's between us could really happen," she fumed. "Instead, you're all about protecting yourself,"

"Tess, that's not fair. You are brilliant, with so much to offer, and I know how life is. I don't want you caught in a situation that will wear you down, and I can't bear to have Cassie grow close to you and lose you. She doesn't need that."

"And neither do you," she said, looking right at him, eyes blazing.

"That's right, neither do I. I don't want to be hurt again, I don't want to hinge my dreams on someone else and be disappointed."

"And you're certain I would disappoint you?"

"No, I'm not certain, but it feels risky. Look, Tess, I'm sorry. I understand how confusing these past weeks must have been for you. I hurt you, but I didn't mean to. I was trying to protect you, and myself, I guess. I should have let you in; I wanted to, I was just afraid of overwhelming you, that it would be too much."

"I assure you, it would not have been too much," Tess snapped. She crossed her arms, but the ice was still there. "Maybe you've done a good job of protecting yourself from disappointment, Jake, but you sure haven't protected me." Her bright eyes narrowed. "The first time we got close, you said I was safe with you. It hasn't felt very safe to me at all, and that has everything to do with the way you've behaved."

Jake felt as if she'd knifed him. "Tess, I'm sorry. I've been thinking of you for weeks, waiting to get a break from all the stress. I just wanted to be able to enjoy each other without any pressure. That was what today was supposed to be about, lame as it is."

He could still see the clouds of hurt in her eyes, and he wanted to pull her close, hold her, offer her comfort. He stepped closer, but Larry was circling the next cow and Tess motioned him forward.

"Well, Jake, you're right, it was lame. But I guess at least you tried, if only a very little bit."

Resignedly, Tess began to swab JM294-12.

*****

Tess had finished inoculating over one hundred and fifty heifers when Cassie rode up on Sparky, all bundled up in her red jacket, and little fringed chaps covered her legs. "Hi, Daddy, Hi, Dr. Tess," she called, her high-pitched voice cheery.

"Hey, little girl," Jake said affectionately.

"Hi, Cassie," Tess smiled.

"Daddy, Tilda said it was okay for me to ride out to see you guys." Tilda stood near the horse barn on the distant knoll in boots and a warm coat.

Jake waved. "That's right, Cassie. Dr. Tess and I will be done in an hour or so, then maybe we can all take a trail ride. You want to ride Sparky around the pasture, so I can keep an eye on you?"

"Sure, Daddy, Sparky needs a workout. Dr. Tess, Tilda and I just checked on Rhiannon," Cassie said importantly. "She's in her box by the stove in the mudroom. No signs of puppies yet, Tilda said."

"It's going to be another week, Cass," Tess answered. "Right around Thanksgiving. But they're getting ready. Every day those puppies are growing bigger and stronger in their mama's belly, ready to make their appearance.Soon you'll be able to play with them and help them learn what they need to know."

"Daddy, will you hold Sparky? I want to give Dr. Tess a hug." Jake took the reins, and Cassie swung off her pony. Tess knelt down to be close to her, feeling a rush of love for the little girl and Cassie wrapped her hands around Tess's neck, squeezing. "Ooo, I've missed you so much, Dr. Tess."

"I've missed you, too, Cassie. And your hugs. You give the best hugs," Tess said, wiping her eyes quickly, wondering if Jake would ever get his act together.

"Tilda is making roast chicken for dinner, and Daddy wants to take a trail ride. You're staying, right?" Cassie asked.

Tess glanced at Jake. He smiled at her anxiously, , willing her to say 'yes.' His eyes were troubled, a yearning look on his face. "Sure, Cassie, I'll stay."

"Great! On our trail ride, we'll take you down to the creek and show you the dam. You'll really like it, I promise. I have my English saddle on Sparky today, Dr. Tess! Watch me post."

*****

To: Sam.Bam@vmailcom
From: Tess.Bam@vmailcom
To: Sam.Bam@vmailcom
Date: Wednesday November 14, 9:15 PM

Subject: Puppy Tails

Sinful Sammi: Took a trail ride on the ranch today and stayed for chicken dinner. Rhiannon's puppies will be along soon~ Cassie is over the moon. Will stay here for Thanksgiving. Thanks for everything and REALLY sorry to miss your sure-to-be-terrific cranberry sauce and those low-fat mashed potatoes. Are you starching Archie's shirts in your spare time?

Love, Tortured Tess.

*****

To: <u>*Tess.Bam@vmailcom*</u>
From: <u>*Sam.Bam@vmailcom*</u>
Date: Wednesday, November 17, 8:46 PM

Subject: Still Delicious

Tortured Tess:
    I'm doing my best to get Archie OUT of his shirts, and when I do, I fully expect he won't be the least bit starchy. . . I want him very, very . . . stiff. . . He's a perfect gentleman, but his kisses knock me sideways. We're headed to a movie right now~ Sure hope Jake figures out how to put the yahoo back in my favorite cowgirl!

Love, Sensationally Saute-ing Samantha

*****

A fierce November wind slapped Jake's face as he and Larry hoisted the metal ramp back into the cattle carrier just before noon on Friday. His thoughts had been spinning for days, weeks really, always coming back how he'd felt seeing Tess with Aaron, Brett and Stuart at the Jackalope, how right it felt to have her in his arms. Since Wednesday, he'd been plagued by her words.
    She deserves the best, which I could give her, if I just knew she wasn't going to wind up frustrated here and resentful about her limited career options. He'd given himself a headache, trying to think it through, considering all the angles. He just couldn't get the best of it. *Maybe it's the coming storm, but something just*

doesn't feel right. The fat Hereford yearlings they'd unloaded were down at the creek, breaking through the ice to slurp the water, already pawing for hardy pasture grasses beneath a thin cover of snow.

Rubbing his leather gloves together, Larry slammed the cattle carrier doors shut, eyeing the dense stratus cover moving in from the west. "We can just about beat the first big snowfall of the season if we leave now. Looks like it'll hit hard, wherever it hits."

"Yep, let's get out of here. It'll be snowing hard by the time we get back to town," Jake answered. "Spike can manage this herd all right."

The engine on the big truck started with a chug and a whine as Jake climbed into the passenger seat. Larry pulled out and he eyed the dim sky to the northwest. "Cassie wasn't feeling real well when I left her at school this morning. Tilda said she'd grab her, but I'd like to get home before school's out, if we can make it."

"It might already be snowing up at the ranch," Larry answered, nodding towards the snowcapped mountains obscured by cloud cover. Highway 17 was a straight-shot due north. After forty minutes on the road, they stopped for fuel and sandwiches.

As Jake handed the girl at the register the money, his cell buzzed. The dread and anxiety he'd felt all day quickened when he saw the number on his display."Mr. McGreer, this is Principal Thompson at Green Junction Elementary. Cassie came into the nurse's office with flu symptoms earlier and Nurse Beatrice sent her home. Is she there with you?"

A chill stabbed at Jake as the cashier handed him change. "No, Ma'am. I think our housekeeper, Tilda, would have called if Cassie had come home sick. You sent her home, you said? Are you certain?"

"It appears her mother signed her out, Mr. McGreer," Principal Thompson admitted quietly.

Immediately in a panic, Jake grabbed the bag and shot through the door, sprinting across the parking lot to the eighteen-wheeled cattle truck. "Mrs. Thompson, I left a copy of the new court order with your office last week. Cassie only spends supervised weekend time with her mother now. You're saying Vicki picked her up?" He motioned for Larry to hurry as he slammed the door shut.

Shooting Jake a look of alarm, Larry accelerated onto the highway. Principal Thompson's voice collapsed. "Oh, Mr. McGreer, I'm so very, very sorry. We've had a spate of the flu the past two days, and Nurse has had her hands full. I'm afraid the records in the health office still show Cassie's mother's number as a first contact. Vicki signed Cassie out an hour and a half hour ago. This matter just came to my attention. What shall I do?"

As the truck picked up speed, Jake felt his chest collapse. He spoke urgently. "I'm on the road still a good two hours south of Green Junction, Mrs. Thompson. To be honest, I'm worried sick. Cassie's mother is suffering from a drug addiction. Please call Sergeant Fuller and ask him to make certain Cassie is safe, and recuperating at her mother's."

"I'll call Sergeant right away, Mr. McGreer. And I am so very, very sorry," Mrs. Thompson said, her subdued voice filled with concern.

In high gear now, the truck accelerated north. Jake pressed speed dial, cold fury pulsing his veins. *No answer on Vicki's cell.* As he dialed the vet clinic, panic squeezed his chest. *Please let Cassie be okay.*

*****

The phone at the reception desk pealed as Tess checked her clients out. Bea and Doc were out to lunch, and Alice was busy in the lab. "Green Junction Veterinary."

"Tess?"

"Jake, what's wrong?"

"Tess, the school nurse accidentally sent Cassie home with Vicki over an hour and a half ago. I'm two hours south of town, and I can't reach Vicki on her cell. Can someone go over to her apartment and make sure Cassie is okay?" her asked frantically.

Tess felt her stomach lurch. "I'll be at Vicki's in five minutes, Jake. I'll call you from there, okay?"

Slipping her arms into her down coat, she grabbed her keys, calling for Alice before racing to her truck.

Vicki's car was gone. Thin autumn sunshine cast bare tree-branch shadows across Vicki's yard as Tess rushed up the sidewalk. Once on the porch, she pounded on the door, frantically calling. Increasingly panicked, Tess ran to the side of the house, desperate for a glimpse of Cassie.

Her breath clouded tall windows as she peered into an empty apartment. In the bedrooms, drawers and closet doors had been left open, clothing strewn on the floor. It was obvious that Vicki had left hastily.

Afraid to give up, Tess returned to the door and continued to knock, calling loudly. Sergeant Fuller's cruiser pulled up to the curb and the passenger window dropped. He raised a hand, motioning Tess into the car. "Nobody here, huh?" he asked.

Washed in cold terror, Tess slid onto the passenger seat as the Sergeant broadcasted Vicki's car description and license number across the scanner. Clipping the mic back onto the dashboard, he turned to Tess. "Cassie must have told her Ma where Jake had gone. Why else would she pull a stunt like this? The highway goes east, west, or south, so those are our options. I don't see Vicki heading to Kansas. It's a rough trip south to New Mexico, and likely she'd cross paths with Jake. I'd say west to California or Arizona is a safe bet. What do you think?"

"I've heard she likes California," Tess said weakly, trying not to let her voice quiver.

"No kid wants to see a policeman chasing her Ma. You coming along?"

Tess nodded, slamming the door shut. Sarge flipped the siren on. They tore across town, then up the on-ramp, entering the interstate at record speed. "I called her Pa. He's filed a missing persons report. He might want to hear from you, though, just so he knows we're going after her." Sergeant Fuller's voice was taciturn and even, his face emotionless, betraying none of the horror Tess felt.

She dialed and Jake picked up immediately. Voice wavering, Tess told him, "We're on Route 50, heading west."

"That's probably a good bet, Tess. Tell Sarge we're heading up 285 and across 114. I can't make anywhere near the time I need to in this big truck, and snow's coming. Vicki's probably past Gunnison, if she went that way. Santa Fe would be the sneaky route, south down 550 at Montrose. Let's hope she hasn't thought of that, though." Tess didn't know what to say, but Jake continued, "Vicki's father is calling the bank. She can't have had too much cash put aside. She'll have to either make an ATM withdrawal, or start using charge cards. Either way, she won't get far."

Though his voice was panicked, Jake spoke with assurance. *He's trying to comfort both of us.* Mountains and trees and creek beds sped past as they raced west. Sergeant Fuller was a good driver, Tess gave him that. *If I weren't so freaked out, this might be fun*, she thought giddy with nerves, trying not to think about the panic Cassie must be feeling. *And she's sick, poor little thing.*

They made it to Gunnison in twenty minutes, and then it began to snow. Icy freeze hit the cruiser's windshield and swirled across the highway. Fueled by fear, Tess thought of a speeding Vicki, possibly drug-addled, losing control of her car on the slick snow and flying off the road.

The Curecanti National Recreation Area encompassed Blue Mesa Reservoir. Tess had never seen the big, blue lake before. It stretched for miles under both sides of the road, its edges frozen. The skin on the back of her neck crawled as she looked over the guardrail, searching the water for the breaks in the ice or the glacial hunk of Vicki's submerged white sedan.

As they passed through Montrose, Sergeant Fuller called Jake. "We'll head north up to Delta and then on to Grand Junction and Clifton if we have to. After that, it's the Utah state line." Tess heard Jake say something in reply. Sarge nodded. "Well, she had a good hour and a half on us. I've closed the gap some. I figure she's between here and Delta if she came this way, or south on 550 if she headed for Santa Fe. All the APB's are out, and the state troopers are combing the key intersections, Jake. We have to hope this snow will slow her down some, and she doesn't get out of the state."

It was past three o'clock when they turned northwest on 550, but Tess's breakfast still churned in her stomach. *This could take hours, yet. If we find them.* She heard a trooper page Sergeant Fuller, and then a dispatcher buzzed into the Sergeant's cell phone.

As he spoke on the phone, Sergeant Fuller accelerated. Grainy ice particles snapped against the windshield and hood of the cruiser, and a pleased grin crossed his placid face. "They've got Vicki pulled over, five miles south of Delta," he told Tess. "We'll be there in a few minutes. I'll keep the lights on until we're in range, but we'll approach slowly. The kid's had enough excitement for the day."

Her heart swooping with relief, Tess's fingers wobbled as she hit speed-dial. "They've found Cassie, Jake," she said, her panicked voice barely a whisper.

"Thank God," Jake breathed. "You'll stay with her, Tess?"

Tess's voice was shaky with emotion. Steadying it, she said, "Once we have her, I won't let her out of my sight, Jake, I promise you that."

"Larry and I are almost to Gunnison. We'll wait for you there."

"I'll give her a big hug from her daddy," she promised, feeling tears coming.

"Thanks, Tess," Jake choked.

Fifteen minutes later, Tess saw three Colorado State Police cars, all with lights flashing, surrounding the white Acura pulled to the shoulder. Just as he'd promised, Sergeant Fuller switched his lights off and slowed. Pulling off the highway, he stepped out of the cruiser and walked over to confer with the troopers surrounding Vicki's car. Tess saw Cassie's brown hair in the back seat, her head bobbing as she strained to see what was happening. *Oh that poor, poor kid!*

The cop standing nearest the driver's seat motioned for Vicki to step from her car, and Sergeant Fuller returned for Tess. "I told them you know Cassie real well. They asked if you'd come get her, help her stay calm. It's probably best."

Jumping from the car, Tess hastened to the white Acura. An officer opened the rear door, and Cassie launched into her arms. "Doctor Tess, I was so worried! Where's Daddy?"

Tess bent, touching Cassie's feverish red cheek. Scooping the little girl up, she turned her away from the scene with Vicki. "He's waiting for you just back in Gunnison, not far away. Sergeant Fuller will take us to him, okay?"

"Is Mommy in trouble?" Cassie asked anxiously, looking over her shoulder to where the cops clustered around Vicki.

Tess swallowed hard. *Please don't let her see them put handcuffs on Vicki.* "I think she's just talking to the policemen, Cassie," she said, as calmly as she could. "It's cold out, and you're not feeling well. C'mon, we're almost at Sergeant Fuller's cruiser. How 'bout we sit inside and call your dad?" Clinging fiercely, Cassie clasped Tess's neck, wrapping her legs around her waist. Ice particles pelted them as Tess hurried them to warmth and safety.

Once she'd gotten them tucked inside, Cassie laid her blistering forehead against Tess's cool throat. "I have to see my Daddy. He's probably worrying."

Sergeant Fuller came up with Cassie's bag, left it on the seat beside them, and shut the rear door. The feverish little girl snuggled against her as Tess dialed Jake, handing the phone to her.

"Mommy surprised me at school, Daddy. I know it was different from the schedule, but my tummy hurt and I just wanted to get out of there. I'm so sorry." Cassie burst into tears, and Tess stroked her hair. "I don't know why she wouldn't just let me sleep at the apartment. I didn't want to go to California, I told her that. She said the beaches there are warm and sunny, but I like it at the ranch with you."

Jake calmed Cassie, who handed the phone to Tess and settled against her. "How am I ever going to thank you?" he asked.

"Shhhh, you don't have to," she whispered. "We'll see you in a few minutes."

After Tess tucked the phone back into her purse, Cassie held the fingers that poked from her cast. Her little voice weak and tired, she said, "Daddy's waiting for us a little ways back, just like you told me. I'm so glad you came for me. I don't ever want something like this to happen again, Doctor Tess. I knew I was safe when I saw you."

*****

Jake's heart was still pounding when the cruiser pull into the rest stop in Gunnison. He climbed into the backseat to find Cassie nestled against Tess, almost asleep. "Hi, Daddy," she murmured, drowsily tucking her fingers into his palm.

"Hi, Cass," he breathed. He took her up in his arms and buried his nose against her neck, inhaling the sweet, baby-shampoo goodness of her.

Cassie threw her hands around his neck. "I'm so glad I'm with you again, Daddy," she said, cuddling against him. "Thanks for sending Dr. Tess. I didn't like all the fuss and I really don't feel very good at all."

"There has been an awful lot of fuss, baby girl," Jake said, holding her close as he set her on the seat, clasping the seatbelt around her waist.

Sergeant Fuller pulled onto the highway as Cassie rested her head on his chest. He folded an arm over her shoulders. "Your boots are dirty, Daddy," she yawned.

"So they are, little girl," Jake agreed. Recovering from his panic, he shot Tess a look of gratitude. *What would I have done without her?* Reaching over Cassie's head, he touched a finger to one of Tess's curls and felt his eyes brim. Taking up his fingertips, Tess held them to her mouth, kissing them gently. Tears of relief snuck down his cheek.

It was after dark when the cruiser swung into Tess's driveway and Larry pulled the big truck in along the curb. Putting a finger to her lips, Tess slid off the seat through the open door. The cold air woke Cassie. Starting, she fussed, clutching at Tess. "Dr. Tess, please don't go! Rhiannon's lonely at the ranch, she wants you there, and so do I! I don't want to be all by myself while Daddy does night check."

"Shhh, honey, you won't be alone," Jake soothed. "Tilda is there, waiting for us and Larry's going to do night check tonight. C'mon, you're not feeling well." Nestling his daughter in his twill-clad arms, he grabbed for her backpack. "Sergeant Fuller's got some work to do, and Tess does, too."

"Dr. Tess, please!" Cassie called beseechingly, eyes suddenly wide.

"I can follow you up, Jake," Tess offered quietly, patting Cassie's leg. "My truck is right around the corner."

"You sure it's not asking too much?" he asked, waving to Sergeant Fuller as he pulled out.

Tess quirked an eyebrow. *Haven't we been through this?* her eyes asked. Patiently, she said, "It's Friday night, and it's Doc's turn in clinic tomorrow. Cassie's had a terrible scare, and I hate to see her any more upset than she already is. I'm free if you need me."

"Sounds like you and Cassie have it all figured out, then," Jake smiled, waving Larry on, too. Tess let them into her warm apartment, and he laid Cassie on the sofa, which had been new the last time he'd been there. "Give me your keys; I'll go get the truck." He turned to Cassie, "Stay with Dr. Tess, darlin', I'll be back in a minute."

Tess had an overnight bag packed by the time Jake returned. Climbing into her truck next to Cassie, she whispered, "I brought my work clothes, Cass, so I can take calls from your house tomorrow. I'm yours as long as you need me."

"That's good, Dr. Tess. That makes me feel better," Cassie mumbled drowsily, patting Tess's arm. When Tess took Cassie's hand, she wished she'd never have to let go.

*****

It was after midnight, when a tap on the guest bedroom door woke Tess. Jake's voice came through it, tense and low. "Tess, I hate to disturb you, but you're the closest thing I have to a doctor right now. I need some help with Cassie."

In a flash, Tess was out of bed, grabbing for the plush terry robe from the back of the door. Jake stood in the hallway. "Cassie's not keeping the Tylenol down, and her fever is worse. I'm worried, Tess. She's pretty out of it."

"How much has she thrown up?" Tess asked, hurrying down the hall.

"There's nothing left in her stomach, I'm sure of that. She's had nothing but dry heaves for the past thirty minutes."

"The poor little bugger! I'll grab water and some washcloths, and go sit with her. Why don't you run a warm bath?"

When Tess got to her, Cassie was listless, flushed with heat. Soothingly, she said, "Cass, we need to bring your body temperature down, okay? This is just a washcloth soaked with water, but it's going to feel real cold. Your daddy's running a bath to help you cool off."

She laid a cool cloth on Cassie's head, another on her arms. Dazed and weak from vomiting and exhaustion, Cassie shook her head, whimpering, her lips red and swollen with fever. Jake came through the doorway. "I've got the bath ready." She nodded, and he scooped Cassie up.

Following him to the master bath, she dropped her hand into the tub. "It's the perfect temperature." He lowered Cassie into the tub, pajamas and all, holding her armpits to help her stay afloat. The feverish little girl squirmed, restless and uncomfortable.

"She's so out if it, she might get lost in there," Tess murmured, dropping the robe and climbing into the tub in the panties and chemise she'd worn to bed.

Keeping her casted arm above water, she scooted under Cassie. Once in her lap, the little girl settled against her, nestling to her chest. Kissing the top of her head, Tess stroked her back, humming a little tune to calm her.

"Count on Dr. Tess to work miracles," Jake exhaled. Exhausted, he put his chin on an arm resting on the tub, and stared at her in admiration. "Tess, what would I have done without you today? Thank God you're here with us."

"You're finally talking sense, Jake," she smiled. "This kid will need somebody to hang onto for awhile, maybe a long while, until she starts to feel safe again. I've got my hands full, here. How about you turn the bubbler on?"

After twenty minutes in the tub, Tess handed Jake a much cooler, calmer child. Gently, he toweled Cassie dry, slipped her into fresh pajamas, and carried her to his bed. Tess peeled her wet underwear off and wrapped herself back in the robe, tying it at the waist. After squeezing the wet ends of her hair in a towel, she twisted water from her panties and chemise and hung them on a towel bar.

"Can I stay here, Daddy?" she heard Cassie murmur from the broad master bed. "I feel better now."

"Yup, I can keep an eye on you this way. What do you think about more Tylenol, Dr. Tess?" Jake asked.

"Let's take her temperature."

Jake held the thermometer in Cassie's mouth. "100.6. You do work miracles, don't you?"

Shrugging her shoulders, Tess smiled and took a seat next to Cassie on the bed she'd shared with Jake that one night, weeks before. "It's not me. Her fever broke. The worst should be over. Let's hold off on the Tylenol. Once her tummy's settled, I think she'll be okay."

Jake dimmed the lamp on his nightstand and took the leather recliner across the room, near the window. Humming a lullaby, Tess stroked Cassie's back until the little girl fell into a slumber and Jake had dozed off, too. Exhausted, she returned to the guest room, crawling between the cream flannel sheets and down comforter.

She tiptoed in to check on Cassie the next morning in fleecy leggings and a turtleneck. The sun was streaming in Jake's picture window. Cassie was buried in the comforter, still sound asleep. Haggard and unshaven, Jake dozed in the easy chair in worn jeans and a sweatshirt, his feet up on the ottoman. The sunlight caught his profile. Tess was reminded of the stunning cowboy she'd seen that first day in Green Junction, and her heart ached.

Jake roused and glanced her way. "Tess, your feet will freeze on this cold floor," he whispered, opening the bottom drawer of the bureau that ran the length of his room. He tossed her a pair of woolen crew socks.

"Thanks," she said, taking the leather ottoman. "I forgot to bring socks."

He leaned to touch her shoulder and whispered, "Tilda's making breakfast downstairs. I don't want to leave Cass alone, though. How 'bout I go grab a tray for us and bring it up? Will you wait here?"

"Sure."

By the time Tess heard Jake's soft tread come back up the stairs, Cassie had woken. "Dr. Tess, you're here!"

"You didn't think I'd leave, did you?"

Rhiannon padded into the room behind Jake. As he set a breakfast tray on his dresser, the plump mother-to-be circled the bed and took a spot on the rug closest to Cassie, groaning a little as she flopped down.

Jake flashed a smile. "I don't usually let the dogs upstairs, but I thought this might be a special occasion, considering the company."

Turning onto her tummy, Cassie stuck her head over the bed, dangling a hand down to pet the dog's silky coat. "How are you feeling, Rhiannon?"

"Probably better than you are, darlin'," Jake answered. "Tilda sent up cinnamon toast and weak tea, with a little sugar and a splash of milk. How's your tummy?"

"Okay, Daddy, I just think it was that yucky medicine."

"Oh, I think it was more than the medicine." Jake said, setting a mug of hot coffee and a warm, honey-soaked half grapefruit in front of Tess

"I didn't eat much yesterday. I'd like some toast please," Cassie said, in her company voice.

"Okay, but only if you take it real slow. Sit up, and keep this napkin in your lap." Jake set a plate of toast on his nightstand and held the mug for Cassie while she sipped. After he'd taken up his own mug, he carried a plate of walnut and raisin sticky buns to the small table near Tess.

"Yum, Tilda's sticky buns?" Cassie asked.

"The buns will be here after lunch, Miss Tummy-ache. Tilda's making some chicken soup down there, too. Let's see if you can keep the toast down, first."

Cassie downed two pieces of toast, brushed cinnamon from her hands, wiped her mouth on the napkin, and asked if Tess could get her puppy books. Cuddling up, Cassie attempted to read aloud to Tess. Then they played checkers and Candyland.

After a lunch of chicken soup and a last game of checkers, Jake walked Tess to her truck. His sober eyes met hers. "There's no way I can thank you for what you've done for Cassie and I, Tess."

"It's alright. I'm just glad I picked up when you called the clinic yesterday, Jake. There's no place else I would have ever wanted to be."

Tess hugged him quickly and climbed into the truck, which he'd warmed while she'd said good-bye to Cassie and Rhiannon and Tilda. Holding the handle of her door, his tired eyes gazed into hers, a little lost.

He reached in, touched her cheek, brushing away a stray curl. Straightening up, he put his hands in his pockets and cleared his throat. "I love you, you know."

Tess did a double take. "What?"

His face bereft, he smiled, a forlorn half-smile. *Like the boy who lost his mom when he was only ten.* "I know you think I've behaved like a cad, so I'm coming clean. I love you, Tess. I have for a long time. I ache for you Every morning I wake up, wishing you were in my arms. Back when Cassie was at her mom's, I was relieved to be thinking about you and not her so much anymore, until I realized it meant that I was in love with you. I fell for you that first morning, when I saw you coming out of the garage with Dave. I couldn't tell you the other day, with the cows, but I wanted you to know." He leaned in and kissed her cheek. "Maybe I have been protecting myself, but mostly, I wanted to protect you."

Tess fell into him, wrapping her arms around his neck and finding his lips, pulling him in for a real kiss, letting him know what he meant to her. They kissed for a long time.

When it broke, he dropped his gaze, then looked up, meeting her eye. His voice low and earnest, he said, "You have no idea how much I want to adore you, Tess. I'm crazy with it. I want you like nothing I've ever wanted in my life."

"I want that, too, Jake," Tess stammered, utterly blown away.

With his sad, half-smile, he kissed her forehead. "I'll see you later, okay?"

"Sure," Tess said, and he closed the door. She watched him walk towards the house, shoulders hunched against the cold, hands in his pockets. On her way down the cold mountain, she remembered the words Jake had spoken when they'd first gotten close. *"You may not know how it feels to have your life turned inside out by someone you tried to love."*

He'd been right; she hadn't known how it felt, then. *Maybe that's the hard part of love, staying vulnerable, willing to trust. Even when it's turning you inside out and upside down, you have to stick around... see it through.*

Her cell buzzed. "Want to ride with me to Tree Lighting?" Alice asked.

"Sure, Al. I can't imagine Ron is still up for this dance."

"I hope not, after all that nonsense with Jake."

"Is it okay if I tag along with you and Lotts?"

"We'd love to have you, Tess."

At her apartment, two emails were waiting in her inbox, one from Penn and one from Colorado State. Reading through them, Tess smiled with satisfaction, then wrote to her father, filling him in on the upsetting scene with Cassie and Vicki. *"I'd like to help make her world safe again, like the world you and mom created for me. Her little face lights up when she sees me, Dad. If I could help her trust again, even just a little, it would be worth it."*

Tess felt more vulnerable than she ever had, remembering Jake's words, aching for Cassie. Slipping into snow pants, she grabbed the snowshoes he'd left her all those weeks ago. The snow pack on the trail was almost a foot deep, and Tess climbed briskly, trying to clear her head. In the afternoon sunlight, the little town below looked like a Christmas village. Sun bounced off bright snow and colorful rooftops, sparkling against doors and windows already decked with wreaths.

After her visit with Jake and Cassie, the evening at the dance alone—or, god forbid, with Ron—was daunting. *I'll muddle through it somehow, and Alice and Lotts will be there after they close the bar. Wonder when I'll hear from Jake next?*

10

"Dance the Night Away"

From: <u>*Richard.Bam@vmailcom*</u>
To: <u>*Tess.Bam@vmailcom*</u>
Date: Saturday, November 20, 5:46 PM

Subject: My Big Little Girl!

Daughter Tess,

 Sounds like you've found something very special there. The opportunity to be a parent has been the most precious gift of my life, and I'm both humbled and thrilled that you are thinking the way you are. Bide your time, keep your eye on the prize, and one way or the other, you'll know if it's right. Sure is nice thinking there is still a way for me to make it all better for you~ I'm always trying. And don't worry about me. I'm on the mend.

Love, Your Dad

PS. Your sister has struck up a friendship with Archie Lawson, and there seems to be a real spark between them. Glad some good has come of her time here, nursing dear old dad.

  The dress Noelle had chosen hung in Tess's closet; a gold, strapless satin sheath with a sparkly beaded tulle overskirt in paler gold that hit just above the knee. A matching bolero jacket was on the hanger, too, encrusted with gold and crystal beads. Noelle had talked Tess into patent gold sandals with four inch heels as well. The entire get-up was completely impractical, but she had not even bothered to argue. Her mother also insisted Tess borrow the heavy crystal encrusted, faux-sapphire jewelry she'd always dressed up in as a little girl.

Tess loved the way the striking deep blue sparkled against the gold, like ice on fire. She fussed with her hair, clipping it up loosely with a barrette that matched the earrings and choker, curling bits with an iron, allowing tendrils to fall.

After she pulled on sheer sparkly gold hose, the dress and jewelry, she looked in the mirror, glad that the bolero jacket mostly covered her cast. She'd agreed to the outfit to make her mother happy, knowing that if she had the chance to wear it with Jake, she'd feel like a goddess. *Even with the cast, this is way over the top for Green Junction.*

Dreading the prospect of an evening with Ron, Tess stroked her cheeks and eyelids with pale, sparkly gold powder, rimmed her upper lids with dark blue, and tucked a sheer lipstick in the little gold evening bag she'd borrowed from her mother. Slipping her sandals into a bag, she pulled on white faux fur boots and her white wool coat and wrapped a scarf around her head. At the first sight of Alice's little blue wagon, she was out the door. The note with the tickets had simply said, "Meet at Green Forks after Tree Lighting", so she'd just have to keep hoping Ron wouldn't dare show up.

The dark night was cold, but the evergreens in the square in front of Town Hall had been decorated by various civic groups for Tree Lighting and they sparkled with lights and ornaments. With everyone milling around, dressed in holiday finery, it looked like a magical village.

Tess caught a glimpse of Jake and her heart skipped a beat. He cut such a handsome figure in his long dark overcoat, even her mother would be impressed. *Cassie must be better, but why would he leave her?*

He waved, flashing an eager smile and the heat in his eyes as he walked towards them bolstered her spirits. Standing next to her, he reached for her gloved hand and squeezed it.

As they watched the high school chorale perform, Tess nervously glanced his way. Jake offered a quick, shy smile, then broke into a grin, wrapping his arms around her waist. Unable to help herself, she snuggled against him. When the music was over, he walked them to Alice's car. "I have to go check on Cassie," he said, running a gloved finger down her nose. Nodding, she smiled back at him.

Hanging their coats at Green Forks, Alice exclaimed, "Zowie, Tess, you look gorgeous. Ron's eyes are going to pop out of his head when he sees you in that dress!"

"I sure hope nothing else of Ron's pops out. It's a bit much, but my mother insisted. Do you think he'll get the wrong idea?"

"Ah, you can set him straight. You look like an angel, absolutely scrumptious. You do that ethereal mystic look so well."

"Thanks, sweetie. I might fool some, but you know the real me." Tess squeezed Alice's shoulder. "You look pretty smokin' yourself. I love the mink."

Alice's deep blue velvet dress hit just above the knees. Its long sleeves clung to her arms, and the low neckline exposed plump cleavage. She'd accessorized with blue sheer stockings, sky-high navy sued pumps, and a vintage mink choker and cuffs.

"Not many girls would think of wearing mink as jewelry that way. It's very chic."

"This was from my grandmother's coat. My inheritance. You got Grandma's Angliotti's Italian linens, I got Grandma Rustevik's Russian mink. Lotts finds mink on bare skin very sexy. Just wait, this will make him nuts."

"That man has fashion sense."

"Hah, I don't think so! Lotts' fashion sense is just beneath his belt buckle," Alice giggled. "But I can't say I mind."

Tess was floored to see Lotts behind the bar in tails. "Wow, Look at you." His deep blue velvet bow tie and cummerbund exactly matched Alice's dress.

"We turn it up around Green Junction every once in awhile," Lotts joked.

"I'll say," Tess grinned. "Nothing very 'green fork' about that penguin suit, especially next to your lady in velvet and mink."

"I don't often get to dance the night away with the woman of my dreams, you know," Lotts answered breezily, laying an arm on Alice's shoulder.

"Yes you do, I'm just usually not wearing the velvet dress," Alice quipped.

Tess laughed out loud, and Lotts asked with a grin,]. "What will it be, tenderfoot?"

"How 'bout a champagne cocktail with cognac, Tess?" Alice asked.

"Sounds delish."

"Open some champagne, Lotts," Alice said with a wink for Tess."Let's get this party started."

Right after he popped the cork, Lotts said, "Jake called. He said to tell you he'll be here any minute."

Tess didn't miss the 'shut up' look Alice gave Lotts. *My date is with Ron. Why is Lotts bringing up Jake?*

People had begun to meander in from the Tree Lighting,   so Tess took a seat at the bar, watching nervously for Ron. Brett and Stuart came in with their dates and sat at the bar near Tess. Neither girl was one of Vicki's friends, Tess noticed with relief. They introduced themselves and made small talk, and Tess was happy for the company.

*****

When Jake spotted Tess at the bar he felt an electrified. She was incredible in her gold dress and sandals. Even her toenails were painted pale gold. "Look at you," he said, bursting with pride.

"Hi, Jake," she smiled nervously, fussing with her purse.

He kissed her cheek. "Sorry to keep you waiting, Tess."

She flashed a look of surprise as he folded his coat over the back of her barstool. Leaning into her, he tucked his nose in her curls, speaking softly. "Cassie's doing just fine. I couldn't wait to be here with you." *God, she's so beautiful.* He'd always been stunned by his attraction to Tess, but dressed like this, she was mesmerizing. He took the barstool next to hers, and Lotts poured him a whiskey. He sipped it while she looked around apprehensively."How about another cocktail, Crash?"

"Mmm, thanks, I better not."

"Waiting for someone?" he joked.

Her eyes wavered, but she smiled resolutely. "Ron Karachek gave us tickets. Are you going to the dance, too?"

His brow furrowed. "I thought I was going with you. I mailed tickets to your office when you were in Philadelphia. Didn't Alice tell you?"

Tess's jaw dropped and her eyes got round as saucers, sparkling like the jeweled choker around her neck. "*You* mailed tickets?"

"I did." He could barely hide his annoyance. "The message said, "Meet at Green Forks after the Tree Lighting." You're seriously going to this dance with Ron? How's that going to work? I just saw him in the cruiser over by town hall."

"Alice called me at my parents to tell me there were three tickets in an envelope, marked Lotts, Alice and Tess. The card wasn't signed. Since Ron had mentioned the VFW Dance at Jackalope, we assumed they were from him. My date is with the guy who wrote, "Meet me at Green Forks after Tree Lighting.""

Jake grinned, shaking his head. "Oh, Crash, we crossed signals again. I figured you didn't mention the dance this morning because you were still annoyed with me. I didn't want to push it."

He watched Tess's smile get bigger. As the tension between them melted, he put his arm around her shoulders. Kissing her sheer, sparkly lips, he murmured, "Will you be my date tonight, darling, ravishing Tessie?"

*****

When Tess felt Jake's cool, firm lips on hers, the uncertainty of the past four weeks melted down her back and formed a puddle at the floor, replaced by a warm, contented buoyancy.

"You didn't think I'd let you go to the social event of the year with anyone but me, did you?" Jake asked. His brown eyes were amused.

"How was I to know?" she giggled. "I really do think I could use another drink." Alice was finishing up behind the bar. "Alice, Jake sent us the tickets."

Alice's jaw dropped and a look of disbelief crossed her face. Eyes flashing, she told Jake, "Dude, next time sign the card. Do you know the trauma you caused around here this week? Lotts, open another bottle of champagne, we've got more celebrating to do here."

Whooping, Alice poured a glass for every patron in the bar, then came over to hug Tess and Jake, toasting them wildly.

Jake's next kiss brought Tess up off her stool. Arms around his neck, the wool of his blue suit mashing against her bare shoulders, her knees went weak, and she let her fingers coil in his dark curls. The longing she'd kept buried through long dreary weeks unfurled. Desire coiled in her belly, making her toes curl. *Remember what Daddy said. Take it slow this time.*

Jake grabbed her hand. "C'mon, gorgeous, you and I have a dinner date. I'll pull the car around and meet you in back."

Tess went for her coat, Alice right behind her. "What a relief," Alice raved as Tess slipped into her boots. She held Tess's coat and squeezed her arm. "Lotts and I will see you at the dance. Enjoy dinner."

Out in the dark frosty night, Jake held the door to a vintage silver Mercedes sedan. Light snowflakes fell sparingly as Tess climbed into the heated seat of the cushy leather interior. "Where did this come from?"

"I couldn't have you arriving at the dance in the ranch truck. This was Uncle Albert's. Aunt Olivia keeps it in her garage. She insisted I take you out in style."

"How does it handle in the snow?" Tess asked curiously, as Jake climbed into the driver's seat.

"A Mercedes with snow tires is as good as a tank. We can go anywhere, as long as we go slowly," Jake replied. A slow, satisfied smile spread across his face, and he brushed the exposed nape of her neck with his fingertips, sending chills down her spine. Leaning over, he kissed her mouth and said, "I'd never let you go to this thing with anyone but me, not in a million years."

He tasted cool and firm and masculine, with a hint of whiskey, and as his admiring eyes burnt into hers, she settled back into the comfortable seat. "You've surprised me twice today, you know. And both were very pleasant surprises."

He took her hand, touching her fingertips gently. "Good. I'm hoping to surprise you once or twice more tonight, as well."

She quirked a brow. "Are you?"

It was fun being able to flirt with him again. "Thanks for telling how you felt, earlier today," she smiled. "I'm really glad to be with you tonight, Jake,"

Gazing at her, the heat deep in his eyes, he said. "I wanted to do something special for dinner. I'm taking you to Steadman's, but we'll be at the dance by the time Alice and Lotts get there."

"Perfect,," she said, enjoying the sensation of his warm palm cupping her cool fingertips. He brought them to his mouth, kissing each tenderly. A thrill shot up her arm as another wave of longing coursed over her. *Pace yourself, girl. Things worth having are worth waiting for, so stop thinking about skipping dinner and taking him back to your place to tear his clothes off.*

*****

Jake was pleased that he'd thought of Steadman's, a classic French restaurant serving the finest cuts of free range regional beef and game, with seafood shipped directly from Louisiana.

"This is lovely, Jake," Tess murmured, as the maitre d' led them to a table.

"Got to give my Philadelphia girl as much swank as can be had, west of the Mississippi," he whispered into the curls above her ear. *It's worth it to make this happen for us, even if she still wants to leave.*

A harpist played in the center of the dining room. Once they were seated, he ordered a split of champagne. After the steward poured a vintage Cristal, he raised his glass to her. "I've got some work to do to make up for the three hundred heifers I stuck you with on Wednesday."

"You do," she agreed, clinking her glass gently against his. After they sipped, her smile turned saucy. "But you came clean today."

"I sure did," he admitted. His sheepish smile brightened at the look in her eyes. "You didn't mind sticking around after lunch today for two more games of Candyland?"

The server was bringing their salad course. "Candyland is my favorite, especially when I can play it with you and Cassie."

He took her hand across the white linen table. "Do you know how lucky I feel every time I'm with you?"

She smiled at him for real then, her eyes soft and sparkling, her face radiant. *I've waited to see that glow. I want to see it all the time, and I'm willing to earn it, every day.*

After salad, the waiter set a shrimp and petite steak before Tess, and the rack of lamb in front of Jake. They chatted through dinner, and he was pleased to see the light remain in her face. The confusion between them had cleared, and the heat was back. The valet brought the car around, and he helped Tess in.

"Are you warm enough?" he asked from the driver's seat.

"I'm fine. Thanks for a lovely evening, Jake. This is really special," she said, flashing an encouraging smile.

"Thanks for setting me straight on Wednesday," he said gravely, touching her cheek. "You know how I feel now, but I wish I'd spoken earlier."

Smiling, Tess put her hand to his neck and pressed her soft pink lips to his, in a sweet, understanding, tender kiss. He took her cheeks in his palms. The blue eyes looking into his were steady, and he knew he'd been forgiven.

"Look, Tess, if you think there's a chance for us, I want to give it another shot," he said determinedly.

"You do?"

"I do, if you'll still have me. Honestly, a girl like you only comes along once in a lifetime. Please, I know I've screwed up, but can we try this again?"

She closed her eyes for a moment, almost overcome by joyful relief. When she opened them, her eyes glowed in the dark. "I'd like that, Jake. I can't imagine anything being as much fun as the times I've spent with you and Cassie."

Alice and Lotts were boogieing on the dance floor when he led Tess into the VFW hall. Jake took her in his arms, pulling her close, and she folded her cold hands inside the panels of his suit coat. Planting his right hand on her waist, he took other hand in his left. She moved like molten gold, sparkly and radiant. Inhaling, he breathed her hair and kissed her cheek, willing her to feel safe, to trust him again..

It was eleven when he returned from the punch bowl. Handing a glass to her, he said, "Honey, Tilda left a message on my voicemail. Rhiannon is in labor, but she doesn't want our evening spoiled. She's happy to handle it, if you want to stay."

"Oh, Cassie will never forgive us if we let her miss the birth of those puppies! We've had our fun, can't we go get Cassie and take her up to the ranch?" Tess asked, setting the glass punch cup down quickly.

He smiled at her eagerness. "Sure. I'll get our coats and call Olivia, let her know we're on our way." *She's always thinking of how to make Cassie happy.*

*****

Her boots on, Tess hurried our as Jake pulled around. "Can we go to my apartment, first?"

There, she grabbed her emergency kit and a change of clothes. Cassie was in her coat and hat and mittens at the door of Aunt Olivia's tall white Georgian when the car swung up the drive. Jake held the passenger door, and Olivia hurried out in her nightgown and overcoat, holding Cassie's hand.

"Oh, Dr. Tess, isn't this exciting! And you still have your dress on, let me see!" Cassie peered over the seat back. "Your hair is so pretty! You look like a fairy princess."

This kid is so incredible. A lump formed in Tess's throat. "Thanks, Cassie."

Olivia leaned in. "I'm sorry this has interrupted your evening, Tess. You look just lovely. Thank you for what you've done for Cassie these past few days. We're deeply indebted. Will you join us on Thursday for our Thanksgiving feast?"

"I'd be delighted to, Olivia, thank you so much."

"Stella and I will prepare everything, so just bring yourself. We'll dine at three," she intoned, regal as ever, despite her nightgown and galoshes.

"Wonderful. I'll look forward to it."

"I won't keep you; I know Cassie is excited about this adventure." Shutting the door, Olivia waved, stepping back towards the house.

As Jake backed down the driveway, Cassie piped up, "Daddy, will we get there in time? I think Rhiannon will need us to help her. It's not easy to have puppies, you know."

Smiling at his daughter in the the rear view mirror, Jake reached for Tess's hand. "I imagine it isn't. I'd call Tilda, but she probably has her hands full right now."

"Rhiannon is having six puppies, Cass, we'll be there in time to help, don't worry," Tess said reassuringly, turning to Cassie's sparkling eyes.

"I can't wait!" Cassie said excitedly. "And I'm so happy you are with us, Dr. Tess. It's always a lot more fun when you are around. Did you like dancing with Daddy?"

"We had a wonderful time, Cass."

"I like his suit, don't you?"

"I sure do. Thanks for sharing him with me tonight."

"That's okay. You make him happy, I can tell."

Jake's dark eyes penetrated the darkness, and he flashed a smile just for her. Tess leaned against the comfy leather seat back and sighed. *This evening has turned out so much better than I expected. Just goes to show, you never can tell.*

*****

The lights twinkled from the wide porch as Jake pulled up to the ranch house. Cassie leapt from the car, heading for the mudroom andTess hurried close behind, clutching her emergency kit. Grinning at their eagerness, he grabbed Tess's overnight bag from the trunk and followed them in.

Two new puppies were already in the whelping box and Cassie squealed delightedly at the births of the remaining four. Much later, after they'd changed into jeans and slippers and sweatshirts and cleaned up the puppies, after Tess got Rhiannon comfortable and Jake helped Cassie settle into bed, they cuddled on the cushy leather sofa in front of the fireplace. "I opened a bottle of Uncle Carlo's Chianti to celebrate tonight," he said. Pouring from a decanter, he handed her a globe of deep red wine.

Tess smiled at him, her eyes glowing with happiness. "This was such a perfect night," she said, "After yesterday, I never would have imagined things could work out so well for us."

"It's been intense," he said, sipping from his glass. "Uncle Carlo's Chianti always helps to put things in perspective."

She settled against him and he rested his arm on her shoulders, playing with her hair. She'd unpinned it, and it fell over her shoulders in tousled waves. Wine glass in one hand, her casted fingertips rested on his thigh. After a long moment, he said, "About that job at New Bolton, Tess, I think you should do it. We'll manage somehow. I don't want you to miss an opportunity you'll regret later."

Her pale eyes glistened in the firelight. "I've been thinking about that, too, Jake, especially after yesterday. If I were working in Philadelphia, I'd be thinking about what I was missing here, you and Cassie, her ponies and the ranch. She'll grow up quickly. I'd miss out on so much if I left. I've decided I want to do another year here, working for Doc. He suggested I contact Colorado State about their PhD program in microbiology. He's spoken to some colleagues about me, and they've inviting me to apply. With recommendations from New Bolton, he's almost positive I'll be accepted. I've set up a tour of their facility the week after next. It's only three hours away."

He touched her curls. "Tess, that's great. You'd consider the program at Fort Collins?"

"Well, as Doc pointed out, if I'd want to concentrate solely on livestock care, CSU has the best program."

His heart leapt. "So if that plan works, you'll stick around?"

"I'm planning to be here summer and next year, too. I'll apply for the program at CSU next fall for admittance the following year. It will be a good balance for me, another year here for practical experience, then research and a PhD, but only three hours away." She patted his thigh and smiled. "I'm really happy with the plan. I'll be able to pursue a bigger career, and stay close to the people I care about."

Thrilled at her news, Jake thought of what Alice had told him earlier while Lotts and Tess were dancing. *"There's more at stake here than you realize, Jake. If you are serious about Tess, you better not let more time pass. You need her here and so does Cassie. She doesn't want to leave, I hope you know that. You should ask her to marry you. You know that's what you want."*

"Don't you think that's rushing things a bit?"

"Only if you don't want to give her a reason to stick around. What's to wait for?"

They drank their wine, and Tess relaxed against him, sighing with contentment. He stroked his fingertip along the silky smooth skin of her collarbone, just above the neck of her sweatshirt, and took a deep breath. "After the past twenty-four hours with Cassie, Crash, I don't know what we'd do around here without you."

She sat up and looked at him, her eyes like saucers. "You mean that, Jake?"

"I do. I love you, Tess," he said, touching a finger to her lips. She let the tip of her tongue press against it, and a flaming sensation shot up his arm.

"I love you, too, Jake. And Cassie. So much. I was so worried about coming back from Philadelphia when I hadn't heard from you. I didn't want to think about life in Green Junction without you."

He set his wineglass down, and kissed her deeply. "I never meant to cause you heartache, y'know."

She kissed him back, giving everything she had. He flamed with familiar heat and desire, but the certainty and trust he finally allowed himself to feel was all new. *She's everything you could ever want. Let her make you and Cassie happy, because she will.*

"Wait here a minute, Tess, will you?"

"Sure, Jake."

*****

Tess sat by the fire, a blanket over her shoulders, bathed in complete happiness. *Things might actually work out for us, after all. He really loves me.*

She watched Jake come back down the steps, towards her, illuminated by the firelight. Her heart welled with the rightness of what was between them as he sat close, and she curled against him. Taking her chin in his hands, he kissed her, deep and long and slow, and she leaned into him, her hand on his heart, feeling it beat, strong and safe and steady. *No one else could ever make me feel this way. I can't imagine ever wanting to be with anyone as much as I want to be with Jake.*

Gently, he ran a finger along her jaw, tracking a line down her neck. "I meant what I said earlier, about wanting so much to be able to adore you, Tess. I want to, everyday, and I've been thinking about how to best let you know how much I believe in us."

He touched her left fingertips. They fluttered from her cast, papery white in the fire light, and he nestled them against the strong bulk of his chest. "Tessie," Jake murmured, kissing her cheek, her eyelids, her forehead. "I called your Dad while you and Cassie were finishing up with the puppies." She felt something cold against her palm and looked down to see a diamond flashing there. "This is my mother's ring. We'll pick one out for you, if you'll have Cassie and I."

He slipped out from beneath her and got down on one knee. The fire blazing around the outline of his shoulders, he asked, "Will you marry me, Tess?"

Astonished, she looked into his eyes. They were sober,, but in them she could see, profound and deep, the promise of a lifetime of love and adoration. Choked with emotion, she said, "I'd really like to marry you, Jake."

"So you will?" he asked, breaking into a huge grin.

"Of course."

Slipping the ring on her left finger, he kissed her fingertips, then took her in his arms, kissing her lips with a passion that resonated to her core. After the kiss, he said, "I love you so much, Tess."

"I love you, too, Jake. No life could offer me what I can have here with you and Cassie. I can't imagine wanting anything as much as I want a life with the two of you."

*****

Jake's heart lept. As he kissed Tess again, she responded hungrily, and he pulled her to the soft rug on the floor. "I've missed you, baby. I've so wanted you for mine."

"I'm yours now," she smiled, so he kissed her again, overwhelmed with the desire to have her completely, this woman who would be his wife. Peeling back the layers of separation that had kept them apart, they stripped each other to the flesh, eager to move beyond hurt and pain.

Naked, her nipples erect, Tess offered herself to Jake with complete abandon. Unable to hold back, he wrapped her legs around his waist, and plunged deep into her sweet ripeness, and she responded with freedom and conviction. Consumed by fervor, they were lost in the ecstasy of their togetherness, stripped bare of everything but their desire to sanctify their commitment. The heat rose in waves as he thrust himself into her again and again, whispering his love for her in a voice that grew hoarse with passion.

As they climaxed together, Tess clasped his back with strong fingers as she writhed and bucked in ecstasy beneath him, crying out for him.

They lay quietly together until their breathing slowed. Beneath the blanket, he ran a finger down her naked side and she looked up, her eyes clear and gentle, happier than he'd ever seen her. "It's never been this way for me," she whispered.

"Me neither," he said throatily, letting his lips wander over his face, feeling his heart break open even wider for her. "And that was just the first time, my darling sweetness."

He folded her against him and carried her gently to his bed. They rested, touching, caressing, but neither could sleep. She turned to him, her mouth was hot and ready. Nuzzling her breast, he suckled, so she moaned and widened for him. As he entered her, she cried out passionately, and they joined together, sealing their devotion to each other once more.

*****

Tess heard tiny feet padding across the floor and felt a small cold hand reach under Jake's down comforter to touch her arm. She opened her eyes.

Two little amber orbs peeped at her face, and a thin voice whispered. "Dr. Tess, what are you doing in Mommy's spot?"

"Morning, Cassie," Tess whispered back. The rising sun glinted on the white bare bark of the tall aspen outside Jake's window.

Taking Cassie's small cold hand in hers, she smiled at the sweet face of the little girl, who would soon be her stepdaughter. The warm bulk of Jake's leg pinned her down, his arm over her naked waist under the covers.

What am I wearing? She took careful mental inventory before she whispered, "It's cold, Cass, you should have your robe and slippers on."

"I woke up and wanted to see the puppies, so I came in to get Daddy. I didn't think I'd find you here, though, Dr. Tess. You usually stay in the guest room," Cassie said, her little voice tinged with curiosity. "Did you have a sleep over?"

"We did. Let's let Daddy sleep a while, Cass. I'll take you downstairs," Tess whispered. "We'll go see what Rhiannon and her puppies are up to. You go get your robe and slippers, and I'll meet you in the hallway, okay?"

"Sure, Dr. Tess."

When Cassie was out of the room, Tess found her bag on the floor against Jake's bureau. *He must have carried it up after the puppies were born.*

Stretched across the bed, Jake opened one eye as she slipped into her t-shirt and jeans. In a sleep-drowsy voice, he said, "You handled that well."

"Thank you. I'm in training, now. I guess we can dispense with the "Dr. Tess" tag though, huh?" she grinned, leaning to kiss his bristled cheek.

Grabbing her, he wrapped his strong arms around her torso and pulled her close. "We can. But it's torture when Dr. Tess leaves my warm bed before the sun is up."

"Get used to it. We've got a kid to raise," she laughed, tickling his chest.

"And we'll do it together, won't we, my gorgeous, radiant, sassy bride?" he asked, smacking her denim clad bottom. "What did you put your clothes on for?" he teased, squeezing her finger just above the ring.

She smiled into his sleepy but very satisfied eyes. Her smile irrepressible, she plastered his face with kisses. "You had plenty of Dr. Tess last night."

"I did get the sweetest of shares of Dr. Tess last night, didn't I? And I will again. Many times," Jake said, his groggy voice assured and very content.

"We'll have plenty of mornings together, Jake. It's Cassie turn now," she whispered, pulling herself away.

Cassie was waiting on the landing, pixie-cute in her fuzzy lime green robe and red wool slippers. "C'mon, Dr. Tess, let's go see

Rhiannon. We should be thinking of names for those puppies, huh?"

"Great idea, Cass."

"I think it was nice that you and Daddy had a sleepover," Cassie said, taking Tess's hand and leading her down the stairs. "He and my mom argued a lot. None of us liked that very much. Tilda isn't here on Sundays, and Daddy and I make pancakes. Sometimes we put blueberries in them or chocolate chips with banana. You can have pancakes with us this morning, if you want, Dr. Tess. Do you like pancakes?"

"I do like pancakes, Cassie."

"Let's take care of the puppies, and then we can have pancakes. You should stay over tonight, too, Dr. Tess. Daddy's really happy when you're around, I can tell, and I like seeing him smile like he does when you are here. We really like it when you are around."

*****

To: <u>Richard.Bam@vmailcom</u>
From: <u>Tess.Bam@vmailcom</u>
Subject: Re: That's my girl!
Date: November 20

Dear Daddy,

I'm truly the happiest girl in the world!

Thanks for your love, advice and understanding, and most of all, your blessings! I can't tell you how thrilled I am~how happy we are~together, finally!

I'm so glad you are feeling better ~ Jake and Cassie and I can't wait to see you and Mom and Sam and Archie at the ranch for New Year's Eve~ A puppy for every lap!

Thanks for helping me stay on course, always, Dad. I have so much to be thankful for ~

Love, Love, Love,

Tess.

*****

To: Tess.Bam@vmailcom
From: Sam.Bam@@vmailcom
Subject: Girls in White Dresses
Date: December 25, 1:05 AM

Tactful, Tasteful Tessie,

Break into the wine cellar, Yahoo Cowgirl, and let Aunt Olivia go wild for your Bridal Spectacular in July at McGreer Ranch, because Archie and I will be keeping Mom busy with our December Nuptial Event at the Four Seasons in Philadelphia~
Diamonds truly are a girl's best friend, especially when I get to share all that sparkles and shines with my super sweet sister! Who would have thought things could get so glamorously glittery for the Bam Girls?? So many weddings, so little time! (And such perfect husbands, to boot!!)
Can't wait to see you next week and meet Jake~ Let's plan a New York White Dress Whirlwind ASAP. Merry Christmas, my darling sister, and enough Love, Love, Love to fill the Planet, or at least, get us all from Philadelphia to Green Junction and back!

Your Sensationally Satisfied Sis, Sam

PS. Can I borrow Cassie? I'll need a flower girl!

*****

6 McGreer Lane
State Route 359
Green Junction, CO, 68432

May 3, 2012

Rancho Nuevo Rehabilitation Center
3851 Rancho Blvd,
Denver, CO 80205

Dear Tess,

Thank you for bringing Cassie by last week for her visit. I was glad we had a minute to talk. It's six months that I've been here now, and I leave soon for Los Angeles. I'll do outpatient treatment there and find a job, staying with my mother to begin with, probably for awhile. It means a lot to me that you and Jake have stuck by me. I know how terribly I behaved in so many ways.

As much as I hated Green Junction, I know now that it was really myself I was hating, too. Though if I never see another snow capped mountain, it will be too soon.

I've talked to my therapist a lot, about how I hurt you, and Jake and Cassie. I keep remembering watching Cassie leap out of my car that terrible day into your arms. I saw the way you held her. I think it's right that you two are together.

I wasn't really ever a very good mother. From the time Cassie was a baby, I felt overwhelmed. I blamed it all on Jake, but now I see what the problem was. I was taking pills to cope, even then. I didn't know how else to manage. Everything was always too much for me, from the time my parents divorced. Before then, even. I hated you from the time I saw you, probably because you had so much going for you, but I know better now.

Cassie seems happy. I guess I always knew she would be at the ranch. I'm trying to start over with a clean slate, and I just want to say I'm sorry about what I did to Cassie and about your arm, too.

I know Cassie's life is much better now. You're a good mother for her, Tess, better than I ever was, and she's lucky to have Jake as a dad, too. I'm really, really glad Cassie is with you both. I want to make a good life for myself, but I still have a lot of work to do. I hope Cassie will be a bigger part of it, someday, and I hope I can count on you to help with that when the time comes.

I feel like you might even be willing to be a friend? I hope I can earn that so I can count on you, too, the way Jake and Cassie do. It would mean so much to me.

In gratitude,
Victoria Scalamagotti McGreer (Vicki)

Author's Note

I remember the jaw-dropping wonder I first felt traveling to Colorado. It was fun to capture the natural beauty of Tess's adventure in that gorgeous place as she emerges from a care-free thrill seeker to a loving partner and committed stepmother.

I'm always available for book-signings, readings and appearances, especially to benefit my reader's favorite animal shelters and rescues. Please visit my website www.LillyChristine.com , contact me at LillyChristine13@gmail.com or find me on Facebook !

Reader Reviews are Important!

If you enjoyed Crashing Into Tess, please post a review on Amazon and Goodreads and "Like" the Crashing Into Tess FaceBook Page

Coming Soon. . .

Visit the next pages to read excerpts from the McGreer's #2 novella, "Crazy On Daisy", which includes "Right Kinda Bull" about Jake's cousin Ty McGreer, to be released in early 2014 on Amazon!